SACRED TARGET

SCOTT MATTHEWS

VINCI
BOOKS

By Scott Matthews

The Adam Drake Series

The Assassin's List
Oath to Defend
Dark Trojan
Call It Treason
Special Counsel
Soft Target
Sacred Target
Tipping Point
Coverup
The Deterrent
The Skysage Affair
Black Dragon
False Target
Conspiracy to Spy

Vinci Books

vinci-books.com

Published by Vinci Books Ltd in 2025

1

Copyright © Scott Matthews 2018

The author has asserted their moral right to be identified as the author of this work in accordance with the Copyright, Designs and Patents Act 1988. This work is a work of fiction. Names, characters, places and incidents are the product of the author's imagination or are used fictitiously. Any resemblance to actual persons, living or dead, places and incidents is entirely coincidental.

All rights reserved. No part of this publication may be copied, reproduced, distributed, stored in any retrieval system, or transmitted in any form or by any means, including photocopying, recording, or other electronic or mechanical methods, nor used as a source for any form of machine learning including AI datasets, without the prior written permission of the publisher.

The publisher and the author have made every effort to obtain permissions for any third party material used in this book and to comply with copyright law. Any queries in this respect should be brought to the attention of the publisher and any omissions will be corrected in future editions.

A CIP catalogue record for this book is available from the British Library.

Paperback ISBN: 9781036701246

Printed and bound in Great Britain by Clays Ltd, Elcograf S.p.A.

Chapter One

THE MAN SITTING in the parked green Prius watched the dark form stealthily run down the sidewalk on the other side of the street. It was two o'clock on a drizzly Sunday morning in Portland, Oregon's Nob Hill district. Printed notices were being stuffed in the doors of random residences and businesses in the area.

He knew the area was chosen because it was just west of St. Patrick's Catholic Church. He also knew what each notice said. He'd drafted the warning.

In the name of Allah, the merciful, full of grace. You who are not believers will be beheaded in three days in your house.

You must choose one of the following to stay alive:

1. Convert to Islam.
2. Pay the jizya (religious tax) for protection.

If you choose to ignore this warning and do not make one of the two choices you're being offered, you will be beheaded.

Do not expect the police to prevent your murder or save you from death.

Several of the catholic churches in the city had received an earlier notice to convert or die nailed to their front doors. Now the next phase of the plan was being implemented to create fear and panic among the Catholic parishioners of St. Patrick's, as well as in the minds of the owners of a few of the trendy Nob Hill boutiques and restaurants in the area.

It had taken him just a year to develop his plan and find the person who would carry it out. From there, it took another year to recruit the other members of the group and test them to ensure their professed pledge of loyalty was sincere. He found that young Americans were easily attracted to the idea of violent jihad. Few had the ability, however, to fully embrace the sacrifice and commit their lives totally to the cause. Fortunately, the leader he had chosen had the fire and the ability to do both.

She also had the natural gift of leadership. The acolytes she chose obeyed her without question. When she'd required them to go far beyond the societal norms they were accustomed to, they hadn't hesitated. Her final test for each of them was to behead a sheep in the dark of night in some farmer's pasture and bring the sheep's head back to her.

He was shocked when she told him about her final test, but he was not surprised. He had recognized her psychopathic personality soon after she enrolled in his entry-level computer science class at Portland State University.

He'd been fascinated by how she charmed and manipulated the others in class. But he was fully convinced of her psychopathic personality by what she offered to do when he was being reviewed for termination by the administration. One of his students was a loud-mouthed football player who voiced anti-Muslim sentiments one time too many in his class. He'd made the mistake of responding out loud to the bigoted lout in class. When the student's well-known and wealthy alumni father persuaded his Catholic church to protest the anti-Christian and discriminatory outburst toward his son, he'd been called on the carpet by the administration and terminated.

That's when his chosen had offered to take care of the loud-mouthed student for him, if he wanted. She had flirted with the football player and embarrassed him by calling him out as gay when he rejected her advances. When he tried to get back at her for embarrassing him, she offered to go to the police and claim she'd been raped. If he didn't like that idea, the football player thought he was such a stud, she said she was willing to castrate him and let the world know about it.

The young student delivering the notices this morning was a new member and hadn't been fully tested. That's why he was interested in how she delivered the last items on her list. In her backpack remained three items; a stencil for gang-style graffiti in bubble letters for the word "ISIS", a black can of spray paint and a gallon Ziploc bag with a small wooden cross soaking in sheep's blood.

He watched approvingly as she ran up to the front door of the turn-of-the-century Victorian home toward the end of the block. She took her backpack off and set it at her feet. From inside, she took out the stencil and the can of spray paint. Holding it up against the heavy solid oak front door, she sprayed the word "ISIS" in gang-style bubble letters onto the door. She replaced the stencil and spray can in her backpack and took out the Ziploc bag. Carefully opening it, she lifted out the wooden cross dripping in sheep's blood and laid it on the front door welcome mat. With a quick survey of her work, she replaced the Ziploc bag, slipped on the backpack and jogged down the sidewalk and turned left up the street. Her ride was waiting one block away.

When she turned the corner at the end of the block, her watcher started the Prius and followed her up the street. He was now satisfied that he had a cell of warriors with the capability to carry out his plan.

Chapter Two

ADAM DRAKE MADE a note in the margin of a copy of the complaint he was reviewing that had been filed against Puget Sound Security, where he served as its special counsel and attorney. A former PSS client had sued them for negligently failing to prevent a theft of its intellectual property.

The former client suspected one of its employees of selling proprietary information to a competitor. It felt that PSS should have discovered the possibility of the theft if they had conducted a thorough background check on the individual. The client apparently had forgotten that the individual was the nephew of the company's CFO and that his recent financial difficulties had been reported but overlooked, due to his relationship to the CFO. Drake smiled at the thought of deposing the CFO and asking about her role in the hiring of her nephew.

It was Monday morning and he'd driven in from his farm and vineyard to get a start on the stack of files on his desk. The one day a week he was spending in Seattle working for his friend, Mike Casey, the CEO and major shareholder of Puget Sound Security, was taking more of his time than he'd anticipated.

Drake finished his review of the complaint filed against PSS and walked down the stairs from the loft in his office to get a fresh cup of coffee. Paul Benning was coming down the back stairs from the condo he rented from Drake above the law office.

"Morning, Paul."

"You're here early."

"Your wife made an indelible impression on my ego last week, telling me I wasn't the attorney I used to be. I thought I'd prove her wrong."

"She does have a way of getting us to do things her way, doesn't she?"

Drake walked to the break room to refill his coffee cup. Benning followed him.

"How's your new PI case for the archdiocese going?"

Benning waited until Drake stepped back from the new Moccamaster coffee maker. "If you have a minute, I'd like to talk with you about that."

"Sure, grab a cup and join me."

When they were seated upstairs in the loft, Benning sat back in the black leather side chair in front of Drake's desk and recounted the phone call he'd received that morning.

"The archbishop's executive called me at seven thirty. One of their parishioners found their front door had been spray-painted gang-style with the word 'ISIS' and there was a bloody wooden cross left on the welcome mat. There was also a notice beside the cross warning that if they didn't convert to Islam or pay a religious tax for protection in three days, they'd be beheaded in their home. It was the same notice the owner of a boutique dress shop nearby found stuffed in the door when she opened up this morning. The archdiocese wants to know how they should handle these new threats to its parishioners."

"Does the archdiocese have any idea who's leaving these notices?"

"They've reported them to the police, but there are no leads so far. The Vatican sent out a general notice based on similar threats and notices in Europe two years ago, in Sweden, I think. Nothing came of those threats and police there attributed it to a lone-wolf ISIS wannabe follower. Law enforcement here is responding the same way."

"Is the FBI or DHS involved in this?"

"Not actively, as far as I know. The Portland Police Department says it hasn't received any intel from the FBI that identifies any locals who might be doing this."

Drake sat his coffee cup down and sat back with his hands clasped behind his head. "The archdiocese is asking you if these are serious threats, not just the general threats ISIS has repeatedly made worldwide to nonbelievers."

"That's pretty much what they're asking."

"I don't know what to tell you, Paul. Portland Police and the FBI could try to work with the local mosques and ask for help, but they haven't had a lot of success with that in the past. Radicalized lone wolves are hard to spot until they reveal themselves online or by making threats that someone reports. The big thing will be to keep the parishioners advised of what's going on and give them assurance that everything possible is being done to protect them."

Benning cocked his head. "Even when it's not?"

Drake knew his friend well enough to know he hadn't just stopped by to brief him on his new P.I. case. There was something else. "What are you thinking?"

"This is the first time this kind of terrorist threat has been made in America. The FBI has to know more about this than they're telling us. I think they might share more if they're sharing intel with someone they like and know."

"You know that person isn't me?" Drake smiled.

"I've come to understand that. When do you go to Seattle this week?"

"I'll drive up tomorrow night, work Wednesday and drive back Thursday morning. But Liz isn't there yet. She's still wrapping things up in D.C."

Benning got up and raised his coffee cup. "Okay, just a thought. Then say hi to Liz for me the next time you talk with her."

Chapter Three

DRAKE WATCHED his friend leave and thought about the change in his demeanor and attitude since he'd decided to retire from the Multnomah County Sheriff's Office.

Benning had been with the MCSO for twenty-five years and worked as a senior detective for the last eighteen. He was eligible for retirement with full benefits but wasn't planning to retire for another ten years. After being diagnosed with stage-two prostate cancer recently and having had surgery, however, he was reconsidering an early retirement. Seldom leaving the condo and suffering a debilitating bout of depression, he'd lost interest in just about everything.

That ended when he'd agreed to help Drake for a client with business in Nicaragua. A confrontation with a rogue Russian general there and being captured by an Iranian terror cell had revived his fighting spirit. It had also led to his decision to retire from the MSCO and begin a career as a private detective working out of Drake's office.

That decision was serving him well. Working out of Drake's office where Benning's wife, Margo, was the office manager/paralegal/executive assistant and, yes, ran the place, allowed him to see his wife more often and establish a new line of work. Benning was a skilled detective and solving cases was something he was good at.

This case for the Archdiocese of Portland was different than the cases he was used to working. If the threats were genuine, and ISIS was behind it or promoting it, then advising the archdiocese on how to respond to the threats wasn't going to be the end of it. He knew Benning would keep after it until the terrorists were identified, arrested and behind bars for the rest of their lives.

That worried Drake, not only for his friend's sake but for the sake of his friend's marriage. Margo was resigned to *his* "adventures" as she called them but still hadn't forgiven him for involving *her* husband in Nicaragua. It wasn't hard to imagine her reaction if her husband started chasing terrorists who were threatening to behead people in their city.

Drake decided not to wait until he saw Liz in Seattle.

"Hello, good looking. Got a minute?"

It was eleven o'clock in D.C. He knew she normally returned to his father-in-law's senate office following the morning's hearings she attended and then left for lunch. Liz served as the senator's liaison with the intelligence community because he was the chairman and ranking senator on the Senate Select Committee on Intelligence.

"How are preparations for your move out west going?"

"I'm getting there. The condo sale is pending in escrow, I have an offer to sell my car and a mover lined to move my things. It's all the little things, like getting in touch with people I know I won't see for a while."

"When you tell people you're moving, how do they react?"

"Usually they're shocked that I'm giving up what I have here to move across the country. Working in the capital is the penultimate achievement for most of the people I know here."

"Are you having second thoughts?"

"Not one. Is that why you called, to see if I've changed my mind?"

"No, I wanted to hear your voice and get some advice. Paul Benning has a case that I think you know about. He asked me this morning if I would run something by you."

"For the Archdiocese of Portland? His first case that you told me about?"

"That's the one. They're getting more serious threats and the police don't seem to be taking them very seriously. This morning someone spray-painted 'ISIS' on the front door of a residence and left a bloody cross and a warning. The warning said convert to Islam, pay a religious tax or die in three days. The explicit threat was that they would be beheaded in their own home if they made the wrong choice."

"Wow. Is the FBI involved?"

"Paul says they are, but they're not sharing anything. The archdiocese wants to know if these are genuine threats and what precautions they should take, if they are. Do you know someone in the intelligence community who might be able to help Paul evaluate these threats?"

Drake waited while Liz considered his request. She knew a lot of people, but he was hoping she had a close relationship with someone with the intel to take a hard look at the threats.

"There is someone I trust and have lunch with occasionally. But's she very careful about discussing her work, except in general terms, unless there's a good reason for doing so."

"Would a request from Senator Hazelton be a good enough reason? He represents Oregon and his state office is in Portland. The archdiocese is a constituent of his."

"Relax, Counselor, I can fill in the blanks. Her name is Marta Halim. She's a senior analyst with the National Counterterrorism Center at Liberty Crossing. I'll invite her to join me for a late lunch or a drink after work and see if she'll help."

"Thanks Liz. I hope this turns out to be someone's idea of a sick joke, but I want to help Paul in any way that I can. He seems to like working as a P.I."

"Is Margo okay with his new career?"

"Hey, she's your new best friend. Maybe you should ask her, as chummy as you two are now. That's a subject I'm not willing to bring up right now. It's been a little chilly in the office since Paul helped me with that matter last month in Seattle."

"You're still curious about the girl-talk we had in your office, aren't you?"

"What? No, why would I be?"

"Maybe I'll tell you why you should be, if you'll come see me."

"That sounds like blackmail."

"You *are* a smart attorney."

Drake knew he was losing this round. "Why don't you call your analyst and see if you can do something to help your new best friend's husband?"

He knew she was grinning as she said goodbye.

Chapter Four

DRAKE WAS in the office break room pouring his second cup of coffee for the morning when his secretary came down the stairs from the Bennings' condo. He watched until she sat down at her desk to judge her mood before he greeted her.

"Good morning, Margo. Want a cup of coffee before I go upstairs?"

"You're in early."

"Need to get caught up on a few things. You sure you don't want some coffee?

"I had a cup with Paul before he rushed down to see you, thanks."

When she slipped on her glasses and reached over to check her phone console for messages, he got the message that the office chill was still on and would probably last for the rest of the day.

In the ten years they had worked together, there had only been two other occasions when she had frozen him out like she was doing now. There had been one long week after

Kay had died when he'd come to the office each morning hung over and unable to get much of anything done. The other occasion was earlier this year in Nicaragua when she'd flown down to be with Paul after he'd been kidnapped and beaten by a Hezbollah terror cell.

Each time, he had waited patiently for her to come to him and voice her complaint. When she would finally tell him what was bothering her, and knew that he was listening, things would return to normal. He hoped it would happen that way again.

Drake worked without interruption at his desk in the loft until noon. When he went downstairs to see if Margo wanted something from the nearby deli that was a favorite of hers, she wasn't at her desk. She wasn't in the break room and the door to the restroom next to it was partially open and he could see the room was empty. She'd left without saying she was leaving, something she never did.

Perhaps it was time to ask Liz to talk with Margo. If he'd made a mistake by offering to let her husband work out of the office, there had to be something he could do that would restore order and tranquility in the office.

He was headed out the door to go get something for lunch at the nearby Little River Café on the RiverPlace Esplanade when his cell phone buzzed in his pocket. It was Senator Hazelton, his father-in-law.

"Good afternoon, Adam. I just flew to Portland this morning. Have you had lunch? I thought I'd have something delivered, if you can join me in my office?"

"I was just leaving to grab something to eat myself. Would you like me to bring you something? I'm getting a cranberry chutney turkey sandwich."

"Sounds great."

"See you in twenty minutes then."

Senator Hazelton was rarely back in his home state these days. As chairman of the Senate Select Committee on Intelligence in the U.S. Senate, he was one of the busiest senators in Washington.

He also no longer had a home in Portland, after terrorists blew it up with a rifle-launched thermobaric grenade a couple of years ago. He still owned the property on Lake Oswego but had purchased a townhouse in Alexandria until he and his wife decided if they wanted to rebuild their family home.

On the short walk to the café, Drake called in their order and twenty minutes later was in the elevator riding up to the senator's office in the Edith Green-Wendell Wyatt Federal Building on S.W. 3rd Avenue.

The receptionist smiled and waved him on to the senator's office. "Nice to see you again, Mr. Drake."

"Nice to see you too, Cheryl. How's your son doing?"

"He's at football camp this week, so it's nice and quiet at home."

"What position does he play?"

"He plays tight end."

"Good choice. I used to hate those guys."

He had been a linebacker when he played at the University of Oregon and taken more hits from tight ends than he cared to remember.

Senator Hazelton opened the door to his office and waved Drake in.

"Would you like something to drink?"

Drake glanced at the round conference table on one side of the office and saw there were water glassed beside the plates.

"Water's fine, thanks."

He waited until the senator sat down to put their sandwiches on their plates and sat across from him.

"Liz usually lets me know when you're going to be in town. Is this an unscheduled visit?"

Senator Hazelton smiled. "I'll have to make sure she delegates that chore to someone before she leaves in a couple of weeks. Wouldn't want to deprive you of having a mole in my office."

It was Drake's turn to smile, thinking of Liz as a mole in his father-in-law's senate office. She was fiercely loyal and had never shared anything with him that the senator didn't want him to know.

"The answer to your question is, yes. The archbishop called me about the threats his parishioners have received. He's being stonewalled by the FBI and he's concerned they know something they're not telling him."

"Did you know Paul Benning left the Sheriff's Office and that he's working out of my office as a P.I.? He's already investigating these threats."

"I told the archbishop to hire him, after Liz told me what he was doing now."

"Why didn't you ask the FBI what's going on?"

The senator unwrapped his sandwich and took a bite while he considered his answer. "I know you've heard about the "Deep State"; influential employees of the government and the military who secretly manipulate government policy and undermine elected officials. They're brazenly flexing their muscles with the election of the new president. It seems they want to embarrass him anyway they can. Being slow to investigate threats to the Catholic Church, after his successful visit with the Pope, might be a way. After all, if you listen to some of the progressives in Congress, the

Catholic Church deserves payback for being murdering Crusaders nine hundred years ago."

"Right. What can I do to help?"

"When you agreed to act as a trouble shooter for Secretary Rallings and me originally, it was because you could act unofficially for us, in your position as an attorney, and not attract a lot of attention to a problem a constituent was having, like you did when Martin Research was testing its new chemical agent detection system and being targeted by terrorists. I still believe we need you in that capacity, perhaps even more so now.

"The government isn't functioning very well these days. Leaks are happening every day and our security is being threatened by them. Important initiatives never get off the ground. That cannot continue.

"I'd like you to be available to work directly with me and a few elected officials I know and trust. For now, investigate the threats to the Catholic Church here in Portland. Find out why the FBI is holding back. Everything in government is being politicized, even in the FBI, to the point that nothing is getting done. We can't keep operating that way.

"It's unacceptable to have citizens who are being threatened and targeted in their homes for their religious beliefs. It's even more unacceptable that the FBI seems to be sitting on their hands about these threats. Call Liz if you need any help we can give you in Washington."

Drake left Senator Hazelton's office after promising to do whatever he could to help.

Chapter Five

PROFESSOR ARI AHMADI stood at his black quartz breakfast bar drinking a small, thimble-shaped cup of Arabic coffee. Boiling the simple mixture of water, lightly roasted coffee mixed with ground cardamom seeds for precisely seventeen minutes was a morning ritual he'd learned from his late father. Savoring the slightly bitter and unsweetened coffee reminded him of his Arabic roots and helped him focus on the work ahead.

He had chosen the chic and modern condo in the trendy Sullivan Gulch neighborhood of Northeast Portland because it was near Portland Community College Cascade where he taught computer science. It was also a neighborhood of young singles and married couples and provided a perfect cover for his other activities.

Ahmadi turned at the sound of footsteps coming down the hall from his bedroom. He was always amazed at how innocent and beautiful his young naked lover looked when she got up in the morning. She'd spent the night training the young women she'd recruited to be Muslim warriors before she came to his bed and still had found the energy for a rather torrid hour of sex.

"You look lovely. Ready to try some Arabic coffee?"

"A Venti double shot on ice is the only coffee I drink. Mind if I smoke on the balcony?"

"Put something on first."

Samantha Taylor, called Sam by those who knew her, was a bit of an exhibitionist. Five feet six, buxom with a figure that turned heads, it wasn't her nudity that concerned him. He had a reputation as a middle-aged swinger; seeing a naked coed on his balcony wasn't something that would shock anyone close enough to see her. It was the tattoo of the Egyptian goddess Isis whose wings spread from side to side under her breasts that concerned him.

Some would pass it off as just another fan of the pop star Rihanna, who had a similar Isis tattoo. But some might also recognize it as the tattoo of female followers of ISIS, the terrorist group he had pledged to support. That was something he couldn't allow.

Ahmadi's covert support of ISIS involved tutoring young hackers referred to him for advance training as ISIS social media experts and online recruiters. That's how he came to know Samantha. But he'd quickly discovered that her desire to support ISIS went far beyond her willingness to be a recruiter of young women in America. She wanted to be more than a 'cheerleader' for ISIS; she wanted to be an active operative.

The desire probably had its origin deep within her psychopathic personality. It had also developed, in part, from her love of taekwondo, the Korean martial art. She started practicing it when she was a freshman in high school as a means of self-defense. She was fully developed by the time she turned fourteen and was bullied by the older girls in her PE classes. In two years, the minimum time taekwondo allowed, she'd earned her first-degree black belt. When the older girls learned the hard way not to mess with her, it became the older boys who wanted a piece of the feisty underclassman their girlfriends were all talking about.

They also had to learn the hard way. Two senior boys had grabbed her one day after last class and pulled her into the boys' bathroom. When she walked out, three minutes later, they were both moaning on the floor with their hands cupped between their legs, praying the pain didn't mean they would never be fathers.

Her father was a casino security guard and her mother was a blackjack dealer in Reno, Nevada. They both worked nights and didn't have time to recognize the warning signs that signaled the development of a dangerous young psychopath. Samantha was seldom home at night and became fond of leading young men on and when their passionate blood was about to boil over, crying rape and beating them severely. She never reported what she thought of as attempted rapes and, of course, the men never reported being assaulted by a five-foot-six young female weighing maybe one hundred and fifteen pounds.

Samantha left home when she turned seventeen and hitchhiked to Portland. She worked as a waitress, bicycle courier, and then as a nanny for a Muslim family. She converted to Islam to curry the favor of the wealthy parents. After one year working for them, they helped her enroll at the nearby university and got her involved in the activities of their mosque.

That's where Ahmadi first heard of her when he learned that she appeared receptive to radicalization. Later, when she was a student in one of his computer science classes, he'd taken her as his lover.

Ahmadi finished his coffee and joined Samantha on the balcony. She now wore a thin white tank top he could see through that didn't reach below her navel. Her legs were crossed and her feet rested on the top of the balcony half-wall.

When he sat down facing her in the other chair on the balcony, she dropped her feet to the floor and turned toward him, grinning with her legs spread apart.

"You are quite mischievous, aren't you? What do you hope to gain with this display?"

"Oh Professor, you know what I want. I want to see that you appreciate me."

"Wasn't last night proof of that?"

She stood up and took his hand. "That was last night. It's a new day."

Chapter Six

LIZ MET HER FRIEND, Marta Halim, at Coastal Flats in the Tyson Corner Center Mall for an early dinner. It was a chain seafood restaurant and a place that was inconspicuous for a meeting with an NCTC analyst.

Marta was a Coptic Christian whose parents fled Egypt when President Nasser began to impose an Arab identity on the country that had always considered itself different than other Arab countries. Her parents were both professors at the American University in Cairo. They recognized the persecution that was sure to follow for those who rejected Arab nationalism and arranged sabbaticals so they could travel to Europe and America. They never returned to their native homeland and watched in horror at the atrocities committed against their church and their family and friends still in Egypt.

Their daughter, Marta, was born in Virginia where her parents taught Arab history in the international relations and cultural diplomacy areas of study at Georgetown

University. She followed them in her own academic career but chose to become an intelligence analyst instead of being a professor. She had decided she could do more to prevent what her parents had experienced in Egypt as an intelligence analyst than as a college professor.

Liz watched her friend walk to her table as she entered the restaurant; black hair worn shoulder-length, large brown eyes and a wide smile showing off her perfectly white teeth. Marta was beautifully exotic in appearance and more than one male head turned to watch her walk by.

When Marta slipped into a chair across from her, Liz reached across the table and shook her hand.

"Thank you for coming."

"Aside from the lure of the grouper fingers they have here, how could I pass up the opportunity to hear about the latest concerns of the Senate Select Committee on Intelligence?"

A waiter arrived and asked if they wanted to order something to drink.

Liz ordered a glass of sauvignon blanc and Marta said she'd have the same.

"How's work at the NTCT? Are you still liking it?"

"I am, very much so. I'm allowed to focus on Egypt and that gives me a lot of satisfaction. There's a growing terrorist presence there, as you know, and it's become even more dangerous there for the Coptic Christians."

"Isn't ISIS just in the North?"

"That's where it's the worst, in the Sinai Peninsula, but they've attacked churches in Cairo and elsewhere."

"Do you still have family there?"

Marta nodded and looked away."

"I'm so sorry. I wish there was more we could do."

"Destroying ISIS is all anyone can do and you're helping with that."

The waiter brought their glasses of wine and they ordered dinner; grouper fingers for Marta and a lobster salad for Liz.

After a short period of silence as they sipped their wine, Liz told her friend about her decision to leave Washington, D.C.

"He must be quite a guy for you to give up everything here."

Liz smiled broadly. "He is. In fact, he's the reason I invited you to dinner. Have you come across any intel about threats being made against the Catholic Church in Portland, Oregon?"

"Nothing, why?"

"Someone is copying the threats made in Sweden to Christians—convert to Islam, pay a tax or die. Notices were posted on parishioners' doors. One home had 'ISIS' spray-painted on its front door and a bloody cross left on the welcome mat."

"Has anything been done to follow through on these threats? As I remember, nothing happened in Sweden other than the threatening."

"Not yet. The notices were discovered early this morning. They were given three days to make a choice or they would be beheaded in their homes."

"How is your guy involved in this? I would think the FBI would be all over this."

"He has a friend who works out of his office as a P.I. His client is the Archdiocese of Portland. To answer your question, the FBI appears to be taking a wait-and-see approach to this. Since the threats in Sweden didn't amount to much, they must be thinking this won't either."

Marta finished one of her grouper fingers and then a forkful of coleslaw. "You know churches in America have been advised to become more security conscious due to the threats and attacks on churches in Europe. And you know that ISIS has encouraged followers to kill Christians wherever they find them. So far, nothing has come of it. From the stuff I see, however, I think it's only a matter of time before there are attacks on churches here."

"I agree, but why like this? A lone gunman walking into a church service with an AK-47 would be hard to stop. With a three-day warning, they have to know there's a chance they'll be identified before they can act."

"Maybe their goal is just to terrorize Christians? The choice of converting or losing your head is something American Christians haven't had to make."

Liz closed her eyes for a moment and shook her head. "As bad as this may sound, I hope that's all they're trying to do. The first time an American is beheaded in their home holy hell will rain down on Muslims living here."

"That could be another thing they're trying to accomplish. When Muslims think they're being persecuted, when a drone goes off course and there's collateral damage, the picture of a weeping mother is worth a hundred new recruits."

They finished eating and Liz asked Marta if she wanted another glass of wine.

"Thanks, but I think I'll go back to work. If I turn something up, I'll call you tonight."

"You don't have to work late for me on this. Tomorrow's fine."

Marta's grin made Liz ask, "Are you seeing someone at work?"

"Trying to. He's working late tonight, and I don't mind

being able to say I'm working on something that's time-sensitive."

"Any time I can help a friend."

Liz waved to the waiter to bring their check, gave Marta a hug and sat down to text Drake.

Chapter Seven

SAMANTHA TAYLOR STEPPED out of the shower in the bedroom and walked to the den drying her hair. Ahmadi was sitting at his desk in the den staring at the screen of his laptop. When he saw that the only thing she had on was the towel she was wrapping around her head, he closed the laptop to give her his full attention.

"After your afternoon classes, will you need me for anything tonight?"

"Not tonight. I'm sending out the individual email reminders that the parishioners have two days to make a choice."

"How did you get all of their email addresses?"

"You've been in my class. How do you think I did it?"

"You hacked the church?"

"The archdiocese actually."

"Can they ever trace these emails back to you?"

"I'm using an anonymous email service, so it won't be easy. But the government will be able to eventually. That's why I'm using the anonymous service and sometimes the college library. I don't want this to look like too sophisticated an operation."

"You want them to think it's some Muslim student playing a prank."

"Sort of. They won't consider it a prank after tomorrow night, if you and your lady warriors are successful."

"Don't worry, Professor. We will be."

Ahmadi watched her cute little behind march to the door and turn down the hallway.

There was more to his email operation than Samantha knew. In addition to losing his position at the university, he had taken a substantial salary cut when he moved to a community college. He planned on getting more than simple revenge on the Catholic Church; he was going to recoup his financial loss as well.

The information he obtained from the records of the archdiocese on each of the parishioners gave him more than enough to allow him to steal their identities and access their bank accounts. That was the tricky part of his plan. When the FBI and the other law enforcement agencies were trying to find the terrorists behind everything, he intended to be far away enjoying his retirement earlier than originally planned.

Samantha and the others wouldn't be so lucky, unfortunately. They wanted to be martyrs for the jihad and probably would be. But that was a price they were prepared to pay. It wasn't a price he intended to pay, however. He'd already paid enough.

Ahmadi saved the draft of the email he was going to send out tonight and closed his laptop. As soon as Samantha left, he would have time to catch the lunch special at his favorite Vietnamese bistro in Sullivan's Gulch.

SAMANTHA WATCHED across the street from Ahmadi's condo for his green Prius to pull out of the building's underground parking on his way to the community college. When he turned the corner a half a block away, she took the hand of the young man named Jamal next to her in the bookstore and walked out. She slipped her arm around his waist and led him to the entrance of the condo across the street, using the key card she borrowed from Ahmadi to let them in.

When they entered the fourth-floor condo, she stopped pretending to be the man's lover and jumped up on the kitchen island to face him.

"Have you learned anything more about his assignment? There's something he's not telling me."

"My friend at the mosque knows that his mission is approved and blessed. But they don't know the details."

"Does he communicate with someone online?"

"He might, but I don't think so. The high-level stuff is handled face-to-face whenever possible."

"Then he has to have someone here he's meeting. Can you follow him and find out?"

"I've taken one of his classes, he'd recognize me. But I might be able to find someone."

"Well, find him fast. We only have two more days before the church people let him know the choices they've made. I'm not keen on going into just a couple of their homes and cutting off heads. I like our plan better."

"How are your girls doing? Have they learned to shoot yet?"

Samantha jumped down and shoved Jamal hard in the chest. "Don't call them girls! They're tougher than any of you and sure as hell better shots."

"Take it easy, Sam. If they are as good as you say they'll get the chance to fight as real warriors. I just wanted to know how they're doing with their weapons training."

"They get to practice on full auto tonight. It's the last time they'll get to use the AK-47s, but they're ready. Just find out what else Ahmadi's up to. After we take care of the lawyer tonight, there's no turning back."

———

AHMADI CLOSED his laptop and let out a long, slow breath. So that's what Samantha was up to. She was too clever for her own good and it was going to get her killed. He would make sure of that.

When he'd watched her going through his desk one morning, he'd known she couldn't be trusted. That's why he'd wired the condo with hidden cameras and microphones. Obviously, she didn't have a clue they were there. His young lover thought she was clever and smart, but she wasn't nearly as smart as he was.

Chapter Eight

DRAKE WOKE up with sun streaming in the window and Lancer, his German Shepherd, licking his face.

"All right already. Give me a minute and we're off."

He sat up, rubbed his eyes and swung his legs out of bed. Lancer's head was a foot away from his, looking directly into his eyes with his big tail wagging from side to side.

Drake leaned forward and rubbed behind each of the dog's ears. "So, what's it going to be, the hill route or the run down to Dundee and back?"

Lancer barked once.

"I was afraid you'd choose the hill route."

After dressing for the run and stopping in the kitchen for a big glass of cold water, Drake led them out the back door of his old, stone farmhouse and into the bright sunlight.

His farm and soon to be fully restored vineyard consisted of forty acres of rich Jory soil that sloped down to the road below in a southeasterly direction. The farm had been planted with pinot noir and chardonnay rootstock and then abandoned four years later when the dentist from New Jersey decided that farming wasn't as glamorous as he'd imagined it to be.

When he and Kay were married and looked for somewhere to live in the country, a realtor friend of Kay's brought them to see the farm. It was rundown and overpriced, as all the land in the area capable of growing grapes was, but Kay fell in love with the place. Her dream had been to restore the farmhouse, replant the vineyard and raise their family in the pastoral hills of Dundee, Oregon.

Two years after they bought the farm, Kay was diagnosed with a late stage and aggressive breast cancer. Twelve months later, as she was dying, Drake promised her he would fulfill her dream of restoring the farmhouse and vineyard.

As he jogged down the driveway to the road below, he felt proud as he looked at the carefully prepared soil and micro-irrigation system he'd put in. The vineyard was ready and waiting for planting of the Dijon clone pinot noir chardonnay rootstock he'd ordered yesterday.

Drake used his morning runs with Lancer to clear his mind for the day ahead. He focused on his rhythmic breathing pattern of inhaling for three steps and exhaling for two. When his mind and body were synchronized, he relaxed and enjoyed the run. Tomorrow, he would reverse the course so the uphill climb would come at the end of his run and he'd have to switch his breathing to a three-count pattern to attack the hill. As much as he sometimes dreaded getting out of bed early in the morning, he knew it was easier to stay in shape than to get back in shape.

When they reached the three-mile point of their run, Drake turned and headed back to the farm.

"Come on, Lancer, let's head back before you wear yourself out."

Lancer looked up at him and sprinted forward wagging his tail. Like a horse in a pasture hearing grain poured into a bucket and galloping to the barn, Lancer delighted in running ahead of him when they made the turn and started back to the farm.

Drake picked up the pace and chased after his merciless friend.

When they got back and he stepped into the kitchen, sweating lightly, his cell phone was vibrating on the counter and playing his new CCR "Up around the Bend" ringtone.

"Good morning, Liz. Making sure I'm running each morning like I told you I was?"

"Right on. I'm not moving across the country to spend time with some guy who's fat and flabby."

"Remind me to take you for a run when you're here."

"I look forward to it. I had dinner with my friend last night. She went back to the NCTC after dinner to research ISIS and its war against the Catholic Church. She just called to tell me there wasn't anything that mentions something planned in America."

"If this is something new, did she think ISIS has the same goal here as they did in Sweden? Create a backlash against Muslims to make it easier to recruit young men to fight for them?"

"She thinks it's a possibility. She reminded me that, in 2015, ISIS declared an all-out war against Christianity when they beheaded twenty-one Coptic Christians on the beach in Libya. ISIS has always talked about taking back Rome, meaning the Pope and the Catholic Church. She says it's difficult to separate the usual blustering from hard intel without something concrete to base it on."

Drake let a soft sigh slip out. "She didn't find anything, then, that would help Paul know what to advise the archbishop?"

"I'm sorry, Adam. She promised to keep digging. If this was serious, as usual it'd be all over the social media sites that ISIS uses. Then NCTC might have something to work with."

"I feel like I did in the D.A.'s Office when I had to tell someone my hands were tied until a crime was committed. Now there's an actual act of terrorism being committed with these threats but nothing that identifies a person or group the FBI can arrest."

"Do you want me to reach out to one of my friends in the FBI?"

"It can't hurt. Paul's talked with them on behalf of the archdiocese, but they say they don't have any leads. They might not tell him if they did, but they might tell you. Someone might also feel the Church deserves these threats and needs to sweat a little, payback for the Crusades or something."

"I hope that's not the case. It's not the FBI I worked for anyway. I'll see what I can do. Call me tonight, I like hearing your voice."

Drake promised that he would and looked down at Lancer sitting patiently at his feet.

"I wish I could be as patient as you, Lancer. But something tells me this isn't some jihadi prankster trying to scare people. Sooner or later, one of these nut jobs is going take the next step. Waiting until that happens isn't my way of protecting this country."

Chapter Nine

PAUL BENNING FINISHED his protein smoothie and looked across the table. Margo held her coffee cup in both hands in front of her mouth, staring transfixed at the marina across the RiverPlace Esplanade below their condo.

"Margo, would you like to go to the gym with me after you finish work?"

When she turned toward him with a blank look on her face, he knew she hadn't heard what he'd said.

"What?"

"Are you okay?"

"Of course. What did you say?"

"I asked if you wanted to go to the gym with me after work. I could use some encouragement. Getting back into shape after the surgery is harder than I thought it would be."

"It's only been six months, Paul. The doctor hasn't cleared you yet for strenuous exercise. I don't want you overdoing it."

"Then come and keep an eye on me."

"Maybe. How's the case for the archdiocese coming?"

"Not much to tell. No one has a clue who's behind the threats. Everyone's hoping this is just a prank."

"But you don't think it is. Is that what's worrying you?"

Benning didn't answer right away. "I'm not sure what's bothering me. I keep thinking about the people who got the warning posted on their doors and what they're going through. If they take the notice seriously, will any of them consider converting or paying the tax? I grew up in the Catholic Church, but I've never really thought about how strong my faith was until now. Did you ever hear the story of the eight hundred Martyrs of Otranto?"

"No."

"No reason you should have. I wouldn't expect you to have heard stories about Catholic martyrs growing up in a Baptist Church. Otranto is a city in southern Italy. In 1480, an Ottoman army of soldiers ended a two-week siege of the city and slaughtered everyone in their path. When they got to the cathedral, it was filled with people praying with the archbishop. The Ottomans commanded the archbishop to throw away his crucifix and convert to Islam. When he refused, they cut off his head. As was the custom, the priests were all murdered as well and the cathedral was stripped of all Christian symbols and turned into a stable for the horses.

"The surviving people were captured as slaves. The Ottoman Pasha ordered the 800 men of Otranto to be brought before him where he told them they had one chance to convert to Islam or die. One man, an old tailor, stepped forward and called out, saying he was ready to die for Christ a thousand times. At this, the men of Otranto cried out with one voice and said they too were willing to die for Christ.

"The next morning, the eight hundred prisoners were

marched up a nearby hill. The old tailor was the first to be beheaded. One by one, the rest of the men were also beheaded and their bodies dumped in a mass grave. The Ottoman army then left and marched on Rome, but the delay of its advance gave Rome a chance to defend itself. The Martyrs of Otranto are remembered for saving Rome.

"I lie awake at night wondering if I have the courage of the men of Otranto."

Margo got up and walked behind her husband to kiss his cheek and hug him. "That's a terrible story, but that could never happen in America."

"It's happening every day in Syria, Margo, anywhere area that ISIS controls. It could happen here, like it did for the French priest. ISIS has been encouraging followers to kill people of the cross wherever they find them. What if someone here is following the command?"

"Then we find them and stop them. Have you talked to Adam about this?"

"I did yesterday. I suggested that he call Liz and ask her if she'd heard anything. I'm going over today to see an old friend, Dan Ramirez, at the MSCO. He works with the FBI's JTTF and might have something that's helpful."

Margo kissed his cheek again and stood up. "I need to get to work, honey. If you still want me, I'll join you at the gym tonight."

"Thanks Margo. I'll see after work tonight."

Benning called his friend and arranged to meet him at Dan's favorite coffee shop, the pink Voodoo Doughnut on NE Davis Street. Cops and doughnuts were a joke for some, but his friend was dead serious about the shop's Memphis Mafia doughnuts.

Ramirez was already seated when Benning got there

with a half-eaten doughnut in his hand and a half a dozen more doughnuts in an open box.

"I'll let you get us coffee, amigo. I couldn't make you pay for my doughnuts, but you can get the rest. Black, cream and sugar."

It had been several months since Benning had seen his friend. The extra calories from his doughnut fetish didn't seem to have increased the size of the pants he was wearing. Ramirez was five six or seven and still trim and fit. Divorced twice and single again, he ran marathons twice a year and captained the annual one-hundred-and ninety-nine-mile Hood to Coast run for the MSCO team.

Benning came back with two coffees and took a doughnut from the box. "What's in this?"

"Ah, savor and enjoy. Fried dough with banana chunks and cinnamon covered in a glaze with chocolate frosting, peanut butter, peanuts and chocolate chips on top."

Benning sampled the doughnut and nodded his approval. "Tasty."

"So, what can I do for you, Detective?"

"Are you still working the JTTF assignment?"

"I attend the meetings and the briefings, why?"

"Parishioners of St. Patrick's found 'convert or die' notices stuffed in their doors when they woke up yesterday. One home had 'ISIS' spray-painted on the door and a bloody cross left on the welcome mat."

"I haven't heard about it. How are you involved?"

"You knew I resigned from the SO. I'm working for a friend as a P.I. to see if I like it. The archdiocese is a new client of mine. They asked for advice on how they should respond."

"What does the FBI say?"

"That they're looking into it."

"I wouldn't expect them to know much after just one day. Unless they have someone inside."

"Have you heard about any new terrorist activity in Portland?"

"Not specifically here, but I do know that ISIS is recruiting teen girls online in America. They're also doing the same thing on college campuses. Did you see the story about the guy who posed as a fundraiser for American Friends of Hamas at Portland State University? He got donations after telling students the group wanted to fund operations against Israel so they could hit soft targets like cafés and schools. What universe are these kids living in?"

"Unfortunately, ours. Our media rails against Israel on a nightly basis. The Palestinians are 'freedom fighters' and the Israelis kill babies. Do you think they're actually recruiting, not just protesting, on our college campuses here?"

"It's probably happening. The FBI tries to monitor it, but it's a big chore with all the universities and colleges we have. I doubt they catch all of it."

"No, I don't suppose they do. Dan, if you hear anything about these 'convert or die' notices, will you let me know?"

"Sure thing. You do the same."

Benning got up and found a napkin to wrap his doughnut in. No use letting it go to waste since he'd be going to the gym tonight and could work it off.

Chapter Ten

SAMANTHA and two of her crew waited in a rented van parked on the west side of SW First Avenue. It was one block away from the World Trade Center complex in Portland where the attorney had his office.

Every day of the week, Monday through Friday, he walked one block north to Paddy's Bar and Grill at precisely six o'clock in the evening. Paddy's was an elegant Irish pub, the oldest in the city, and a popular place to have a drink at the end of a work day.

Her number two had a pair of compact binoculars focused on the Trade Center's entrance.

"That's him. Blue suit and yellow tie. Right on time."

Michael Brennan was sixty-two years old and one of the top lawyers in the city. His firm was known to boast that its twenty-five lawyers were the smartest in town because they were all Harvard law grads. The firm's clients were among the biggest business in the Northwest and included the Archdiocese of Portland.

Samantha didn't know why Ahmadi had designated him

to be the first. She assumed it was because he was the archbishop's friend and the attorney for the archdiocese. She had argued that the first one singled out should be a priest, but he'd been adamant that it had to be the attorney.

It didn't matter to her. This is what she dreamed of doing.

She took the binoculars from her number two and handed her a street map of Portland. "Remember, you're lost and just want directions to Pioneer Place. When he stops to tell you where to go, don't hesitate to use your stun gun. It won't take him long to give you directions before he walks on."

Number two was eighteen and the first person she had recruited. Allacia was the first member of her black family to go to college and was a top student. She'd been an easy convert to Islam, rejecting her parents' Christian upbringing and world view as soon as she got to college. She said she wanted to achieve something more than just a college degree and a job, and radical Islam, as taught to her by Samantha, had provided just what she was seeking.

Michael Brennan crossed SW Taylor when the light changed and started toward the van. When he was fifteen feet away, Allacia got out and approached him.

"Excuse me, sir, could you help me? I'm trying to find Pioneer Place, but these one-way streets have me turned around."

Brennan smiled at the attractive young girl wearing a short, blue summer dress and holding a map in her hand. He came closer and held out his hand for the map.

"These one-way streets can be confusing. Here, you're three blocks away. Take SW Taylor and go west, that way."

Allacia said thank you and when the lawyer started past, she brought the hot pink stun gun up from behind her back.

Turning with him, she jammed the stun gun in his right side and brought her left hand with the map around to his back.

She counted one thousand one, one thousand two as she discharged eight million volts of electricity into his body. The reaction was immediate: intense pain and muscle spasm then a stunned and dazed mental condition followed by a loss of balance.

The third member of Samantha's crew jumped out from the side of the van to help Allacia. "He's having a heart attack! Let's get him to a hospital!"

Together they helped him into the side of the van and pulled the door shut. There was no one else on that side of the street and no one to hear why the man was being taken away.

As soon as she pulled away from the curb, Samantha praised her crew and instructed them to stabilize their victim.

"Use the flex cuffs on his wrists and ankles like we practiced. Allacia, give him the propofol so he doesn't wake up. We have time to kill before he goes on display tonight."

Propofol is the nonbarbiturate intravenous anesthetic used in surgeries, and Samantha had no idea how Ahmadi got his hands on it. She would have liked to keep the lawyer awake so she could see the terror in his eyes when he understood his predicament. But they had six hours before they could sneak into the botanical gardens where the lawyer would be discovered tomorrow.

Ahmadi had planned well, she had to admit. With the email each parishioner was going to receive tonight, telling them they had one more day to choose to convert or agree to pay a religious tax, they couldn't say they hadn't been warned. The shock they would receive when they turned on their televisions in the morning would jolt them into making their choice quickly while they still had time. If it didn't, she would make sure Ahmadi's threat was ultimately carried out.

It wouldn't be the way he had warned. It would be more effective and spectacular, with a much higher death count. When the world learned she was responsible for the massacre, she would soon be as revered as Nusaybah Bint Ka'ab, the first woman warrior of Islam.

Chapter Eleven

PAUL BENNING FOUND Drake working in his office loft at six thirty Tuesday evening.

"Margo said you might still be here. Big case?"

"Trying to keep up with your wife. When I finish something, it's back on my desk before I'm halfway through the next thing on her list. My one day a week in Seattle for Puget Sound Security and the drive up and back is like a vacation."

Benning laughed. "I thought you were the boss around here."

"Right. If you'd like an end-of-the-day drink with me, grab a couple tumblers and ice down in the break room."

Drake finished the dictation on the last file on his desk and opened the door of the credenza behind his desk. When he turned around with a bottle of Jim Beam Black in his hand, Benning was back.

"Here we go, two tumblers with ice as ordered."

After pouring two fingers over the ice, Drake sat back and raised his tumbler. "Cheers."

"I met with a buddy from the Sheriff's Office today who's assigned to the JTTF. The FBI hasn't briefed the task force yet on the church threats. He said he'd pass along anything he hears."

"What have you told the archdiocese?"

"Not much. I told them I was talking with everyone I knew who might have information about the threats. I also advised them to bring in security for the parishes. The problem is the archdiocese has one hundred twenty-four parishes, twenty-two missions, one seminary, forty elementary schools, ten secondary schools and two Catholic colleges. They can't bring in security everywhere. They've asked their attorney for advice, but they haven't heard back from him yet."

"What are they telling the people who received the notices?"

"They counseled each of them and ask them not to discuss the notices they received. They're trying to keep a lid on it to prevent everyone from panicking. With the FBI suggesting all this might be a hoax, they're hoping nothing more comes of it."

"I hope they're right."

"There is one thing I thought of that might help. My buddy at the Sheriff's Office mentioned that ISIS is focusing on recruiting teenage girls on social media in America. Do you think Mike would let Kevin McRoberts do his thing and see if there's anything on social media anywhere about these threats?"

"He might. I'll ask him."

Drake held up his tumbler. "Want another? I have to drive home, but you don't."

"No thanks. I should be going. I invited Margo to go to the gym with me tonight and she said yes for the first time."

Benning got up and picked up both their tumblers to take downstairs. "Are you driving up to Seattle tomorrow?"

"First thing in the morning. I'll let you know what Mike says about using McRoberts."

Mike Casey, the CEO of Puget Sound Security, and his best friend and former Delta Force partner employed one of the top hackers in the world. If anyone could troll the dark world of jihadi websites and social media and find something, young Kevin McRoberts could.

Thinking of PSS and Seattle reminded Drake that he'd promised to call Liz tonight. It was ten o'clock in D.C., but he knew she'd still be up.

"Hi beautiful."

"Hi handsome."

"How was your day?"

"Frustrating, to tell you the truth. I'm interviewing for my replacement and there are a lot of qualified applicants. But I haven't found anyone I think will get the job done for the senator."

"You're not going to find anyone as qualified as you. Maybe you're setting the bar too high."

"I don't think so. The problem is the people I really want are safely employed in agencies safe from elections and changing administrations. Senator Hazelton is a Republican serving in a blue state. Sure, he's a senior senator, but why risk it if his state turns against him? Remember the 'Tiger of the Senate', Oregon's Wayne Morse? He served four terms and lost to a novice when he opposed the war in Vietnam."

"You'll find someone. You know he'll still rely on you even after you leave."

"I hope so."

"Did you learn anything from the FBI?"

"Only that they're not devoting much manpower to the threats against the church. One of the good guys I know at FBI headquarters was transferred to the Portland office right after the election by the director. He thinks it was because he went to school with the new president's son-in-law or because he was too vocal about some of the things the agency wasn't investigating. Anyway, the forensic evidence from the notices and the bloody cross didn't provide any leads."

"You think they're waiting until something happens?"

"They're classifying this as a hate crime, not terrorism. They just don't have anything to work with."

"All right, thanks for trying. Anything special going on this week for you?"

"Only your calls."

"Then sleep well and I'll call you tomorrow. I'm driving to Seattle tomorrow. Do you have anything you want me to tell Mike?"

"Tell him I'll be there by the end of the month as promised."

"Will do. If you happen to wrap things up a little early, come on out and I'll show you a little more of Oregon."

"What do you have in mind?"

"No more river rafting. I thought we might take a short vacation somewhere."

"That sounds wonderful. I'll see if I can push up my departure by a week."

"Now that sounds really wonderful."

Drake knew what he wanted, a surprise she wouldn't see coming. She was going to love it.

Chapter Twelve

AFTER HIS RUN the next morning, Drake was fixing an omelet in his kitchen when a breaking news banner flashed across the screen of his small, wall-mounted flat screen.

...this morning early visitors at the catholic shrine and botanical gardens just minutes from downtown Portland, Oregon, discovered the crucified and decapitated body of Portland attorney Michael Brennan. The wooden cross his body hung on was propped against the base of a 110-foot cliff next to the rock cave in "Our Lady's Grotto". The shrine is closed and the FBI crime-scene experts are combing every inch of the 62-acre shrine and botanical gardens. So far, no one has claimed responsibility for what the FBI is calling the most heinous hate crime of the century. Brennan was a Catholic and attorney for the archdiocese of Portland. An FBI spokesman said Brennan was probably killed because he was a prominent Catholic in Portland, Oregon.

Drake grabbed his phone and called Benning.

"Do you have your TV on?"

"Yeah, I got a call from the archdiocese half an hour ago. They're in panic mode."

"I don't blame them. They're saying no one is claiming responsibility."

"Not true. Brennan had a 'convert or die' notice stuffed in his mouth. The notice is identical to the ones posted on people's doors."

"I'll bet the archbishop is giving the FBI holy hell, excuse the pun, for not taking these threats more seriously."

"As well he should. I had a feeling this wasn't a prank by a jihadist wannabe."

"Anything I can do before I leave for Seattle?"

"You might ask Mike if he'll let Kevin McRoberts search the social media sites. I need to get out in front of this and come up with something for the archbishop."

"You got it. I'll call you as soon as I know anything."

Drake set the eggs he was mixing for an omelet back in the refrigerator and called Liz.

"Have you seen the news?"

"My friend at the NCTC called five minutes ago. It's awful. This is the kind of atrocity ISIS has been shocking us with in Syria and Egypt. I never thought I'd see it here."

"It was bound to happen, sooner or later."

"Did you know the man?"

"I've run into him at the courthouse and bar luncheons. I didn't know him personally."

"I wonder why they singled him out. Had he done something that would make someone want to kill him?"

"Not that I know of. I'm sure the FBI will investigate that angle pretty thoroughly."

"Are you still going to Seattle?"

"There's nothing I can do here to help Paul. He wants me to ask Mike to turn Kevin loose on social media sites and see if he can come up with anything."

"Call me when you get there. I may have something

more by then. I'm going to call the Special Agent in Charge of the Portland FBI office on behalf of the senator and demand to know what the hell is going on."

"Let me know what you find out."

Drake got the eggs back out and finished preparing his omelet. The news channels were all repeating the same information when he finished his breakfast and got ready to drive to Seattle.

AHMADI WAS PREPARING his morning cup of Arabic coffee when Samantha strolled into the condo's kitchen. There was something different about the look in her eye he couldn't put his finger on. She had got back at two thirty in the morning, said the attorney was dead and that everything had gone well. After a long shower, she'd climbed into bed without saying anything more.

He'd thought she was having a hard time with the killing and didn't want to talk about it when she returned. But the look in her eyes suggested that something else was going on. It wasn't arrogance; it was more a look of contempt. He'd seen the same look whenever a student came into his class at the beginning of a term and thought he or she knew more than the teacher. He took great pleasure in showing them very quickly how wrong they were.

Samantha was new to the world of jihad, but her ambition to be a great woman warrior of Islam was blinding her to the subtleties of the war they were fighting. He already knew that he couldn't trust her. With this new attitude, he would have to be even more careful with her.

"Do you want to talk about it?"

Samantha was rummaging through her backpack and didn't look up.

"What's there to talk about? I cut his head off and we got him up on the cross. Getting the damn thing stood up was the hardest part of the night. Next time, I don't want them drugged when I cut their heads off."

He watched silently as she took her pouch of cannabis, rolling paper and lighter and went out on the balcony to smoke.

He followed her out and stood leaning against the frame of the sliding glass door. "I want you to take your fighters and go to the safe house until the weekend. The FBI doesn't have anything that leads to us, if you carried out the mission as we planned. But I don't want to run the risk that someone will slip up between now and then."

She inhaled deeply and held her breath longer that she usually did. When she turned to look at him, for a moment her eyes were slightly squinted and her lips were pressed firmly together. Then her face relaxed and she smiled.

"I'll need some cash for groceries and stuff."

"You'll have it. Take the Ford Excursion I keep in the storage unit and whatever you need. I want you on the road before noon. I'll go to the ATM downstairs and get the cash for you."

Ahmadi left the condo and took the elevator down to the lobby of the building. On the way, he opened the app on his cell phone to monitor Samantha in the condo above. As soon as he left, she was on the phone.

"He wants us out of town. What do you want me to do?"

Chapter Thirteen

DRAKE WAS on the road by eight o'clock. He was driving his company car, the gray Porsche Cayman GTS his friend had leased for him as an incentive to work as the company's special counsel. That and stock options, plus a relationship that dated back to their service as a hunter-killer team for the 1st Special Forces Operation Detachment-Delta (1st SFOD-D), had done the trick.

Since leaving the army, Mike Casey had purchased a controlling interest in a then-small security company when its founder retired. His parents had sold their Montana ranch and offered to loan him the money to purchase the stock as an advance on his inheritance. The company had slowly expanded, and when he and Casey had taken down the head of the Las Vegas-based International Security and Intelligence Services in their second post-army adventure working together, it expanded more rapidly.

After word got out that PSS had been responsible for the demise of the much larger security firm, many of its clients became new clients of PSS and Casey had to rapidly expand the company to service their needs. PSS now had offices in twenty countries around the world and employed nearly eleven thousand people to provide its mainly corporate clients security and risk management services as well as VIP protection, investigation and intelligence services. Cyber security was a major concern of most of its clients, and Casey had the good fortune due to the bad fortune of a young hacker by the name of Kevin McRoberts.

Microsoft was a PSS client and had been hacked by a young Kirkland, Washington, high school sophomore. At Casey's request, Microsoft agreed not to prosecute and McRoberts became an indebted employee of PSS. Now twenty years of age and a renowned "white-hat" hacker, young Kevin was an invaluable and trusted member of the PSS home office team.

At ten thirty Wednesday morning, Drake pulled up to the employee gate at PSS headquarters and punched in the forty-eight-hour security code. When the gate pulled back, he drove across the guest parking lot and down the ramp to the gated-entrance for employee underground parking and entered the security code a second time.

His reserved space was next to Casey's in the middle of the first row and next to the stairs leading to his office on the fourth floor. Grabbing his new 5.11 Tactical Rush Delivery bag that carried his laptop, his Kimber .45 in a quick-draw compartment, tactical flashlight and travel toiletries, he ran up the stairs, two at a time, to the executive floor.

Casey was standing in front of his assistant's desk when Drake walked down the hall. When he saw him, he swung his wrist up and checked his watch.

"Counselor, glad you could make it today."

"I could fly, but then you'd have to send a Gulfstream down for me each week. You're saving money this way."

"That's one way of looking at it. Grab a cup of coffee and join me in my office."

Drake walked to his office at the other end of the hall and left his bag on his desk. When he returned to Casey's office, he had a mug of coffee in his hand and leaned against the door frame.

"Anything new on my desk?"

"Two new matters. One file involves one of our defense contractors and another possible theft of its intellectual property. The company they suspect manufactures drones and is controlled by a Chinese holding company. They don't want to take the matter to court; they want us to come up with a more *creative* approach.

"The other matter concerns the request for security and protection for one of our contractors that wants to bid on the Navy's construction of a new naval base on Tiger Island, Honduras. With your experience for Trans World Marine in Nicaragua, I thought you might have some ideas to add to our recommendation."

Drake nodded and sat down in the chair in front of Casey's desk. "I need to ask a favor. Have you seen the coverage on the attorney in Portland who was just found crucified?"

"Hard to miss. It's the only story the major networks are covering this morning."

"Paul Benning was hired by the Archdiocese of Portland to investigate threats against the Church. Monday morning some parishioners found notices stuffed in their front doors telling them they had three days to convert to Islam, pay a religious tax or die. The attorney had the same notice stuffed in his mouth. No one's claiming responsibility and the FBI says it doesn't have any leads. Paul wanted me to ask if perhaps Kevin could take a quick troll through terrorist social media and see if anyone's bragging about it."

"I'll tell Kevin to have a look. Have you talked to Liz about it?"

"I did last night. She reached out to a friend in the NCTC who said the only thing she was aware of was a lot of teenage girls being recruited online by ISIS. They're given a mentor who encourages them to come up with their own terror plot. This could be what's going on in Portland. I'll go see Kevin and then get to work on those files."

Drake left Casey's office and took the stairs to the floor below to the IT/cyber security and intelligence divisions of PSS. Kevin's office was in the far corner of a large, open workspace where employees monitored the IT systems and tested the firewalls of their assigned PSS clients.

The young hacker sat with his hands flying over a clicking keyboard, peering at one of four flat screen monitors on his desk. A can of Red Bull was within reach of his left hand. The sleeves of his light blue button-down collar shirt were rolled up to his elbows and his tousled dirty-blond hair was shorter than Drake had seen it. On the beach, Kevin would look like just another surfer dude.

"Morning Kevin. Got a minute?"

Without taking his eyes off the monitor, Kevin's fingers kept flying. "Just a sec, let me finish this line of code."

Drake waited patiently for him to finish.

With a flourish like a concert pianist finishing a performance, Kevin turned and saw who was standing in his open doorway. He jumped up to shake Drake's hand.

"Mr. Drake, good to see you."

"Good to see you too, Kevin. I have a favor to ask."

Chapter Fourteen

DRAKE WORKED through the morning on the first file on his desk. A PSS client was working on counter-drone technology for the Defense Advanced Research Projects Agency (DARPA), an agency of the U.S. Department of Defense. It was developing a laser-based weapon to detect and destroy small UAVs that could threaten forces and military targets. The suspected drone manufacturer who had lured away one of the client's key employees was believed to be unaware of its Chinese holding company's interest in the client's counter-drone technology.

His solution wasn't all that creative, but it would be effective. PSS had become a business partner in the FBI's CounterIntelligence Strategic Partnership Program (CISPP) after thwarting a sarin gas attack on Seattle's light rail trains earlier in the year. As a Business Alliance partner, Drake would recommend that the client advise the CISPP of its concerns and let the FBI handle the matter.

He had just started on the second file when the young PSS hacker knocked on his open office door.

"There are some sick young people out there, Mr. Drake."

Drake waved him in. "What did you find?"

"That ISIS has a very sophisticated propaganda machine. There are as many as two hundred thousand pro-ISIS messages posted each day on social media. ISIS mass-produces slick videos and action films that target teens and appeal to their sense of belonging and purpose. Girls as young as thirteen are told they can become a 'revered wife' and be loved and cared for. Can you imagine wanting to be the bride of some bearded ISIS fighter in Syria?"

"I can't, Kevin. Anything about what's going on in Portland?"

"There are a lot of posts praising the killing of the attorney but nothing about who did it. The only thing I could find was a thread about someone at a community college in Portland recruiting women for ISIS."

"Were you able to identify the community college?"

"It was abbreviated as PCCC. I think it's the Cascade campus of Portland Community College."

"But there was nothing that tied the recruiting of women who want to be warriors for Islam to the murder of the attorney? Was there any mention of the notices to convert to Islam or die?"

"Not that I could find. Do you want me to keep looking?"

Drake gazed out the window for a moment. "No, that's all for now. Thanks Kevin."

"Any time, Mr. Drake."

He remembered that he had promised to call Liz when he got to Seattle.

"Hi beautiful."

"Let me close my door. I may have something for you."

Drake heard her high heels on the hardwood floor of her office crossing to the door and returning.

"You were right; the FBI knows more than it's sharing with Paul. Michael Brennan had been receiving threats. He represented the archdiocese in the sexual abuse lawsuits against its priests. They think someone abused by a priest is responsible for the threats and the murder."

"That doesn't make any sense, Liz. Why the elaborate hoax of threatening fellow parishioners when the target was just Brennan? They could have killed him without trying to make this look like a terrorist plot."

"That might be exactly why they did it."

"Is the FBI interviewing all of the plaintiffs in the sexual abuse cases?"

"That's the plan."

"And once again the FBI is doing everything it can to avoid saying this might be terrorism. Are they even considering that possibility?"

"My friend said they did before they learned about the threats Brennan had been receiving."

Drake sighed. "Well, at least Paul can tell the archbishop that the FBI doesn't think there's a real threat against the church or its parishioners. Let's pray the FBI is right this time."

"Are you driving back to Portland tonight?"

"I'm taking a file with me so I can get out of here before the traffic is bad. I'll call you when I get home."

"Be safe and give Lancer a hug for me."

He knew this wasn't the first time or the last time the FBI would tell people they didn't need to worry about terrorism at home. He understood the reason for minimizing fear and preventing panic, but there was something callous about the way the FBI had so quickly dismissed the terrorism angle.

There could be a sexually abused person out there with the cunning to plan a murder and make it look like terrorism. If there was, the FBI had made the right choice to investigate it that way. But if there wasn't, and there were terrorists warning Catholic parishioners to convert or die who had killed Michael Brennan, his death wouldn't be the end of this.

Drake was deep in thought when Casey stepped into his office.

"Do you want to get something to eat?"

"What did you have in mind?"

"There's a Thai place that I want to try. We can have it delivered if you want."

"Sounds good. There's something I want to run by you. We can discuss it over lunch."

"Let me go order our lunch and I'll be right back."

When Casey left, Drake opened his laptop and checked to make sure a new employee PSS had recently decided to hire was on the job and ready for an assignment.

Casey returned and sat down in front of his desk.

"How's the new hire from Denver working out?"

"I think she'll fit right in. She's qualified and tough. She has a level one black belt in Krav Maga and she's fearless. I've watched her practice with Morales."

"Did she tell you much about the undercover work that she did in Denver?"

"That's the reason she applied for a job here after she left Denver. She was working undercover, getting close to Sinaloa leaders in Denver. When she came up with enough evidence for the arrest of seven young Hondurans who were bringing in brown powder heroin, they were all released on their own recognizance.

"She was sure she'd been made, but she'd also had enough of Denver's catch-and-release program and quit. If guys say they're indigent in Denver, they release them without bail and make them pinky swear they'll show up in court. They rarely do. The seven Hondurans disappeared and are probably doing the same thing in some other city."

"Her file says she's twenty-seven, five feet five and weighs one hundred twenty pounds. She looks like she could pass for someone ten years younger. Do you think she could?"

"Do what, pass for a seventeen-year-old?"

"Yes."

"Why?"

"Someone's recruiting young women at a Portland community college to become warriors for Islam. I think it might connected in some way to the murder of Michael Brennan and the threats to the Catholic Church. I'd like you to send her in undercover and see what she can find out."

"Will the archdiocese pay for this?"

"If she finds something helpful, I'm sure they will. If she doesn't, I'll pay for her time there."

"All right, I'll have her come up so you can brief her. When she's in Portland, she'll report to you. Will one week be enough or do you think it will take longer than that?"

"I'd like to move fast on this, so one week will hopefully be enough."

Chapter Fifteen

ZAL NASIR WAS a thirty-year-old employee of the Intel Corporation in Hillsboro, Oregon. He had a Master's Degree in Computer Science from McGill University in Montreal, Canada, and worked in the Data Center Solutions division of Intel, its software company. He was a Shia Muslim and founder of the Islamic Revolutionary Council of America, the IRCA.

The members of the Council were young, professional men who were smarter than the old leaders of the Sunni terror group ISIS. But they were also students of the tactics that ISIS used more crudely. They considered themselves to be Persians by heritage and therefore enemies of Wahhabism, the austere faith of Saudi Arabia and ISIS that insisted on the literal translation of the Koran.

He was now Samantha Taylor's real handler, after they had discovered what ISIS and Ari Ahmadi, her professor and seducer, were doing. Ahmadi was good, but they were better. They'd found a way to get past Ahmadi's firewalls when his efforts for ISIS came to the attention of the Council. The professor had sold ISIS on the assault on the Catholic Church as an attack on Christians and the Communist Pope in Rome.

The truth was Ahmadi just wanted revenge for losing his more esteemed position at the university by stealing from the accounts of Catholic parishioners and recouping his loss of income and savings after being fired and having to defend himself at his termination hearing.

Samantha Taylor had been carefully recruited in the same way Ahmadi had first recruited her, with a twist; using her bi-sexual appetite against her. Ahmadi was a pure Wahhabist and didn't tolerate lesbian relationships. When they convinced her they were more tolerant and would continue to allow her to pursue her warrior dreams, she had pledged her allegiance to the Council and agreed to continue posing as Ahmadi's recruit and lover.

But now it was time for Ahmadi to disappear. The Council's plan that Sam had gotten Ahmadi to approve, to post convert or die notices and then later attack the churches, could not be allowed to be traced back to them. With Ahmadi's past relationship with the attorney, it would only be a matter of time before someone made the connection. Then Ahmadi's relationship to Sam would lead the authorities to her, and then possibly to the Council, and that would be a disaster.

Nasir waited for Sam to get off the MAX Blue Line at the Hillsboro station and make her way to his idling black BMW M5. As soon as she was seated beside him, he began her briefing.

"The Council has decided it's time to silence Ahmadi. Take everyone to his safe house across the river in Vancouver then come back tonight. Send him a text message saying that you need to see him. I'll have two brothers meet you at the condo. All you have to do is get them inside and they will do the rest."

Sam turned in her seat to face him. The movement pulled her tight skirt higher, exposing more thigh than Zal needed to see. He was more than aware of the way she used the promise of sex to get her way. She had been trying to get him to her bed since he became her handler.

"What if he won't see me?"

Nasir pointedly glanced down at her bared leg. "I think you'll find a way to make him want to see you."

"Am I authorized to execute the plan next Tuesday?"

"Yes. I'll let you know if there are any changes."

Sam turned to face forward and started to say something then stopped. She nodded once then got out of the car.

Nasir watched her walk back to the MAX light rail station. She exuded sexuality in everything she did; the way she walked, the way she carried herself, the way she dressed and the way she seduced you with her eyes. But he knew her for what she was, a psychopath with a blood lust. But something had changed in her with the killing of the attorney. The wildness he'd seen in her eyes when they'd planned the crucifixion and beheading was replaced with a cold, calm steeliness. She'd become the perfect weapon for America, a beautiful, young seductress who was trained and loved to kill.

He left the station parking lot and drove to the Orenco Taphouse where two brothers were waiting for him. He found a parking space across the street from where they were sitting at an outside table and checked to see if anyone was paying too much attention to them.

Thoroughly Americanized, they were clean-shaven young professionals wearing sunglasses in the afternoon sun.

They had chilled glasses of microbrew in front of them on the table and a plate of nachos.

Nasir nodded to them as he walked by and entered the Taphouse to get a beer. He returned with a glass of his favorite Boneyard IPA and sat down.

"She will go to his condo tonight and let you in. Park somewhere nearby and wait for my call. She'll give him an injection of the propofol he gave her for the attorney. When you get inside, strip him and put him in the Jacuzzi tub he likes so much. Slit his wrists and he'll bleed out before he can regain consciousness. When the police investigate his suicide, they'll find enough on his laptop to link him to the attorney. Any questions?"

"Security at the condo?"

"She will buzz you in. There are cameras. Wear ball caps and sunglasses and dress like college students."

"Does she leave with us?"

"She'll stay to sanitize the condo and then leave. Don't worry; she knows what she's doing."

"She'd better. Tuesday will be a massive blow to this country if she pulls it off."

"If Allah wills it, she will. Meet me at the airport Monday night as planned, and we'll watch the news from sunny California."

Nasir left first and went back to work. The benefit of flex hours, he'd found, was that he could take care of his duties anytime of the day or night. The current mission he'd planned for the Council had taken a year in the planning after gaining the allegiance of Sam and training her.

As far as he could find, there was nothing that connected Sam to him or the Council. Tonight would be the first time she'd met anyone else that she knew was involved with the Council.

They were careful and operated completely under the radar of all the security and intelligence services. All Council members, and now Sam and her warriors, had erased their digital footprint to avoid detection by masking their IP addresses used to connect them to the internet. They'd disabled the tracking software in their phones and knew how to jam the Wi-Fi signals used by surveillance devices.

They were invisible in the land of their enemy and would succeed because of it.

Chapter Sixteen

IT WAS six thirty Wednesday evening when Drake and Carol Sanchez stopped at Stanford's Restaurant and Bar at Jantzen Beach in Portland for something to eat. It had taken her five minutes after hearing about the new assignment to retrieve a backpack from her locker and be ready to go. She said it had everything she needed for a one-week undercover gig in Portland.

Driving down I-5 from Seattle, Drake learned that the backpack was her go-bag. She always kept it nearby in case the Sinaloa cartel ever caught up with her. In addition to clothes, that included a pair of cutoffs she thought would be perfect attire for a student on campus during summer term, the bag contained cash, her Smith and Wesson M&P 9 Shield backup pistol and a CRKT Homefront Tactical knife. With her black belt in Krav Maga, Drake pitied the cartel thug who tried to take her down.

They were seated in a booth looking over their menus when Sanchez set hers down and looked up. "I'm new at PSS, do you mind if I ask you a question?"

"I don't mind. Ask away."

"You and the boss seem to be close. I know you're the company's attorney, but I'm guessing your relationship is more than just the attorney/client thing."

Drake couldn't keep himself from smiling. "You really are new to PSS. I'd have thought Morales would have shared some of our exploits when you two were working out. Mike and I go way back. We were a team in Delta Force before he started with PSS."

"Why did you leave the army?"

"It's a long story. Let's just say we left for some of the same reasons you left the Denver PD."

"Because the system didn't have your back?"

"Because the chain of command didn't."

The waiter arrived with two Coronas and took their orders: fish and chips for Drake and the prime rib for Sanchez. "This might be the last good meal I'll have for a while. Do you mind?" she'd explained.

Drake didn't. It was on the company credit card, and for all they knew she'd be eating ramen noodles for the rest of the week, depending on the contacts she was able to make.

His cell phone started playing *Up around the Bend* by Creedence Clearwater Revival, his new ringtone. Drake took it out of his pocket and read the message before summarizing it for Sanchez.

"You have a reservation at the Best Western at the Meadows. It's a mile or so from the campus and a five-minute walk to a light rail station at the Portland Meadows Race Track. We can get you a rental car if you want it, but you might have a little more freedom of movement without one."

"I'm used to walking. I won't need a car."

"If you're able to identify someone you think is

recruiting for the jihad, get the best facial shot you can to me and I'll get it to Kevin. He can get into the college database and get all the info on the student, if it is a student. He can also run the picture through our database facial recognition software."

"What do you want me to do if I identify our recruiter and she or he heads off campus? Should I follow them?"

"Just get the license and we'll run it. If they leave on foot or take the light rail somewhere, use your best judgment. Kevin will track your cell phone, so we'll always know where you are. Do you have a favorite rescue code?"

Sanchez thought for a moment. "There are enough Korean restaurants in big cities, so how about 'kimchi'? I hate the stuff, so you won't hear it unless it's an emergency."

"Okay, 'kimchi' it is."

Their waiter appeared just then with their orders. "Did I hear you folks want kimchi? I'm afraid it's not on our menu, the chef hates the stuff."

They both laughed and Drake waved off the puzzled waiter. "That's okay. We're fine. Thanks anyway."

The fish and chips were excellent and Sanchez appeared to love her prime rib, judging by the way she attacked it. By the time he finished his fish and half of his chips, she was forking the last bite of the steak into her mouth. Sanchez was going to fit right in at PSS. The only other person he knew who ate with such relish was Mike Casey, the CEO.

With their dinner tab paid plus a healthy tip for the puzzled waiter, Drake followed the GPS directions in his Cayman GTS over the two-point-one-mile route to the Best Western Inn at the Meadows.

When they stopped under the porte- cochère of the motel, Sanchez hopped out and reached back to get her backpack. "Will you be the only one here in Portland on this?"

"I will be your primary. A P.I. in my office will help if we need him. He's the one who asked us to look into ISIS recruiting at the college. He's a recently-retired sheriff's detective. You'll like him. Check in with me when you head over to the campus and then tomorrow every two hours."

"Good to know. I'll get my stuff in my room then I'll head over to the campus tonight to get the lay of the land."

"Happy hunting, Sanchez."

Drake waited until she entered the motel without looking back before he drove away. Regardless of what she found at the college, he was impressed with the newest PSS hire.

Chapter Seventeen

ARI AHMADI SAT in the living room of the Mountain View Suite in the Embassy Suites Hotel at Portland Airport. His laptop was on the coffee table in front of the sofa, next to a bottle of Johnnie Walker Blue Label he'd ordered from the bar.

He was watching the video feed from his condo. When he'd checked the feed from the safe house in Vancouver and saw that Sam and her warriors weren't there, he knew it was time to pack a bag and get out of town. He didn't know what she and her friend had in mind, but the fact that she'd disobeyed him was enough of a warning.

What bothered him the most wasn't her betrayal, it was that he'd misjudged her and thought she wasn't capable of it. He knew she was a pathological liar lacking remorse, that she was cunning and manipulative and promiscuous in her sexual behavior. But he was the one who helped in her radicalization and introduced her to jihad. As far as he knew, he was the only contact she had with anyone in the jihad. Apparently, he was wrong.

If she was taking orders from someone other than him, it meant he was no longer trusted. And that meant ISIS would deal with him sooner or later, the same way it dealt with infidel Christians, homosexuals and traitors.

He wasn't interested in hanging around until the axe fell. By morning, the software that he was running would deliver the money from the accounts of the wealthiest parishioners from the one hundred twenty-four parishes of the archdiocese into his off-shore account and he'd be able to live the life of an Arab prince. He wasn't a prince, of course, but with the work he'd done he deserved to live like one.

Ahmadi poured another two fingers of Scotch into his glass and continued watching the video feed from his condo. He owned the condo free and clear and no one would know that he was out of the country if he kept paying the utilities. He'd been paperless with all the companies that expected a payment from him and mail wouldn't be piling up in his mailbox in the lobby. Someone might wonder if he still lived in the condo, but by then it wouldn't matter.

What would matter was what Sam knew about him and his work for ISIS. That was the loose end he had to decide how to tie up.

SAM TAYLOR LEFT the safe house across the Columbia River in Vancouver in Ahmadi's Ford Excursion to drive to his condo. She didn't go back to the house she rented off campus for one of his favorite dresses because she wasn't sure that he'd buy her story about why she wasn't at the cabin. If he didn't believe her once she was in his condo, it wouldn't matter.

She would miss the sex. The professor was a good lover. But the Council had planned all along for him to be blamed for the attacks on the Catholic Church and the killing of the attorney. He was, after all, a Sunni Muslim and had served his purpose in the Council's plan.

She parked the big SUV on the street a block away and checked the time on her cell phone. She was ten minutes ahead of schedule and had time for a smoke before she called the men Zal was sending to help her with Ahmadi. Enough time for a good hit of weed.

Taking the joint she'd rolled before she left the safe house out of her black clutch, she lit it with her Bic lighter and inhaled deeply. First the head rush and then she started feeling the chill. It was too bad she never got the professor to smoke with her. He would have enjoyed the high.

After five minutes, she sent a text message to the number Zal gave her.

In place.

Within seconds, she received a reply.

Go.

She checked her clutch one more time to make sure the cap was secure on the syringe loaded with propofol and stepped down out of the Excursion. The black mini skirt she wore with high heels that exaggerated her gait made walking the block to the condo building take a little longer. But if the professor took a good look when she buzzed him, she knew he wouldn't be able to resist seeing her.

She was used to using the key card he'd given her to get into his condo. But this time she decided to be a little more cautious. If he was angry because she wasn't at the safe house, she wasn't sure what he would do and didn't want to take a chance. By buzzing him from the lobby, she would be able to gauge his mood.

Sam entered the condo building and walked across to the call box guests used to gain admission. Two men wearing blue windbreakers and Trail Blazers hats entered the lobby behind her and walked toward the elevator.

She entered the number for Ahmadi's condo and pushed the buzzer. "Professor, it's me. I need to see you."

She took two steps back so that she was fully in view of the security camera above the call box and waited.

There was no answer.

She stepped back to the call box and tried again.

"Please, Professor, I have to see you. Don't you want me anymore?"

She stepped back again and flirted with the security camera.

After a long minute, she walked over to the two men standing out of range of the security camera. "He should be there. He rarely goes out at night. Do you want to go up? I have a key card. He could be in the shower or something."

The men looked at each other while deciding. The shorter of the two nodded.

"Lead the way."

When the elevator reached the fourth and top floor, she led them down the hall to Ahmadi's condo and took out her key card. She inserted the card in the key card door lock and waited for the green light. When it flashed, she pulled down on the lever and opened the door.

The men rushed in before her, pulling pistols from the small of their backs, and searched the condo.

Ahmadi wasn't there. His laptop wasn't either.

It was on the coffee table in his suite at the hotel at Portland Airport where he was watching Sam and the two men in his condo.

Chapter Eighteen

CAROL SANCHEZ WALKED onto the Cascade campus of Portland State Community College early the next morning. Her destination was the College Center building she'd located the night before that housed two coffee shops and the Women's Resource Center.

Someone at PSS had a sense of humor it seemed. The registrar's office had been hacked to enroll her for the summer term in a sociology class called Sociology of Gender. Its focus was how socialization was affected by gender in various cultures.

It was the kind of class they thought she'd be interested in as a young Muslim woman trying to figure out how to survive in the misogynistic society of America. She hoped she could muster up the appropriate rage if she needed it in her new role.

She followed a girl whose eyes were glued to her iPhone with red Beats headphones covering her ears into the coffee shop. Other than the barista behind the counter, they were the only ones in the place.

Sanchez stood in line behind the girl and when she left with her coffee, ordered a cup of chai latte for herself. When she turned around, the girl had left the coffee shop.

Probably for the best, she didn't look like the talkative type. Even if I could get her to tear herself away from texting as fast as her little thumbs could move, that is.

Outside, in the morning sun that promised a warm August day, she wandered over to a bench in front of the Students' Union building. Three students were throwing a Frisbee back and forth, while another was practicing his hacky sack tricks.

Sanchez was beginning to think that the intelligence about teen girls being recruited for jihad here was unreliable. The campus was too laid back and lacked the fervor she'd experienced at the University of Colorado when she attended there. There were no postings for rallies or radical speakers that she'd seen in the Students' Union the night before.

She'd spent time on the social media sites maintained by the college for the benefit of its students; Facebook, Twitter, Instagram and YouTube. There was nothing that even came close to anyone supporting ISIS, much less recruiting for it.

She took her laptop out of her backpack that PSS gave her before she left with Drake and decided to check the sites again. As she was scrolling through the Facebook site, she saw someone approaching in her peripheral vision. She kept her head down, looking at the screen of her laptop, when a shadow stopped in front of her at ten o'clock.

Sanchez looked up and saw that the shadow was cast by the body of a large black man wearing a campus public safety officer badge on his blue uniform.

"Morning, miss. Are you a student here?"

"I am, why?"

"Because I haven't seen you on campus before."

Sanchez forced herself to laugh. "You got me. I enrolled for summer term to get used to it here before fall term. But I'm having a hard time getting to class during the summer. I'm trying to decide if I should drop some classes before the deadline."

"Do you live near here?"

The public safety officer didn't look old enough to have experience in law enforcement, but he was persistent and skillfully interrogating her. She needed to throw him off track and leave her alone.

"Are you hassling me because of my gender or because I'm not black? Either way, I'd like to be left alone."

"Why do you think I'm hassling you, miss? My job is to make sure this is a safe campus for students. I'm not sure you're a student. Do you have your student ID card with you?"

Sanchez smiled tightly and reached for her backpack. PSS had thought of everything, even providing her a current student ID card for the college.

"I'm sorry, Officer. I moved here to get away from treatment like this. I thought Portland would be different."

The ID card she handed him was in the name of Nailah Khauri. It wasn't a common Muslim name but easy enough to identify it as one.

Officer Samson studied the card and then handed it back to her. "Did the treatment you mentioned involve your religion?"

"It did, and, yes, I'm Muslim."

"Then I hope you'll like it here. We have quite a few Muslim students and I think they're getting along fine. Sorry about whatever happened before you moved here."

"You can't have many. I think I would recognize them."

"You will if you're on campus more often. There's a group of Muslim women that hang out in the Students' Union most afternoons. I apologize if I bothered you with my questions."

Officer Samson tipped his black baseball cap with gold PCC lettering and turned to walk away. Then he turned back.

"Miss, you might talk with that girl over there. She's kind of the leader of that group of Muslim women I mentioned in the Students' Union."

Sanchez looked in direction the officer nodded and saw a young woman wearing cutoffs, a tight white T-shirt, and khaki-colored Nike field boots marching east across the campus.

"Thanks, think I will."

Sanchez grabbed her backpack, slipped it on and followed the woman. Whoever she was, she had good taste in boots because Sanchez had a pair of the Nikes herself. She didn't wear them with cutoffs, but then she wasn't nineteen or twenty either.

The woman was on a mission, that was apparent by her pace and focus. She wasn't looking to the left or right, just straight ahead. She shouldered her way around the three Frisbee throwers blocking her path and never slowed.

At the east end of the campus, she turned south toward the Technology and Education Building. From her exploratory visit the night before, Sanchez knew the building housed the Cascade Computer Resource Center, where enrolled students could use over one hundred PCs for classwork. It also housed the offices of professors and part-time instructors on the upper floors.

The woman on a mission entered the building with Sanchez jogging behind to catch up. She slowed when she walked inside and saw the woman walking up a flight of stairs off to her right. Morning classes hadn't started yet and no one was taking the stairs behind the woman, leaving Sanchez no choice but to follow her as inconspicuously as possible.

When the woman turned the corner at the top of the first flight of stairs, Sanchez ran to catch up, taking two stairs at a time. When she got to the top, she caught a flash of white just turning the corner half a flight ahead of her.

Past the second floor and halfway to the third, Sanchez saw another flash of white and heard the door open to the third floor. She ran up and caught the door before it closed, pausing to listen for footsteps down the hall.

When she heard the gripping sound of the lug-patterned soles of the boots marching far enough down the polished vinyl-tiled floor of the hall, she opened the door. The woman was at the far end of the hall, knocking on a door.

There was no place to go other than down the hall toward the woman. Sanchez ducked back, closed the door and started down as fast as she could. When she reached the ground floor, she spotted an empty lounge chair in the lobby and quickly sat down.

By the time she'd taken her laptop out of her backpack and opened it, the woman came down the stairs and walked by, eyeing her suspiciously. Sanchez kept her eyes on the blank screen of her laptop until the woman left the building.

She might have been made, judging by the way the woman looked at her, but it probably didn't matter. If she was confronted, she would tell the truth and hope that it was convincing. She asked the public safety officer about other Muslim women on campus and he had pointed her out. All she wanted to do was talk, but when she saw her knocking on some professor's door, she'd decided this wasn't the time.

With that explanation in mind, Sanchez jumped and followed the woman across the campus to a student parking lot. And she watched the woman get in a late-model, white Ford Excursion and drive away.

Sanchez was close enough to use her phone camera to take a quick picture of the Excursion's license plate.

Chapter Nineteen

SAMANTHA TAYLOR WATCHED the girl who followed her across the campus stop at the edge of the student parking lot. Before she turned out of the lot onto the street, the girl pulled a cell phone out of her back pocket and pointed it at the rear of the Excursion.

Sam yelled and slammed the steering wheel with both hands. She had been so careful on campus that she thought she'd gone unnoticed. And now someone was following her and could link her to Professor Ahmadi if she ran the license plate of his Excursion.

The girl had to be stopped before she could do that.

Sam made a U-turn in the middle of the block and sped back to where the girl was still standing. Rolling down the window, she confronted the girl.

"Something I can help you with?"

The girl looked to be in her late teens and dressed like it; denim cutoff shorts, a white T-shirt tied off at the waist and a pair of ice-blue running shoes.

"I was going to leave a note on your car tomorrow. My name's Nailah Khauri."

"Why were you going to leave a note on my car?"

"I'm new here. I want to meet some students like me. The security guard said you might know some."

Sam looked for signs of deception and didn't see any. If the girl was trouble, it was only because she had the license plate of the professor's SUV on her cell phone.

"What kind of students are you wanting to meet?"

"Students who can help me know how to get along in this city."

"You mean Muslim students?"

The girl nodded and smiled. "Yes, Muslim girls who go to school here."

Sam smiled back. "I'm Muslim and I'm meeting some Muslim friends of mine. Get in and I'll introduce you to them."

The girl ran around the front of the Excursion and got in. Sam reached across to shake hands.

"You said you're new here. Where're you from?"

"Denver."

Sam drove around the parking lot and back onto the street. "Why'd you leave?"

The girl took a deep breath and looked out the window to her right. "I had to get away from my father."

"Was he abusive?

"No, he didn't like my boyfriend."

"Why'd you come to Portland?"

"I heard it was pretty."

Sam threw her head back and laughed. "Yeah, it's pretty, just not so much for Muslims."

"What do you mean?"

"You'll find out soon enough."

They turned onto North Killingsworth Street and drove on without talking until they took the entrance to I-5 North.

"Where are we going?"

"My friends rent a house in Vancouver. It's not far."

Sam smiled at thought of calling Professor Ahmadi her friend after what she had attempted to do the night before. But he did lease the house and several others in and around Portland to use as safe houses for his ISIS activities. And she had been 'friendly' with him.

The girl looked out at the Columbia River as they crossed over it on the I-5 Bridge and seemed to be taking in the scenery.

"Have you been across the river to Vancouver before?"

"No, this is my first time."

They took the exit off I-5 onto East Mill Plain Boulevard and drove east to Northeast 124th Avenue and then turned north. Near the end of the street, they pulled to the curb in front of an older, two-story house. The brown lawn hadn't been mowed in a while and the peeling beige paint had faded to nearly white.

Sam nodded toward the house as she took the keys out of the ignition and put them in her black running belt waist pack. "It doesn't look like much, but it's cheap and has a lot of room. Come on in and I'll introduce you to my friends."

She walked around the front of the SUV and waited for the girl who was hesitant to get out. She waved and flashed a big smile. "Come on, you'll like my friends."

Sam followed her up a cracked and buckling cement walkway and leaned around her to open the front door. As soon as the girl stepped inside, she stopped to stare at a line of women wearing black T-shirts and camo pants facing her. Sam took the syringe of propofol meant for Ahmadi the night before out of her waist pack and plunged it into the side of the girl's neck.

Chapter Twenty

DRAKE WAS in his office Thursday morning, trying to get in another good day's work to get caught up. By nine o'clock he'd finished the pile of files Margo had deposited on his desk when he was in Seattle. When he returned to the break room downstairs from his loft with his second cup of coffee, Margo pointed to another stack of files on the corner of her desk without saying a word.

He grabbed the new files and managed a tight smile. "Slave driver."

"Black woman's revenge. Buzz me when you're ready to go over your schedule for next week."

The office chill had improved a little; from thirty-two degrees to maybe a cool forty-two degrees. Not much, but progress.

At ten minutes after nine o'clock, he heard Paul Benning coming down the stairs from their condo a floor above the office. He didn't stop at his wife's desk but said in passing, "Hold his calls."

After a run up the stairs to the loft, he stood in front of

Drake's desk slightly out of breath. "The archdiocese wants to see us this morning, sooner rather than later."

"What's happened?"

"They're getting calls from panicked parishioners. The first couple of calls came just after six thirty this morning. Some of the parishioners who are stockbrokers checked their personal accounts and found they had zero balances. After the warning they received saying convert or pay a religious tax or die, they asked if the archdiocese thought their accounts had been drained by the terrorists. They were told it was unlikely, with what the FBI had advised them, that it was a hate crime made to look like terrorism. When the number of calls exploded to over thirty, they're not so sure now. They want us to tell them what we think. They've called the FBI and the PPD, so it'll be a lively gathering."

Drake scooted his chair back and motioned for Benning to take a seat. "What do we know about the parishioners with empty accounts?"

"They are some of the wealthiest of the Catholics in the Portland Archdiocese. I don't know anything else about them."

"From what you've told me, the only thing that might link this to the convert or die notices is the option to pay a religious tax within the three-day window. The notices were delivered Monday and the accounts might have been emptied the evening of the third day. That's pretty thin."

"It is, but it's a connection a lot of them are going to make."

"This also could be related to the crucifixion of the attorney for the archdiocese. A plaintiff from one of the clergy sexual abuse cases could have delivered the notices to make this look like a terrorist thing. Kill Brennan the way ISIS has been killing Christians then hack the archdiocese to get the identities of the wealthiest Catholics and empty their accounts to recoup the damages they didn't get in the trials."

"That's pretty thin as well, but it's probably what the FBI will suggest to keep from saying terrorists are behind this."

"Who are we meeting with at the archdiocese?"

"The chief administrative officer. Her name is Kelly Johannsen. She's handling this for the archbishop. Mid-thirties, MBA from the Mendoza School of Business, University of Notre Dame, and tough as nails."

Drake got up and grabbed his blazer from the coat tree and slipped it on over his blue button-down long sleeve shirt and yellow tie with blue spots. "All right, let's go meet Ms. Johannsen."

Benning told Margo where they were going and led the way up the stairs to the secured- parking garage and his new Ford F-150 pickup. It adjoined the one hundred and eighty condominiums that were directly behind and above the five-hundred-feet stretch of retail shops and offices accessed by the esplanade along the river and marina.

The offices of the Archdiocese of Portland, the second oldest archdiocese in America, were located on East Burnside Street. It took fifteen minutes in light traffic to drive across the river on the Hawthorne Bridge to SE 26th, then SE Stark to East Burnside.

The offices of the archdiocese were in an ordinary, two-story brick building that looked like the administrative buildings of a school district. Security was present at the main entrance and Benning and Drake were allowed to enter after their names were checked off a list of approved visitors for the day.

They took stairs to the second floor and were again

stopped by a security guard who checked his list before they were directed to a large, crowded conference room. Three groups of men huddled around a long conference table.

Benning nodded toward two of the groups. "FBI and Portland Police."

Drake nodded to the other group. "U.S. Attorney's Office."

One of the two men from the U.S. Attorney's Office walked over and shook hands with Drake, who introduced him to Benning. "Paul, this is Brady Newman, Assistant Special Agent in Charge of the Portland Field Office. Brady, this is Paul Benning. He's been advising the archdiocese on the notices the parishioners received Monday."

"In what capacity, Mr. Benning, if I might ask?"

"I'm a former MCSO detective, Mr. Newman. Now I'm a private detective working out of Mr. Drake's office."

"What's your involvement, Drake?"

"Sticking his nose where it doesn't belong," a man with a scowl on his face interjected from ten feet away as he approached from a huddle of FBI men.

"Nice to see you too, Rand."

"What are you doing here, Drake?"

"Ms. Johannsen invited me, Rand. She's probably interested in why the FBI hasn't done more to help the archdiocese this week."

The FBI man started forward to invade Drake's personal space, but the other attorney blocked the movement with his right arm. "You two have a history?"

Drake smiled. "I prevented the assassination of the Secretary of Homeland Security a while back and the FBI didn't appreciate it. I guess you could call that an institutional history. Rand wasn't around back then."

"Drake thinks there's a terrorist under every rock

because he was Special Forces in Iraq. There are no terrorists involved in this, Drake, so you can leave now."

"How did you establish that, Rand?"

"The same way we do everything, Drake, by thoroughly investigating the matter. This is a computer crime with someone trying to make it look like terrorism to throw us off. Stay out of it and let the professionals handle it."

"Is that why you're here, Brady? You're computer crimes with the criminal division, right?"

"Yes because that's all we have to go on right now. We're checking to see if the IT system here was hacked to identify these wealthy parishioners."

Just then, a young woman with curly, auburn hair wearing a black skirt and a white blouse entered the conference room. "Mr. Benning and Mr. Drake? Ms. Johannsen will see you now."

Drake couldn't resist smiling at Rand Gibson as he followed Paul Benning out of the conference room.

Chapter Twenty-One

KELLY JOHANNSEN'S office was modern and bright. China-white walls hung with vibrant floral watercolor paintings above a dove-gray carpet. Her desk was a simple glass rectangle sitting on four black metal legs with a rose-colored Mac Book Pro sitting on it.

She stood as they entered and walked around her desk with hand extended. She was a trim five six or seven with short, ash-blond hair and piercing blue eyes. "Thank you for coming, Paul. You must be Adam Drake."

Drake shook her firm, cool hand and nodded. "Pleasure to meet you, Ms. Johannsen."

"Please have a seat and call me Kelly. Would either of you like coffee or tea?" she said as she moved back behind her desk.

"I've had my morning quota, but I can't speak for Paul."

"I'm fine, thanks Kelly. How many calls have you had from parishioners so far this morning?"

Kelly Johannsen sat down with a sigh as she glanced at the screen of her laptop. "Sixty-eight so far. We estimate the combined losses will be around twenty million dollars. This is a disaster that will only be made worse if we find out it's because someone hacked our records here."

"How would hacking your records provide the information for this large a theft?"

"Are you Catholic, Mr. Drake?"

"No, I'm not."

"In addition to the personal information we have about each parishioner, quite a few of our wealthy ones tithe a set amount that comes automatically out of their accounts. I imagine it would be quite easy for someone smart enough to get into our IT system to obtain that information and use it to drain these accounts."

"Have you talked with the FBI yet, Kelly?" Benning asked.

"Only briefly. They're trying to first confirm that our system was hacked and then go from there."

"I know you discussed this with Paul previously, but have they come up with anything new about the notices and threats or the murder of Michael Brennan?"

The archdiocese CAO studied Drake for a moment before she answered. "I'll assume you know about the lawsuits we've had to handle and that we settled them out of court. The FBI seems to believe that some disgruntled plaintiff, who wanted more than he settled for, is behind all of this. I don't believe that. Michael Brennan was a gentle man and dealt with all the plaintiffs courteously and with respect. The FBI doesn't know this, and I'll ask you to honor his memory by not repeating it, but Michael was sexually abused by a priest when he was an altar boy. He had great empathy for the victims."

Drake nodded to indicate the information would remain

confidential before asking, "Who do you believe is behind all this?"

Kelly Johannsen's eyes took on a steely look and her lips pressed together ever so slightly as she locked eyes with him. "I believe it's a jihadist or jihadists following the inciting rhetoric of the thugs from ISIS; kill Christians wherever you find them."

"Are you telling the parishioners that you suspect Islamic extremists are behind this?"

"No, Mr. Drake, we're not. You choose to call them Islamic extremists. Our Pope calls them violent individuals, says that every religion has them, and denies that Islam is a violent religion. As a church, we pray for these individuals and for reconciliation among all religions."

Drake thought he detected a touch of sarcasm in her voice and smiled. "I heard that was the Pope's position. But surely you could warn your parishioners about the 'violent individuals' you suspect."

"I could but not as long as the FBI advises me that this is probably someone with a grudge against Michael Brennan. Besides, the demand was to convert or pay a religious tax. If it isn't someone with a grudge and the individuals responsible for this are 'violent individuals', their demand has been met. Isn't it safe to assume the remaining parishioners are safe and will be left alone?"

Drake couldn't refute the logic of her assumption. "What is it you would like us to do, then?"

"Paul told me about the company where you serve as special counsel and what its capabilities are. I'm inclined to think it's all hyperbole, but with twenty million dollars stolen that we may have some responsibility for, I must do everything possible to get that money back. I'd like to retain you and your company to do that for us."

"Why not save your money and let the FBI handle it?"

"Because someone clever enough to hack our sophisticated IT system isn't going to move the money somewhere the FBI can legally recover it. Restitution, if there's a conviction down the line, isn't a realistic outcome. I need someone who thinks out of the box. If what Paul tells me is true, I believe that's you."

"I'll need Paul to help me, if PSS agrees to take this on for you."

"Certainly."

Drake stood and waited for Ms. Johannsen to walk around the desk and shook her hand. "I'll be in touch as soon as I discuss this with PSS."

Kelly ushered them down the hall past the crowded conference room to the stairs and said in parting, "I look forward to hearing from you. Good luck."

Chapter Twenty-Two

CAROL SANCHEZ REGAINED consciousness and evaluated her situation before she opened her eyes. A slight movement of her wrists and ankles confirmed her impression that she was bound and sitting in a straight-back chair. The bindings were narrow and tight, disposable restraints or zip ties, the kind law enforcement favored.

Wherever she was, she knew she was inside and that it was warm. She could hear voices in the other room beyond a door, judging from the muffled sounds.

It was a good thing it was warm because she was naked.

The last thing she remembered was standing in front of a row of young-looking women in black T-shirts and camo pants. Maybe they were the voices in the next room. The women hadn't looked like a group of Muslim students. They looked more like the pictures of Kurdish women fighting ISIS in Syria.

What the hell did I get myself into? No panic, you've been in tighter spots before. Drake will know I'm in trouble when I don't check in. He can locate my phone and ride to the rescue—if my phone's still around here somewhere.

The noise in the other room died down and the door swung open hard, banging back against the wall. The woman in the cutoffs and Nike field boots marched over and stood with her hands on her hips.

"The college says you're Nailah Khauri, a new student. You say you're Muslim. I don't believe any of it, Nailah, or whoever you are. Recite something from the Koran. Describe the mosque you attended as a kid. Give me something before I hurt you to make you talk."

Sanchez had to decide; be strong to gain their confidence or be weak and needy.

"Who are you and why am I tied to this chair?"

The woman lunged forward and slapped her hard on the left side of her head. "Answer me!"

Sanchez glared at her defiantly. "Care to try that when my hands aren't tied?"

The woman turned to the others who had filed in behind her and laughed. "Oh, you'll get your chance, Nailah. Convince me you're Muslim."

"My father is Egyptian and Muslim. My mother is Spanish and not Muslim. She didn't convert and didn't attend mosque. I didn't either, my mother wouldn't allow it. That's why my father beat me."

"Why do you want to hang out with Muslim women if that's true?"

Sanchez lifted her chin and looked around at the other women. "Because they might have had the same experience with their fathers and understand what's it like to grow up with a man like that."

The woman considered her answer then pivoted on the

heel of her boot and left the room. The others followed her and shut the door behind them.

Sanchez's left ear was ringing and she hoped her eardrum wasn't ruptured. The leader reminded her of the gang leaders she'd dealt with when she was undercover in Denver, always the meanest and most violent to assert their leadership. This woman's eyes were blazing with something extra, though, like the look Mel Gibson would get when he wanted to appear crazy in the role of Martin Riggs in the movie *Lethal Weapon*. Except with this woman, the look probably wasn't acting, more a controlled madness.

She wasn't afraid of her in a fair fight, but didn't think any fight with her would be fair.

SAM LED her warriors to the kitchen at the back of the house. "I don't know who she is, but we can't take any chances. One of you take her phone and drop it in a garbage can on campus. Allacia and Safiya, drive her to Ahmadi's cabin at the coast. Give her some propofol for the trip then throw a blanket over her and put her on the floor behind you. At the cabin, tie her up like she is now and keep an eye on her. Give her water to keep her alive, but there's no need to feed her. When it's time for us, I'll call you. We'll leave her there to die. When they find her, they'll think she's one of Ahmadi's girls.

"In the meantime, I want one of you at the front door and one of you upstairs as lookouts. Get your weapons and rotate shifts among the rest of you every two hours. We won't be stopped, inshallah, but if they come for us, fight as you've been trained. I need to go check on something. I'll be back in a couple of hours."

Ariana raised her hand. "If the police show up before we leave, what do we do with her?"

"If they do, we'll know she isn't who she says she is. Kill her."

Chapter Twenty-Three

DRAKE AND BENNING waited until they got into Benning's truck before they discussed their meeting with Kelly Johannsen.

"What do you think?" Benning asked.

"She's in a tough spot. She thinks this is terrorism; the FBI thinks the convert or die notices are a cover for a revenge killing and theft. She can't warn people it's terrorism and have the FBI contradict her."

"Do you think it's terrorism?"

"Aside from the notices and the crucifixion, there's nothing that says the FBI isn't right. My gut says she's probably right. It's a pretty elaborate red-herring to pull off for a cyber-thief when he could just hack the archdiocese and take the money. Why go to all this trouble?"

"Could it be organized crime trying to make us think it's terrorism?"

"Possibly, but why add a capital offense to cybercrime when it's not necessary? There's too much that doesn't make sense."

Drake took his cell phone out of the breast pocket of his blazer and looked to see if Carol Sanchez had checked in. She'd sent him a text before she left to go to the college campus that morning, but he saw that she hadn't sent him anything in the last two and a half hours. She was new, but he was her only backup and she needed to keep him informed.

"Paul, let's swing by the PCC Cascade campus on the way back to the office. Carol Sanchez hasn't checked in since this morning."

As Benning continued driving west on East Burnside, Drake called Kevin McRoberts in Seattle.

"Kevin, Adam Drake. Run a quick check on Carol Sanchez's phone and tell me where she is."

"Just take a moment, Mr. Drake. Umm, she's on the PCC campus, looks like she's just north of the Students' Union in an open area."

"Thanks Kevin. Did you get anything more on social media about ISIS recruiting young women on college campuses?"

"Nothing new, sir, just more of the same."

"All right, Kevin. When I get back to my office, I'm calling Mr. Casey about a new assignment for you. If he approves it, I'll brief you on it. I think you'll have fun with this one."

"Thanks Mr. Drake. Look forward to hearing about it."

Benning turned north on Northeast Martin Luther King Jr. Blvd. toward the PCC Cascade campus. "Are you going to turn Kevin loose to find the parishioners' stolen money?"

"If anyone can find it, Kevin can. I don't care how clever this thief was; he had to leave crumbs along the way. Kevin will find them."

Benning turned west again on North East Killingsworth Street. The campus was nineteen blocks away.

"Drop me off at the southern end of the campus and I'll go find Sanchez. Circle the campus and pick me up where you let me out. I won't be long."

Drake got out when Benning pulled to the curb at the corner of Killingsworth Street and Mississippi Avenue. He walked north onto the campus and asked the first student he met where the Students' Union was. After pulling a headphone out of his ear and taking his eyes off his iPhone for a second, the boy with an adolescent beard hooked a thumb over his left shoulder. "Next building."

The Students' Union was a modern, three-story, soft red brick and dark gray wood-sided building with random floor-to-ceiling blocks of windows across its façade. It faced a large plaza with bike racks and raised beds of evergreen shrubs and clusters of arborvitae scattered around.

Students crisscrossed the plaza with their heads down, holding their phones or occasionally an open book in front of them. Drake stopped at the edge of the plaza, looking for Carol Sanchez. He didn't see her anywhere and called Kevin McRoberts.

"Kevin, I'm standing on the plaza in front of the Students' Union and Sanchez isn't here. Locate her phone again for me."

"It shows her phone is still there, Mr. Drake. Maybe fifty feet northwest of the Students' Union at the edge of the open area."

Drake walked to the western edge of the plaza. The only thing he saw ahead of him was a black metal waste receptacle. He had a sinking feeling that was where he'd find her phone.

"Kevin, I think I know where her phone is. Can you trace where it's been this morning?"

"On it."

The phone was lying under a pile of crumpled napkins and white Starbucks paper coffee cups. Drake wrapped one of the napkins around the phone when he retrieved it in case it had fingerprints on it that could be useful.

Drake's CCR ringtone started. "Her phone traveled from the Best Western south to the campus then moved north on I-205 across the Columbia River to a neighborhood in Vancouver, Washington, then back to the campus where you are now."

"She met someone and took a ride with them. She doesn't have a car. Can you get me to this neighborhood across the river?"

"Mr. Drake, I can get you within five feet of where the car she was in parked."

"Stay on the line, Kevin. Paul Benning drove me here. When I get back to his pickup, you can guide us across the river."

It took him two minutes to jog back to the pickup point where he told Benning to meet him.

"You see her?"

Drake held up the napkin-wrapped cell phone. "This was in a trash receptacle. Kevin traced its movement this morning and says it traveled over the river to Vancouver and then back to this campus. Either she ditched it here or someone did it for her. Let's go see what's across the river."

"What if she found the recruiters and she's trying to get recruited?"

"I thought of that. But why leave her phone? It's new. The only person she was to call is me. My number's unlisted. Even if they could find out who I am, all they would know is that she called an attorney. We'll be careful across the river when we get there so we don't blow her cover."

It was eleven o'clock Thursday morning as Benning pulled back onto Killingsworth Street on the way to a neighborhood in Vancouver.

Chapter Twenty-Four

THE DRIVE from the community college campus across the eight-lane Glenn L. Jackson Memorial Bridge spanning the Columbia River to the neighborhood in Vancouver took twenty-four minutes. The house was in the middle of the block and in need of some tender loving care; the paint was peeling in places and the lawn hadn't been mowed for some time.

Drake matched the address to the one on his phone as they drove by. "That's the place. Let's drive around the block and find somewhere to pull over. It doesn't look like anyone's home."

Benning turned left at the next corner and drove around the block. Before turning back onto the street, he pulled to the curb at the corner. The old house was half a block away with a clear line of sight at ten o'clock.

Two curtained dormer windows broke up the west-sloping, gray shingled roofline. As Drake studied each of them, he saw the curtain pull back for an instant in the window closest to them.

"Someone's home. Top window on the right."

Benning took out a pair of Leopold binoculars from the center console and focused on the window. "Looks like a young woman, standing back from the window watching us."

"That's pretty observant to have picked us up on the first drive-by."

"Drugs?"

"Maybe. Sanchez was trying to connect with anyone who knew something about recruiting for ISIS on campus. It could be anyone in there."

"What do you want to do?"

"She hasn't checked in and doesn't have her phone. I need to make sure she's okay, even if I screw things up. Pull in front of the house. I'll just knock on the door and make something up."

Benning drove Drake to the house and pulled to the curb beside the buckled cement walkway. "If you're out of sight, how will I know if you need help?"

"If I go inside and don't come out in three minutes, come in after me."

Drake opened the door and stepped down to the curb. He took out his cell phone as if he was checking to make sure he had the right address and started toward the front door. He was halfway up the walkway when the upstairs dormer window shattered and the barrel of a rifle poked out.

Instinct took over and Drake spun around, running for safety behind Benning's big Ford F-150. The familiar sound of an AK-47 on full auto and a wild spray of 7.62x39mm bullets chased him.

Benning was already crouching behind his pickup when

Drake swung around the rear and joined him. "Think she's in there?"

"I hope not. When the police get here, there'll be a shootout or a hostage negotiation. Either way, if she's in there she'll be in danger and I put her there."

"You said she's been undercover before. She knew the risk."

Drake looked down the street and saw a group of kids standing on the sidewalk watching them. He waved them back and yelled, "Stay inside."

The kids stepped back on the lawn behind them but didn't go inside. Sirens were racing toward their neighborhood and they had a front row seat for all the action.

The rifle barrel wasn't visible in the window any longer, but there was no way of knowing if it would reappear momentarily or when the police arrived.

"If there's one AK-47 in there, no telling how many more there might be. What do you want to tell the police?"

Drake poked his head up for a quick look and ducked back down. "You're recently retired from the Sheriff's Office, you do the talking. You might know some of these guys. Tell them you're investigating threats made against the archdiocese and had a tip someone here might have information that could be helpful."

"When they ask what the tip was, what do I say?"

"Tell them the truth. A student at Portland Community College by the name of Nailah Khauri told you about this place. You hoped to be able to talk with her here."

Benning nodded and pointed over Drake's shoulder. "Here they come."

Drake turned to see two police cruisers racing up the street toward them.

He pointed over Benning's shoulder. "Here come two more."

The four approaching cruisers slid to a stop, blocking the street. They were nose to nose, thirty yards away on each side with uniformed officers piling out with guns drawn.

Drake and Benning knelt and raised their hands above their heads.

Benning shouted, "I'm Detective Paul Benning, Multnomah County Sheriff's Office. The shots came from that window. AK-47, full auto."

An officer to Benning's right looked over the hood of his squad car with a bull horn raised. "How many are inside?"

"We don't know."

"SWAT's on the way. Can you roll your truck this way and use it for cover?"

"Yes."

Benning rose on one knee and turned to open the driver-side door. Drake rose in a crouch and moved to the back of the F-150, keeping it between him and the house. Benning opened the door, reached in to move the shifter to neutral and grabbed the steering wheel with his right hand. With his left, he signaled to Drake and began pushing the vehicle toward the nearest police cruiser.

The F-150's front bumper was two feet from the left rear of the cruiser when it rolled to a stop. Benning and Drake darted around behind the cruiser and knelt beside the officers.

Benning did the talking and explained why they were there. While he did, other officers spread out and moved down the street on either side to warn residents to stay inside and away from their windows.

A police helicopter flew in and hovered to the west of

the house. It reported to the officers on the ground within ten minutes that thermal imaging cameras reported no signs of anyone inside.

A search of the house also confirmed that the house was empty and there were no weapons inside. Empty AK-47 shell casings, however, littered the upstairs floor beneath the broken dormer window.

Chapter Twenty-Five

ZAL NAZIR, Samantha Taylor's handler, sat at a window table in the Copper River Restaurant and Bar waiting for her to arrive. She was ten minutes late. The angry roar of her high-revving motorcycle engine he heard, as she raced into the parking lot, told him she knew she was late or that she was angry and her new Triumph Street Cup motorcycle, with its classic café racer looks, had been ridden hard on the way to their meeting.

Her skin-tight black leather pants and jacket caused two men at the next table to turn and stare as she straddled her bike and pulled off her black helmet. When she unzipped her jacket low enough to reveal that she was only wearing a black bra under it, they kept on staring. The woman was an incorrigible exhibitionist and the modesty requirements of her new religion hadn't sunk in yet, Nazir thought, if they ever would.

He watched as she made her entrance, stopping just inside the front door to look around and run her fingers through her hair. When she saw him, she walked toward him without ever taking her eyes off his, brushing against a waiter on the way before she pulled out her chair and sat down.

"We have a problem."

"Lower your voice and compose yourself. You've already attracted all the attention we need here."

Sam glared at him and sat back in her chair with arms folded across her chest.

"Now, pick up your menu and tell me quietly what our problem is as you select something to eat."

"Someone followed me on campus. She says she's Muslim, but I didn't believe her. I brought her to the safe house and wanted to question her when you summoned me here. After I left, two men showed up at the safe house. One of my warriors fired on them and then they all had to escape out the back. The police arrived and searched the place. Someone knows about us."

"Know about us or about you? Who is the person who followed you? Do you know her?"

"No, I don't know her. I'll find out when I get to Ahmadi's cabin at the coast."

Nazir shook his head and signaled for a waiter. "I think you've overreacted. The only problem you have is getting rid of the woman you kidnapped. Regardless of who she is, she can't be allowed to identify you to the police. Tell one of your warriors to take care of it. I have something more pressing I need you to take care of."

When their waiter finally made his way to their table, Nazir ordered a seared ahi salad for himself and a cheeseburger and fries for Sam. He also ordered two Apocalypse IPAs, hoping that he could get her to relax a little as he outlined her new assignment.

"I have a contact in the local FBI office. He's a counterterrorist expert. He takes me to lunch and pumps me for information about terrorists I might have encountered at my mosque. I play along because he also likes to talk about big cases the Portland office is handling. This week it's the murder of your attorney. They're trying hard not to call it terrorism and investigating anyone known to have had a grudge who might want revenge. Sooner or later they will learn that Professor Ahmadi had a reason to kill him. We need to give them someone else who had a reason and provide enough evidence to shut down their investigation."

"How do we do that?"

"I've found the perfect person. He was one of the plaintiffs who sued the Portland Archdiocese claiming sexual abuse when he was an altar boy. Brennan defended the church and proved the kid was a cross-dressing gay and it ruined him. The ultimate settlement was a pittance and the guy's been in counseling since the trial for severe depression. He works for the city's IT division and has the skills to have hacked the archdiocese and drained the accounts of the parishioners. He's going to commit suicide and beg forgiveness for what he did."

"What do you need me to do?"

"He lives alone. Take the executioner's sword you used and some of the rope that bound him on the cross. Hide it in his apartment and leave the suicide note I wrote for you on his computer."

Their lunch arrived and they tasted their beers until the waiter left.

"Use the propofol you used on Brennan. Give him enough to kill him. All the information you need is in the envelope I'll give you when we leave. Do it tonight."

He watched her pick up her cheeseburger with both

hands and take a big bite before she nodded. Her smiling eyes told him she was relishing the night ahead, more than the half-pound cheeseburger she was devouring.

Chapter Twenty-Six

WHEN THE VANCOUVER police were satisfied with Benning's story that he and Drake had come to meet with Carol Sanchez, a potential new client, and didn't know anything about her or the people in the house, they were allowed to leave. On the drive back across the river, Drake called Mike Casey at PSS Headquarters.

"Mike, we may have a situation here. Carol Sanchez is missing."

"Kevin McRoberts gave me a heads-up when you asked him to track the movements of her phone. What have you learned?"

"We found the house. When we drove up, someone opened up on us with an AK-47. By the time the police arrived, whoever was inside had escaped out the back. Carol wasn't in the house."

"Do we know anything about the people who were there?"

"Not yet. Paul will dig into that when we get back to the office."

"Any chance they're the ISIS recruiters she was trying to identify?"

"It's possible. This was her first morning on the campus. If she identified them this quickly, she's every bit as good as you thought she was or they're not trying very hard to conceal their activities."

"She's done a lot of undercover work and knows how to handle herself. There's no way they could have discovered what she was doing this quickly."

"We need to find her. Anyone jumpy enough to fire on us without knowing who we are or why we were there is trouble. If it's not the ISIS recruiters then it's got to be a gang or someone with a lot to hide. They'll be suspicious of her now, either way."

"Agreed, but finding her won't be a problem. Deciding what you want to do when you know where she is will be the problem."

"Why won't finding her be a problem?"

"Because I didn't want to take any chances when you wanted her to go undercover. She's new, albeit experienced, so I had one of the new GPS microchips implanted before she left with you. It's like a little glass bead, the size of a tiny grain of rice. It's invisible, inserted in the web of her left hand between her thumb and first finger."

"You didn't tell me about that. Send me the coordinates and we'll go see if she's okay."

"You'll have them as soon I can get someone to send them to you. I also want you to wait for Marco Morales to get there in case you need some backup and you need help getting her out."

"Have him meet me at my office. Are you sure you don't want to join us?"

"You're having to deal with Paul's wife worrying about

him working with you. You don't want to add my wife to the list."

Drake remembered all too well how Megan Casey blamed him when her husband had been paralyzed with curare by an assassin outside his hotel room in San Francisco. The assassin traveled the world as an international fashion model and had been sent to kill him. Mike Casey had simply been in the wrong place at the wrong time, but Megan Casey still felt he was responsible somehow.

"Understood. I'll keep you posted."

Benning turned to Drake, shaking his head. "You better not be thinking of leaving me behind. Because if you are, forget it. Margo understands that I'm the one who wants to make this P.I. thing work. She didn't like all the things I did as a detective in the Sheriff's Office, but she understood it was part of the job. She'll get used to this as well."

"I hope so, Paul. You know how much I care for her. I miss her mothering me, keeping me on my toes. But it's not the same in the office anymore."

"We'll work it out. Now, to change the subject while we wait for Morales, how far do you want me to dig into the house we just left and the people living there?"

Drake looked out the window and down at the river as they drove over the Hawthorne Bridge, thinking about where to start. There wasn't much they knew at this point.

"Everything you can dig up. The Vancouver police will be doing the same thing. You might want to see how much they'll give you. Margo's great at public record searches. See if she can find out who owns the place. Maybe that will tell us who was living there. If they're students from the community college, the college might have the address listed for the place and we can identify them that way."

"I'll check with campus security and see if anyone

reported anything suspicious this morning. We know she was there and that her phone ended up there."

"Good idea. Anything will help."

Both men were quiet the rest of the way to the office. Drake couldn't help thinking about how naively he had sent Carol Sanchez undercover onto the college campus. If ISIS did have people there recruiting young women, why had he assumed she would be safe? Had he really thought they would only be young nonviolent people foolishly attracted to the perverse idea of a new caliphate? ISIS was a well-organized and well-funded terrorist organization. Of course, they would have the capability of obtaining weapons and training new recruits to use them.

The thought of college kids hating their country so much they would join something like ISIS made him furious. That ISIS was bold enough to mount a serious recruiting effort on American soil made him more determined than ever to fight the bastards.

He needed to get his head on straight if he hoped to find Sanchez and deal with the people who had taken her. If they were affiliated with ISIS, he was prepared to deal with them as he'd been trained. They weren't criminals who deserved a day in court. They were terrorist enemies who made the mistake of declaring war on the wrong country.

Chapter Twenty-Seven

CAROL SANCHEZ SAT with a black bag over her head in what she thought was a heavy wood Adirondack chair, judging by its wide arms and the way the back was angled. Her wrists and ankles were duct taped to the arms and legs of the chair so that she was hunched forward and couldn't lean all the way back. Her back ached and her head throbbed from whatever she'd been injected with before she was transported to wherever here was.

There were two women behind her in the room, talking quietly but loudly enough for her to hear what they were saying. There were others in another room, but she was unable to hear them clearly. The walls were either well-insulated or maybe made of thick wood, like in a log cabin, which fit with the closed-up smell of the place.

From the damp smell of wet earth, musty moss and fallen conifer needles that carpeted the ground when she'd been walked from the SUV inside, she thought she was in a forest somewhere that got a lot of rain. She was familiar with the forest smells in Colorado where she'd hiked and camped, but this forest smell was different.

The place was quiet, aside from the murmur of voices in the other room and the women talking behind her. No sound of cars or machinery outside, just the occasional chatter of a squirrel and the soft song of a running creek somewhere close. If she wasn't being held prisoner and tied to a chair she couldn't rock or move, she thought she might like this place in the forest.

The sound of a cell phone ringtone behind her startled her out of thoughts of her surroundings.

"Yes, Umara," one of the two women behind her said.

All conversation stopped in both rooms.

"I'll do it. It's three o'clock now; the others can be on the road in one hour and meet you as planned."

Sanchez strained to hear what was being said.

"Get the others ready to leave. You're to stay with me and finish things here."

"Allacia, are we—"

"Yes. Now get the others moving."

Sanchez listened to the other women walk across the wood floor into the other room and instruct the others in hushed tones.

The woman behind her walked around the chair and stood in front of her.

"Who are you, girl? It really doesn't matter to me because you're not leaving here. I'm just curious."

"I told you who I am. That hasn't changed. Who are you? Who are you calling 'Umara'?"

"Do you recognize the name? You should if you're Muslim as you claim."

"I know that Nusaybah bint Ka'ab was also known as

Umm' Umara. She was the female warrior who fought alongside the Prophet, peace be upon him."

"Umara is our leader and she's every bit the fighter her namesake was. She trained all of us. We are new female Muslim warriors for the final battle. It's too bad you won't be around to see how we're going to pave the way for the conquest of Rome."

"I don't understand. Why do you think I won't be around to see what you're planning? Is it something I could help you with?"

Allacia laughed harshly and slapped Sanchez hard with her open hand. "Do you think so little of us that you think you could help us? We are trained fighters for Allah. Do you know how to fire an AK-47 or kill a man with a knife? Have you practiced hand-to-hand combat? Have you ever killed someone?"

"No, I haven't. Have you?"

"Do you remember the attorney in Portland? I—"

Someone entered the room. "Allacia, we're ready to leave."

"I'll be right out."

Sanchez tried to calm herself, left alone in the room with the black bag over her head. It was clear they were planning to kill her. If they did it while she was taped to the chair, there was nothing she could do to resist. Her only chance was to get them to take her outside so they would have to cut her loose to move her. Have a chance get ahold of a weapon. She would have to find a way.

Doors closed and the SUV drove slowly away. Two voices were heard outside, both familiar and near the door the others had left through.

"Take a shovel from the lean-to and dig a grave down by the creek. It floods in the winter and her remains will wind up somewhere downstream. When you're finished, come help me. We have to wipe down the professor's cabin so there's no trace of us here."

Sanchez learned three things in the last hour. The women she'd seen in the house in Vancouver believed they were well-trained fighters for Allah. She didn't know if they were or if the one called Allacia just wanted her to think they were. They were planning something that involved the Catholic Church, judging from the reference to paving the way for the conquest of Rome. And they were planning to leave with her body buried in a grave down by the creek.

Why had she thought leaving law enforcement and undercover work with gangs and the cartels in Denver would allow her to work in the private sector and be safe? At least safer than she had been. PSS was a fine company and the pay was certainly better, but this was more than she'd bargained for.

Next time, she promised herself she would be better prepared and armed, no matter what she was asked to do. She wasn't about to underestimate her adversaries again, especially if they were in any way involved with people who claimed to be fighting for Allah.

Sanchez began to mentally prepare herself for the opportunity she hoped would present itself.

Chapter Twenty-Eight

MARCO MORALES, former long range reconnaissance patrol (LRRP) soldier and Army ranger, now employed by PSS, buzzed Drake's office from the front door off the boardwalk at three o'clock, two hours after leaving Seattle.

Margo Benning checked the CCTV security screen and recognized the young Latino who'd helped rescue her husband from the Hezbollah terrorist camp in Nicaragua a year ago. She buzzed him in.

"Adam, Marco's here."

"Send him up and let Paul know."

Drake was studying the high-resolution satellite imagery from the commercial satellite company PSS used when Morales sprinted up the stairs to his loft.

"Thanks for coming, Marco. Looks like Carol's at a cabin near Jewell, Oregon. It's at the edge of the Clatsop State Forest, about seventy miles from here. It's secluded, with only one way in, an old dirt logging road."

"What's she doing there?"

"I have no idea. Did Mike tell you why she was on the college campus?"

"To find out if someone was recruiting for ISIS. You think they're the ones who have her?"

"That's the problem, we don't know. If she found the people we were looking for and was accepted by them, rushing in to pull her out would compromise her and put her in danger. But she might already be in danger. That's what we need to go find out. What did you drive down?"

"One of the new GMC Yukons we just added to the fleet. I brought weapons and some gear, in case we need it."

Drake checked his watch. "Let's figure two hours to get there, which will make it five o'clock, another hour to hike in and get eyes on the cabin. That's still two and a half hours until sunset. As much as I'd like to have the cover of darkness, we can't wait that long. Go down and see if Margo's called Paul and have him ready to leave in five. I'll grab my go-bag, change clothes and be right down."

Drake closed the door to the loft and opened the teak wardrobe he had built to store his workout clothes, an extra suit, shirt and tie and his go-bag. The go-bag held a new Kimber Master Carry Ultra pistol he'd purchased for concealed carry, his CRKT M16 Tanto folder, a pair of Danner light weight hiking boots and a set of black 5.11 Tactical TDU pants and shirt. He added a black Oregon Duck cap with the gray O for luck. The situations he'd run into over the last two or three years had taught him to be prepared for anything—like rescuing a PSS employee he'd sent into harm's way that he was responsible for.

He kept the tactical stuff in the go-bag, except for the Duck cap, and slipped on a pair of jeans, a dark-blue polo shirt and Nikes. When he came down the stairs from the loft, Morales and Benning were waiting for him.

Margo's eyes were on him while her husband reassured her that he wasn't going to be in any danger. When he finished, she pointed to Drake.

"Paul says he isn't going to be in any danger. Make sure that he isn't."

Drake smiled to lighten the mood and said, "Yes, ma'am."

The icy stare from his secretary told him it hadn't worked.

They left out the front door and turned left and walked the short distance to where Morales had parked the Yukon on the street next to the Kimpton RiverPlace Hotel.

When they were belted in and the coordinates from Sanchez's microchip were entered into the sophisticated GPS navigation all the vehicles in the PSS fleet carried, they headed to the I-5 freeway and its intersection with U.S. Route 26, known as the Sunset Highway.

Morales drove with Drake riding shotgun and Benning sitting in the second row of seats. He'd been quiet for the first fifteen minutes and broke his silence with a question for Drake.

"Which client had us searching for ISIS recruiters on a community college campus? Is this a government thing?"

Drake turned to look at Morales, who kept his eyes on the road ahead. Was he asking because he had something against working for the government as their client or was he questioning the decision to send Sanchez undercover?

"Our client is the Archdiocese of Portland, Marco. The threats made against the Church and its parishioners had the earmarks of ISIS and its repeated threats against American churches and especially the Roman Catholic Church. We have information that ISIS recruiters are working college campuses to recruit young women as ISIS brides.

Specifically, there was chatter that the recruiting was happening on the community college campus we asked Sanchez to check out."

"So, you were looking for some ISIS recruiters that might lead you to the person or persons behind the threats to cut off the heads of Catholics if they didn't convert to Islam or pay a tax. Why isn't that something the FBI is doing? I don't understand why we're doing their work and putting Carol at risk."

There it was. Drake should have seen it sooner. Sanchez and Morales were sparring partners at PSS headquarters. Morales must have developed feelings for her. The Army's reluctance to send women into combat wasn't sexist, per se. It was rooted in the age-old tradition of men protecting the women and children and doing the fighting themselves. The tradition was especially valued in the machismo culture of Latino men like Morales.

Drake decided there would be a better time to explain why he'd also been asked to find out why the FBI was dragging its feet. At the moment, he wanted to reassure Morales that he was just as concerned about the welfare of Sanchez.

"Marco, we're going to get her back safe and sound and back to sparring with you in Seattle because, from what I've heard, you need the work. Rumor is she's been cleaning your clock."

Morales turned and flashed a quick smile with his eyes. "Maybe I've just been letting her win a few times. She is a girl."

Chapter Twenty-Nine

THEY DROVE through the old logging community of Jewell, Oregon, at the junction of Highway 103 and Highway 202 ninety minutes after leaving Portland.

Drake pointed left at the junction. The GPS navigator showed them turning north off Highway 202 onto Beneke Creek Road.

"When we're getting close, find somewhere to pull off. We'll recon in from there."

There were a few scattered houses as they left the highway and drove deeper into the forested land in the upper northwest corner of the state. They crossed Beneke Creek and then passed a sign announcing the state forest ahead; Drake motioned for Morales to slow down.

"Looks like the old logging road that takes off to the west from Beneke Creek hugs the southern end of the state forest. Let's drive by the path into the cabin. They may have a lookout."

Morales turned onto the unnamed one-lane logging road and slowed to twenty miles to drive around huge potholes that cratered the road. The GPS navigator display located the cabin a quarter of a mile west of their position and a hundred yards off the logging road.

The way into the cabin turned out to be a rutted dirt path that cut through the forest between tall fir trees. Fifty yards past the dirt path was a turnout that had been bulldozed so that logging trucks could pass each other coming and going from the logging sites.

They pulled off and got out of the Yukon, being careful to close the doors quietly. Morales walked to the rear of the SUV and swiped his foot under the rear bumper to open the rear lift gate. Inside were two tan tactical load-out bags.

"I didn't know what we might need, so I brought a little of everything; three Sig Sauer P320 pistols, three HK416 assault rifles, binoculars and a Motorola P25 two-way radio for each of us. What's your pleasure?"

Drake selected a pair of Leupold BX-2 tactical binoculars in a carry case, a two-way radio and an HK416. He lifted his untucked shirt to show he had his Kimber in an ITW concealed leather holster.

Benning stepped up and took a pair of binoculars, a two-way radio and a P320 pistol. "I haven't fired the HK416, so I better stick to something I've used. The sheriff's department tested these P320's while they were going through the army's selection process."

Morales was anxious to get going. "Why don't I go ahead and see what we're getting into? It will only take a couple minutes to get eyes on the cabin and let you know what I see. The radios are pre-set, ready to use. One click for eyes on target. Two clicks for come quick."

"Alright Marco, go see if she's in there."

Marco touched the brim of his black PSS cap and slipped into the forest.

"Adam, if this winds up being a hostage situation, how far do we take it before we call for help?"

"As far as we have to if she's in danger."

"Just remember the trouble you had when those three jihadis came after you on your farm. I'm retired and Liz won't be able to bail you out this time."

"I know, Paul. We'll follow the letter of the law and only use deadly physical force if someone is about to use unlawful deadly physical force against her or ourselves."

"You quote Oregon law pretty good for an attorney."

"I'm sure you have it memorized as well."

Drake's radio clicked twice. Time to go.

"Paul, when we can see the cabin, I'll go right, you go left."

They followed the path Morales used as they took off at a jog through the tall fir trees. The thick, soft carpet of needles silenced their approach as they zigged and zagged their way to within thirty yards of an old cabin and stopped behind a large fir, wide enough to hide them both.

It was an old log cabin. The logs were hand hewn and chinked with mortar that had blackened with age. A covered porch ran along the front and the front door was open. An older Subaru Outback was parked next to the cabin with its tailgate up.

Drake raised his binoculars to search for Morales. He found him at two o'clock behind another tree. Morales saw him and pointed to his right down toward a small creek.

Drake turned his binoculars in that direction and saw a woman wearing camo pants and a tan T-shirt digging in the ground. An AK-47 was leaned against a tree next to her. When he studied the ground where she was digging, he saw that it was a trench two-feet wide and five-or-six-feet long. She was digging a damn grave.

He handed the binoculars to Benning and pointed in the direction of the woman digging.

Benning's whispered expletive told Drake he'd seen the grave being prepared.

Drake whispered into his two-way radio. "Marco, can you subdue the woman and find out who's inside?"

"On my way."

Drake took the binoculars back from Benning and watched Morales move silently around and behind the woman. His training as a recon ranger showed as he moved from tree to tree until he was ten feet away.

Drake waited for Morales to move on the woman, applying a choke hold to subdue her and then find out who was in the cabin.

Morales waited too long. The woman threw her shovel down and reached for her AK-47 on her way back to the cabin. As she turned, she saw Morales and screamed.

Morales rushed her and tackled her. As she fell, she fired wildly into the trees overhead.

Morales knocked the woman unconscious with an elbow strike as they fell and wrenched the rifle from her hands.

The silence that followed the burst of gunfire lasted a full minute before a voice from inside shouted.

"Don't come a step closer; I have a gun to her head."

Chapter Thirty

DRAKE PULLED BENNING CLOSE. "Circle around the cabin and see if there's a window with a view inside. Find out how many are in there."

Benning nodded and moved left. Drake stayed behind the tree with a view of the front of the cabin.

The woman shouted again. "Who are you? Why are you here?"

"We're friends of the woman you're holding. We're no threat to you. Let her go and we'll release your friend out here. Then we'll walk away."

"You cops?"

"We're not cops."

"Then who are you?"

"I work for a private security firm. The woman you're holding is the daughter of someone I work with."

"What was she doing on campus?"

"She's enrolled there for summer classes."

"How'd you find us?"

"Like I said, her father works with me for a security

firm. We all have GPS microchips implanted so our employer knows where we are. Her father thought it was a good idea for her as well."

"I don't believe you."

Drake saw Benning wave to him from the side of the cabin and signal that he had eyes inside and held up two fingers. Sanchez and one other.

"If she shows you where the microchip is implanted, will you believe her?"

"Maybe."

"Nailah, let her feel the web between your thumb and first finger on your left hand."

Drake raised his two-way radio and whispered to Morales. "Can you leave the woman with you?"

"She's unconscious. I used her belt and boot laces to tie her up."

"Move to your side of the cabin and see if you can see Carol. Paul, see if there's a back door or some way into the cabin."

Drake laid his HK416 down and stepped out from behind the tree. "Look, this isn't getting us anywhere. I'm coming closer so we can talk face-to-face."

"It won't make any difference. I have my orders. I can't let her go and I'm not afraid of dying."

He walked forward and to his right. Benning had signaled that he had eyes on the woman and Sanchez. He took that to mean that Sanchez was being held closer to Benning's side of the cabin than Morales's side. He just needed to get his own eyes on the woman to be able to decide what to do because the situation was escalating.

He stopped twenty-five feet out from the front porch and to the right of the open front door. A young black woman stood behind Sanchez inside, who was duct taped to an old Adirondack chair. The AK-47 the woman was holding was resting on the back of the chair and pointed down at her captive's head.

Drake raised his hands above his shoulders. "No one is going to die here. Your friend is free to leave just like you are free to leave. Just let Nailah walk out to me."

Looking to his right and left, he moved both hands slightly forward and back, telling Benning and Morales to move in. As he lowered his hands, he gave a slight fist pump with his right hand. Prepare for action.

"My name is Adam. What's your name?"

The only response he heard was a prayer being recited in Arabic.

Drake charged onto the porch and cleared his Kimber. As the barrel of the AK-47 turned toward him, he fired two bullets into the forehead of the woman standing behind the Adirondack chair.

Muffled grunts from under the black hood over her head told Drake Sanchez was okay. He pulled the hood off and ruffled her hair. Before he could take his knife out of his pocket, Morales rushed in with Benning right behind him.

Benning dragged the dead woman away and Morales knelt down to carefully slice through the duct tape binding her wrists and ankles.

Drake stepped back while Morales worked to free her. "Sorry, Carol. I never expected that putting you on that campus would lead to this."

When her hands were free, she peeled the duct tape slowly off her mouth. "She put this on as soon as she heard the shots outside so I couldn't say anything. I wanted to warn you. She was prepared to die. Thanks for coming to get me."

Sanchez tried to stand but her knees buckled. Morales

threw his arm around her waist and led her out onto the porch and away from the blood and gore lying on the floor behind her.

Benning was searching the clothes of the dead woman. "She has a wallet and a burner phone. Her driver's license says she was Allacia Evans, age 20. Student ID for Portland Community College, Cascade campus. The address on her license is a house somewhere near the college. Not much else that tells us anything about her."

"Do you want to be the one to call this in?"

"Sure, but we need to figure out how we're going to explain this to the deputy sheriffs when they get here."

"We'll tell them most of it. It was a lawful use of deadly force. That won't be the problem. The problem will be explaining why we were investigating the possibility of ISIS recruiting young women at the community college and where we got the intelligence that pointed us there. The FBI has already warned us to stay out of their way regarding the threats against the archdiocese. They'll go nuts when they learn about this."

Morales walked in from the porch. "Maybe not when they hear what Carol can tell them. She heard the dead woman say she was the one who killed the attorney that was crucified and that they had something planned for the Catholic churches here."

Drake stepped outside and gave Sanchez a hug. "You okay?"

"I'm okay, just pissed that I let them take me like they did. And hungry. Did you guys bring any food?"

Drake laughed as he remembered the way she put away her steak the night before. "I'll tell Morales to see if there's any food left inside. Either way, I owe you another steak dinner."

Chapter Thirty-One

THREE CLATSOP COUNTY Sheriff's patrol cars met Paul Benning, former Multnomah County Sheriff's Department detective, out on the logging road and he led them into the cabin. Drake, Morales and Sanchez were standing in a line in front of the porch when the three cars fanned out before parking, effectively securing the remote scene.

Benning acted as spokesman and summarized the events of the day, beginning with their search for Carol Sanchez, being fired on in Vancouver and tracking her to the cabin. He carefully detailed the events of the shooting.

Then they were separated and questioned individually. By the time they each had given their individual statements, and the deputies caucused to compare notes, the Sheriff of Clatsop County, Bob Benson, arrived to take command.

Fortunately, Sheriff Benson and Detective Benning knew and respected each other. Because of that, and the consistency of their statements, they were allowed to leave a little after eight thirty in the evening, on the condition they remained in the county overnight. Sheriff Benson wanted their formal statements to be taken the next day and to have time for the forensic team's report to verify their accounts of the shooting.

The second woman had refused to answer any questions and was arrested for her role in kidnapping Carol Sanchez. Drake expected the FBI would arrive by morning to question her as well as themselves.

Drake reserved rooms for the four of them at the Hampton Inn and Suites in Astoria for the night. On the way there, they stopped at Charlie's Chop House for dinner and a chance to talk privately before tomorrow.

Charlie's Chop House was a new steakhouse that reportedly was inspired by old-school Portland steakhouses like the Ringside Steakhouse. When a friend and fellow attorney had recommended it to Drake, he knew he had to eat there the next time he was in Astoria.

He wasn't disappointed. An all-wood interior done in rich red and black colors featured a full bar along the back wall and solid wood tables with comfortable high-back black leather chairs.

When they were seated and a round of drinks was on the way, Drake directed their conversation to the question that had been bugging him. "What I don't understand is why the woman who called herself 'Allacia' would admit to murdering Michael Brennan. If this leader, 'Umara', is training up a band of female ISIS fighters, why take out Brennan? There has to be some connection we're not seeing. ISIS, even if it's inspiring this from a distance, wouldn't order the execution of one man unless it's personal and Brennan was somehow involved with one of them."

"Maybe Brennan knew something about one of them they didn't want discovered," Morales suggested.

Benning shook his head. "I've been through the reports

of the police and the FBI and there's nothing to suggest that. They've been through the files in his office, his personal laptop and his home office. Nothing points to someone with a possible connection to ISIS."

Their drinks arrived, bourbons for Drake and Benning and beers for Sanchez and Morales, and the waiter gave them her recommendations for the evening.

"Our cuts are from prime grass-fed beef with no added hormones and include top sirloins cut block style, bone-in and boneless rib eyes, New York strips, filet mignons and chopped sirloins. They're all the best steaks you've ever eaten."

They all ordered bone-in rib eyes.

Sanchez finished her beer and signaled for another. "From what I saw, this group is very organized and disciplined. They're being trained as fighters and Muslim warriors. They didn't strike me as the online cheerleader types who are supposed to be recruiting young women to be ISIS brides. Someone else must be handling that kind of work. Maybe there's more than one group involved here."

Drake remembered something Sanchez said on the drive to Astoria. "Carol, didn't you say the woman you followed on campus went to see someone in the Technology Building? Is that where they teach computer stuff?"

"Yes, it also houses the computer resource center where there are computers for students to use."

"Did you see who she was trying to see?"

"No. I saw her knock on a door and stomp off when no one answered. I was peeking around a corner at the end of the hall."

"Do you think she's the one who calls herself 'Umara'?"

Sanchez closed her eyes for a moment. "She was clearly

the leader in the house in Vancouver. So, yes, she's probably Umara."

"When we get back to Portland, let's find out who she tried to see and what Umara's real name is. If she's not the one with the computer skills, maybe the person she wanted to see is—someone who has the skills to hack the archdiocese and drained the accounts of the Catholic parishioners. Paul is going to find out who owns the house in Vancouver; Carol, you and Marco focus on Umara and who she went to see."

When their steaks arrived, the conversation abruptly ended. As they enjoyed what Drake conceded was the best steak he'd ever eaten, they all continued to think about the young women who aspired to be fierce Muslim warriors.

They had shown they were capable of extreme violence and a willingness to die for their cause, not only in the murder and crucifixion of Michael Brennan but also the kidnapping and planned murder of Carol Sanchez.

Drake's concern was what the FBI would do with the information about the young women and its reaction to his being involved in another terrorist plot at home. Would they try to sideline him, as they had previously, by threatening to pursue criminal charges against him for killing the woman at the cabin? It was certainly possible. He knew the agents he'd embarrassed before had long memories and didn't want anyone messing around in what they considered to be their exclusive expertise and domain.

What they refused to understand was that he was as good as or better than they were in dealing with terrorists, with his training as a Delta Force operator, and that he would never renege on the oath he took to defend his country.

Chapter Thirty-Two

FRIDAY MORNING, at nine o'clock, Morales drove the GMC Yukon over the Youngs Bay Bridge on the Oregon Coast Highway from Astoria to Warrenton, Oregon to keep their appointment with the Clatsop County Sheriff's Office.

They were again separated and ushered into small rooms with no windows to give recorded statements they would later be asked to sign.

On the way to give his statement, Drake was met in the hallway at the door to a conference room by FBI agent Rand Gibson.

Gibson tilted his head toward the conference room and walked inside.

Drake wanted to continue walking behind the deputy sheriff escorting him in the worst way but knew it would only delay the meeting with the FBI. Two men sat at the conference table and didn't stand when he entered the room behind Gibson. They continued reading open files in front of each of them.

Gibson stood at the head of the conference table and scowled at Drake with his arms folded across his chest. "Well, cowboy, it looks like you've really done it this time."

"Done what, Rand? Rescued a co-worker from being killed and buried in a grave next to a cabin where she would never have been found?"

"No, interfering in a federal investigation. We're considering arresting you and your friends."

"For what, representing my client and trying to find out who hacked the archdiocese and stole from its parishioners? Good luck with that. You may have a law degree, but you don't know the first thing about prosecuting a crime like the one you're threatening me with."

"Maybe, but they do. Why don't you tell us what you were doing sending Sanchez undercover onto the community college campus?"

"Trying to find something that would lead us to the people threatening the archdiocese. You've concluded that this is just a computer crime that someone was trying to make everyone think was terrorism. With the attacks on the Church in Europe, my client was concerned that it wasn't."

One of the men seated at the conference table closed his file and looked up. "I apologize for not introducing myself when Agent Gibson neglected to do so. My name is Wayne Williams from the counterterrorism division. May I ask how you came to suspect that ISIS might be recruiting young women on the Portland Community College Cascade campus?"

Williams was older than Gibson by ten or fifteen years and had the look of an experienced agent. Contrasted to Gibson's dark suit, white shirt and tie, Williams was dressed business casual in a light-blue summer blazer and a cream-colored polo from what Drake could see. He knew most of the FBI agents in the Portland Field Office, but he'd never seen Williams before.

Drake reached across the conference table and shook hands with Williams who stood to meet him halfway. "Have you been in Portland long? I don't believe we've met."

Williams met Drake's eyes ever so briefly before he sat down. "I was transferred to Portland by the former director. Not sure how long I'll be here. Back to my question, how did you suspect recruiting being conducted on that campus?"

There was no harm in telling Williams what he might already know if he worked in the counterterrorism division of the FBI.

"In addition to my law practice in Portland, I'm also special counsel for Puget Sound Security. PSS is involved in the counterintelligence strategic partnership program with the FBI, so we try to keep our ears open. Our IT expert came across a thread that bragged about the recruiting on the campus. Given my belief that the threats against the Church involved terrorism and just not cybercrime, I recruited Carol Sanchez to go look around."

"I wasn't aware of that. I'd appreciate it if you'd be willing to share that information."

"For God's sake, Williams, don't encourage this guy. We've got this covered. You were only allowed to tag along this morning because there was a mention in the sheriff's report that ISIS was thought to be involved. That came from Drake and his people and they have absolutely no credibility in our office."

"Maybe he should, Gibson. He's been right in the past more often than you guys have been."

Williams stood and handed Drake his business card.

"Call me when you're willing to share the information you developed. As far as I'm concerned, we're done here."

"That's not for you to decide, Williams. I have some questions..."

Drake turned to leave and Gibson moved to block his way.

"Let him go, Gibson. Don't make a fool of yourself."

Drake tipped his head to Williams and walked out to continue down the hall with the deputy waiting for him.

By noon, the Clatsop County Sheriff's Department was finished with their interviews and formal statements and let them return to Portland. When they were alone in the Yukon with Morales at the wheel, Benning assured them that the matter wasn't officially closed but that the sheriff had privately told him that he didn't see any charges being brought against any of them.

"He's looking into who owns that old cabin, but said he may need our help. The recorded deed shows that it's a company registered in Panama that paid for it from an offshore account five years ago."

Morales slapped the steering wheel and turned to look at Sanchez in the second row of seats. "I told you it was going to be fun working for this company. In your first month, you've been undercover, kidnapped and now we're hunting terrorists with an offshore account in Panama. Who knows where we'll get to go before this is over?"

Who knows indeed? Drake thought. Before they got any deeper into this mess, he needed to conference with his father-in-law, Senator Hazelton, his friend and CEO of PSS and especially his girlfriend, Liz, and get their input.

He shook his head unconsciously as his mind reacted to calling Liz his 'girlfriend'. She was more than that and the term 'girlfriend' seemed almost degrading somehow. What should he call her? His lover? He knew he loved her, but even that label didn't seem right.

Maybe between here and the drive back to Portland, he'd come up with the right term. For the moment, he was just looking forward to hearing her voice and sharing the way he felt about the life he'd taken that day.

Chapter Thirty-Three

DRAKE WAITED until he was in back in his office in Portland before he started a series of phone calls. He made sure Benning had cleared the way and explained their need to spend the night in Astoria, but the absence of Margo at her desk when he got there suggested she was angry, at him or maybe at both of them. He understood her worrying about her husband's safety, but she needed to get over blaming him for the line of work her husband was pursuing and the risks he was taking.

After stowing his go-bag in the teak wardrobe in the loft, minus his Kimber that had been retained by the Clatsop County Sheriff's Department until their investigation was officially closed, he took out his cell phone and called Liz.

It was six o'clock in the evening in Washington when she answered his call and didn't sound happy. It wasn't the reception he'd expected.

"Why didn't you call me last night?"

He hadn't promised to call her, but he had a pretty good idea who had.

"I'm sorry, I should have."

"Are you okay?"

He was quiet for long enough that she knew the answer. "I can be there tomorrow morning."

"You know I'd like that, but you need to finish up there so you can be here all the time."

"How is Carol Sanchez doing?"

"She's tough, but it'll take some time to really deal with being kidnapped and all. Mike told her he wants her back in Seattle to meet with a counselor, but she's refused and wants to see this through. She's the only one who's seen any of these women."

"Is there anything I can do to help?"

"Did you get a chance to talk with the FBI agent you know in the Portland office?"

"I did. His name is Wayne Williams. He's in the—"

"Counterterrorism division. I met him this morning. I wondered why he made the trip to Astoria."

"Wayne was transferred because he embarrassed the director when he testified before a closed session of the Intelligence Committee. He voiced his concern that the FBI was downplaying the threat of ISIS in America. The past administration wanted attention focused on killing ISIS leaders in Syria and Iraq and not on active terrorist investigations in all fifty states. There's a new president, but it's the same old FBI. He says that's the main reason the Portland office is continuing to investigate the threats to the Catholic Church and the murder of that attorney as a cybercrime instead of terrorism."

"But he isn't buying it."

"That's my impression."

Drake took Williams' business card out of his pocket

and looked at it. "He gave me his card. I think I'll give him a call."

"You sure you don't want me to fly out tomorrow?"

"Fly out before Labor Day and we'll go somewhere special for a little vacation before you start working for PSS in Seattle."

"Promise?"

"I promise."

He sat for a moment, regretting his decision to tell Liz to stay in Washington. But with the hunt for Umara and her crew heating up, he knew where his head was going to be until it was over. And then they could take a break and sort out their future.

His next call was to Mike Casey at PSS.

After he finished with the short version of the last day's events, he listened as CEO Casey asked about his two employees, Sanchez and Morales.

"Marco's fine and eager to track down Umara before she does whatever she's planning. Sanchez is too, but I'll keep an eye on her. She knows they were planning on killing her and would have if we hadn't found her. She was afraid we didn't know that she was in danger and were waiting to see how things played out. She's tough, had to be to do the undercover work she did in Denver. Morales is keeping an eye on her. They seem to be pretty close."

"Is there anything you need from here?"

"There is, two things actually. The money stolen from the parishioners after the archdiocese was hacked went somewhere. The archdiocese wants to retain us to find it. I'm sure the FBI is trying to trace it, but I'll bet Kevin can track it down faster. He can get whatever he needs from the archdiocese; just have him ask Paul to arrange it for him.

"Along with that, the cabin where they held Sanchez belongs to a company registered in Panama and was paid for five years ago from an offshore account. It's possible that offshore account might be the recipient of the twenty million dollars missing from the parishioners of the archdiocese."

"I'll get Kevin on it."

"Paul is finding out who owns the house in Vancouver where Umara grabbed Sanchez and Sanchez and Morales are trying to ID the person Umara tried to visit when Sanchez was following her. When we get those two pieces of the puzzle, we might start to figure out what's going on here."

"All right, keep me in the loop."

The last call was a short one to his father-in-law. As he expected, the senator was still in his office.

"Hello, Adam. Liz just filled me in on your trip to the coast. Sorry it had to end that way."

"I am too, but there was no other way. Even if these jihadists are Americans, they're still way too willing to die for Allah. I don't know how they get them brainwashed so quickly."

"Is there anything I can help you with?"

"You asked me to look into what was going on in the Portland FBI office and why it was dragging its feet investigating the threats against the archdiocese as terrorism. I met an agent who was recently transferred out here from Washington. Can you find out more about him and why an experienced agent from the CTD winds up in a field office on the West Coast? Liz said he testified in a closed session before your Senate Select Committee on Intelligence. His name is Wayne Williams."

"I remember Williams. He felt the FBI was too willing to carry the water for the previous administration's position that we were winning the war against the JV team, ISIS, and that everyone's safe here at home. He was a senior agent or he wouldn't have been in front of my committee. I'll look into it."

"Thanks. Tell Mom hi. Are you coming back to Oregon during the summer break?"

"We'll be at the cabin at Crosswater for Labor Day weekend. Come visit us."

"I'll try. Thanks."

He always found it humorous when the senator referred to his summer retreat south of Bend, Oregon, as a "cabin". It was more like a lodge than a cabin and he had fond memories of the place. It was where he first realized he was attracted to Liz, after she had nearly been killed by a sniper's bullet that was meant for him.

Chapter Thirty-Four

SAMANTHA TAYLOR, called Umara by her band of warriors, followed Tyler Murphy home from the LGBT nightclub to his one-bedroom apartment in the Pearl District of Portland. He was the sacrificial lamb who was going to be so depressed that he killed himself tonight.

The note that he was going to leave behind would admit that he killed the attorney who ruined his life and cheated him out of the settlement he deserved when he sued the Portland Archdiocese for sexual abuse as an altar boy.

Sam didn't feel sorry for the poor schmuck, after watching him sit through the Friday night drag show at the Embers Avenue nightclub. He may have been sexually abused as an altar boy, but being outed as a cross-dressing gay hadn't ruined his life. Anyone who watched him for twenty minutes knew what he was. He was lucky sharia law wasn't the law of the land in America. The pervert would have been thrown off the tallest building in the city years ago.

She followed him from the nightclub to his small but

expensive apartment in the Pearl District and was delighted that he came home alone. She wouldn't have minded killing two perverts, but the suicide note she would leave didn't mention a lover who was also involved in killing the attorney. Improvising to explain the double suicide would have been a challenge.

When he entered the lobby of the modern apartment complex, Sam walked to the corner and then back to give him time to take the elevator to his fourth-floor apartment.

She knew which apartment he lived in and her Android smartphone with its near field communication (NFC) capability had read his key fob when she had flirted with him at the nightclub. No matter that he had pushed her away rather rudely; he would pay for that soon. With her rooted handset that could replay the code from his fob, her phone was now a key that would get her into his apartment.

Sam was dressed in her shortest black skirt, a diaphanous white, see-through blouse and six-inch cross-strap sandals. Tyler Murphy might not be attracted to her, but she knew any other man in the place would be. Unfortunately, there wasn't anyone in the lobby to prove her point.

The elevator ride to the fourth floor was fast and the apartment she wanted was just three doors away from the elevator. Seeing no one in the hallway, Sam walked to his door with her head down, as if she was searching her sequined clutch for her key fob, while she held her smartphone tightly in her left hand.

The human-hair short, black wig she was wearing would help to hide her identity, as would her stylish black-framed, oval glasses. But she was planning on a long career in America and didn't want to have some CCTV camera put an early end to it.

At the door to apartment 409, she leaned close and listened for any sound from inside. The only thing she heard was the muted sound of music playing. With a quick look to her left and right, she held her phone to the door handle and heard it click open.

Sam stepped in and quietly closed the door. The apartment was small, maybe five hundred square feet, and well-appointed. The entry and kitchen with a breakfast bar and granite countertops were dead ahead. Just beyond on the left was the door to a bedroom and en suite bathroom. At the back of the apartment was the living and dining room. She knew because she had studied the floor plan of the apartment Tyler Murphy had leased for the last two years.

She took her sandals off, laid them down on the tile floor and moved to the door of the bedroom. Murphy was humming along to what sounded to her like a musical of some sort and brushing his teeth with an electric toothbrush. Before she continued, she pulled out a pair of blue latex gloves from her clutch.

She slipped through the open door of the bedroom and flattened herself against the wall next to the opening to the closest and bathroom beyond. Tyler Murphy was standing in profile facing a mirror six feet away. He was barefoot, shirtless and still wearing the cream-colored linen slacks.

Sam opened her clutch and took out a syringe, the same syringe that she had used on the attorney. She'd carefully loaded it with five times the dose of propofol that had killed Michael Jackson.

She took a deep breath to steady herself and then sprung through the opening and plunged the needle of the syringe deep into the muscular tissue of the man's left arm.

"You! What the hell did you just do?"

Sam stepped back and watched him crumple to the floor.

The propofol wouldn't itself kill him, but it would stop his breathing long enough for him to die of asphyxiation. She turned him onto his back and dragged him across the tile floor to his bed and hefted him up onto it. When he was positioned on his back, she pulled his slacks off, leaving him in his boxer shorts.

She positioned the syringe in his right hand, lying palm up on the bed, and went into his bathroom to put away his toiletries. When it looked like what a tidy man would leave before committing suicide, she moved to his closet and took out a small coil of rope from her clutch. It would match the rope she used to tie the attorney to his beloved cross when the police found it and had it analyzed.

She had wanted to plant the executioner's sword in his apartment, but she couldn't find a way to bring it along and conceal it within the dress she wanted to wear for the night.

The only thing left was the suicide note on his laptop. She opened it on the writing desk on the other side of his bed, opened Word and quickly typed the suicide note her handler had given her. When she was finished, she stepped back to read it and make sure there were no mistakes and collected her clutch.

In the entry, she slipped on her sandals and looked around to make sure there wasn't any evidence of her having been there. She understood from watching television there would probably be some trace evidence she'd left if the police looked hard enough after deciding this wasn't suicide, but by then her attack on the churches would have happened. She really didn't care if they knew that Umara had also killed the pervert as well as the cross worshippers next week.

Chapter Thirty-Five

AFTER A GOOD NIGHT'S sleep in his own bed and a morning run with Lancer, Drake was drinking a cup of coffee on the front porch of his old, but renovated, stone farmhouse.

He was admiring the forty acres that sloped down from the house to the county road below. It was divided in two sections for pinot noir and chardonnay rootstock he'd ordered and would plant in the fall. The rows in each of the two sections would stretch horizontally from his left to his right across the rich Jory soil, the basalt-based volcanic soil found in most of the vineyards in the Dundee Hills.

He was close to fulfilling the promise he'd made to Kay and he felt a deep satisfaction in honoring her memory in that way.

Lancer raised his head from the hardwood floor at his feet when Drake's ringtone broke the stillness of Saturday morning.

"Morning, Paul."

"Are you coming into the office this morning?" asked Benning.

"I wasn't planning on it. Why?"

"The Clatsop County Sheriff called me this morning. The woman we found digging the grave hung herself in her cell last night."

Drake didn't know what to say. She deserved to be punished for what she'd done and was planning, but she was so young, probably in her teens. How did a young mind get so twisted so early?

"Was the sheriff able to identify her?"

"He's still working on that."

"That leaves us with no leads for finding 'Umara'."

"Not quickly, anyway. I had a friend at the county access the Vancouver recorder's office about the house where we were ambushed. It just happens to be owned by the same company registered in Panama that owns the cabin in Jewell. If we can identify the owner or owners of that company, we might have a chance. This is all connected in some way."

"Kevin's working on that. He probably hasn't slept since Mike gave him the assignment."

"Have you heard from Morales and Sanchez?"

"They were going over to the campus this morning to find out who Umara was going to see when Sanchez followed her."

"Let me know if they find anything."

"Will do."

"I think I'll try to meet with the FBI agent today, the one I met in the Sheriff's Office. Turns out he's a friend of Liz. He didn't seem to be swallowing the 'it's cybercrime, not terrorism' line. He might know something the FBI hasn't been willing to share because, right now, we're at a dead end."

"Relax, Counselor. I'm a detective remember. These things don't get solved overnight."

"I have a feeling, Paul, that this one better be solved sooner rather than later. If Umara is planning something, she won't wait forever with Sanchez rescued."

Drake ended the call and sat stroking Lancer's head lying across his left knee. It was time to go on the offensive, but how?

He patted Lancer on his shoulder and stood up. "Looks like I'm headed back to town, big guy. I'll pick up something good on the way home for dinner to make up for the lazy day we had planned."

Agent Williams' card was laying on his desk in the study. Williams answered on the second ring.

"Williams."

"Adam Drake, Agent Williams. It seems we have a common friend."

"She's the reason I was in the Sheriff's Office when the report of the shooting at the cabin came through. Liz told me you represented the Portland Archdiocese and thought terrorists were behind the threats."

"Do you have time to meet with me today?"

"Sure, but not at my office."

Drake glanced at the time on his Timex Ironman. Nine thirty. "Meet me at McCormick and Schmick's Harborside at the Marina in two hours. I'll buy lunch."

"See you there."

He wasn't sure what he expected to learn from Williams, but something was going on in the Portland office. Sure, it had its past embarrassments with the arrest of Brandon Mayfield, the Portland attorney. They arrested him for being the bomber in the 2004 Madrid train bombings, and the subsequent public apology and humiliating two-million-dollar settlement had left a bitter taste in their mouths. But, since then, the FBI nationwide had generally been vigorously investigating terror threats in the country. It didn't make any sense to him why it would so quickly reject the possibility that the threats against the Catholic parishioners and the crucifixion of Michael Brennan weren't acts of terrorism.

Drake shed his running shorts, sweaty T-shirt and running shoes on the bathroom floor and showered. Twenty minutes later, he was dressed in khaki cargo shorts, a dark-gray Oregon Duck T-shirt with a green 'O' on the front, white Oregon hat and Birkenstocks. People thought the Northwest was all about rain and cool summers, but Augusts in Oregon were usually hot. Today's forecast called for ninety-two-degree heat and plenty of sun, a good reason to enjoy lunch at an outdoor table and dress accordingly.

With the weekend crowds flocking to the wineries and tasting rooms in the area, the drive into Portland from Dundee took an hour in his old silver Porsche 993, the last of the classic air-cooled 911 Porsches. He didn't mind the dawdling pace of the tourists so much, he was used to it, but the 993 was a race horse and preferred a good run to a slow jog. When Liz was finally here, he'd have to plan a day trip to Crater Lake or some distant Oregon treasure to blow the cobwebs out of his baby.

Drake pulled into one of the four reserved parking spaces for his office, next to his PSS Porsche Cayman GTS. He used it exclusively for travel to and from Seattle and appreciated the car, but it was no 993. Still, it was nice not to have to put the extra miles on his classic.

He had an hour before he met Agent Williams and took

the back stairs from the parking garage down to his office. In his loft, he checked his PC for messages and found one from FBI Agent Rand Gibson.

> *Wanted you to be the first to know you were wrong, Michael Brennan wasn't killed by ISIS.*
> *He committed suicide in his condo and left a note apologizing for killing the attorney.*
> *Take a hint and stay out of our investigations.*

Chapter Thirty-Six

AGENT WAYNE WILLIAMS was sitting at an outside table at the Harborside, drinking a pint of beer, when Drake joined him. He looked relaxed in a pair of jeans and a white polo shirt.

Williams raised his pint. "One of the benefits of being shipped out west. You've got some great craft beers."

Drake hailed a passing waiter. "Full Sail Amber when you have a moment."

"I've wanted to ask you, what did you do to get shipped out west?"

"Didn't Liz tell you?"

"I didn't ask her. I'd rather hear it from you."

Williams' lips tightened slightly and he finally nodded. "Okay. No secret really. I disagreed with the former director and made the mistake of doing it publicly."

"Now that he's gone, is there a chance you'll be recalled to Washington?"

"The director doesn't run the FBI, senior staff does.

Most of them are still there and their politics haven't changed, so I doubt it."

A waiter came back with Drake's pint of beer and took their orders. Crab cake and shrimp sandwich for Williams and a cheeseburger for Drake.

"Thought I'd give your crab cakes a chance. Always been my favorite in Washington."

Drake started to laugh at the mention of crab cakes and the innuendo he shared with Liz about enjoying them but stopped when he saw the look on Williams' face. "Sorry, the mention of crab cakes reminded me of someone. Have you been to your office today?"

"I spend as little time there as I have to. Why?"

"Gibson sent me a taunting email a little while ago. One of the plaintiffs in a lawsuit against the archdiocese committed suicide last night, left a note apologizing for killing attorney Brennan."

"Was there a mention of the threats against the Church or the twenty million dollars that was stolen?"

"Gibson didn't mention it."

"Those plaintiffs were altar boys, if I remember correctly. You'd think he'd apologize to his fellow Catholics first then admit his guilt for killing someone he's supposed to hate second. Just when you stumble across this Umara and her gang, this suicide seems a little too convenient a way to end this investigation."

"Maybe the threats against the parishioners and the murder of the attorney are two different things, with two different parties responsible?"

"Could be, but it doesn't feel right. I'll look into it when I'm back in the office."

Their food arrived and both men began eating while

they thought about the news of the all-too-convenient suicide.

Williams put his sandwich down on his plate and wiped his mouth. "Not bad. Dungeness crab is better than I expected. You said you might be willing to tell me where you got the information about ISIS recruiting on the community college campus. Care to share?"

"Since we're both sharing—and we are both sharing, aren't we?—I'll tell you. Liz knows someone in the NSA who said there was chatter about recruiting young women to be ISIS brides on college campuses. PSS has a very skilled individual and went on the dark web and found someone mentioning the recruiting on the Cascade campus. That's why I put Carol Sanchez undercover there to see if she could find out what was going on."

"That's pretty bold for an attorney who just represents the Portland Archdiocese."

"I thought there might be a link between the threats against the Catholics and what ISIS was possibly doing on the campus. I didn't think your FBI was interested in pursuing it, so we did."

"Did you tell us what your guy found?"

"I'm not on very good terms with the local office. I didn't waste my time."

"You should have come to me."

"I hadn't met you."

"Get me the information and I'll check it out personally, compare it with anything we might have."

"I'll see that it gets to you. Now, is there anything you want to share with me?"

Agent Williams finished off his beer before answering. "Let's figure the investigation of the murder of Attorney Brennan will be closed soon. I'm with the counterterrorism division, so I can keep investigating Umara and her followers. What I propose is that I will share whatever I find, if you will do the same."

"Does that mean anything the FBI and the Portland office finds or just what you find?"

"I'll let you in on a little secret; there are two of us assigned to counterterrorism who have any experience. The other guy is Muslim and meets with local Muslims he calls his contacts. From what I can see, he's never produced any intelligence that's worth what he's being paid. If anyone finds out anything about Umara, it will be me."

"Then, with any luck, we'll be meeting more often."

Drake's phone vibrated in his pocket and he excused himself and walked a short distance away from their table.

"Yes, Marco."

"Carol's found the office in the Technology Education Building. It's locked and security isn't being helpful. They won't identify the occupant without knowing why we want to know. They turned three shades of green when I asked if they might just let us in. What do you want to do?"

"Are you at this office now?"

"We're standing in the hall outside with three campus security officers."

"Hold on for just a minute."

Drake walked back to Agent Williams. "Do you have time to help me with something right now? I need you to flash your badge over at the Cascade campus. It'll be the first of our sharing things."

Agent Williams agreed and Drake got back on his phone with Morales. "Marco, stay right where you are and don't let anyone in that office until we get there. Tell the security guys the FBI is on the way. Call Benning and have him meet us there."

Chapter Thirty-Seven

CAROL SANCHEZ WAS WAITING for them on the Cascade campus in Parking Lot One. Wearing khaki shorts, a pink polo shirt and aviator sunglasses, she was standing in front of three parking spots reserved for public safety officers.

Agent Williams pulled into the only empty spot in his white Chevrolet Monte Carlo with its telltale stubby antennae on the roof. When he got out, he walked up to Sanchez and held out his hand.

"I'm Special Agent Wayne Williams. Nice to meet you, Miss Sanchez. Sorry about the time you had to spend with Umara and her crew. If you're up to it, I'd like to get you with a sketch artist later."

"Thank you, Agent Williams, but I don't think that will be necessary. If's she's a student here, I'll be able to identify her from her student ID card photo."

"Right. Lead the way, then, to the office you saw her trying to enter."

Sanchez looked to Drake who nodded for her to show the FBI agent the way.

Drake and Agent Williams fell in beside Sanchez as she led them across the campus to the Technology Education Building. As they walked, she pointed to the bench she'd been sitting on when the public safety officer suggested she speak with the student marching by.

"When I saw the angry look on her face and the way she was dressed, cut-offs and hiking boots, I knew I had to see where she was going. She was the militant type who would know the campus radicals, if anyone would. I didn't know anything else about her at that point."

"You were undercover in Denver, I understand. You had to have been pretty good at spotting trouble to survive that."

Sanchez looked down and shook her head. "Not good enough, it seems."

Drake knew what she was thinking. He was questioning his decision to send her in undercover just as she was questioning her decision to take the ride with Umara to meet her friends. They would both rehash the choices they'd made for a long time.

He reached over and rubbed her shoulder lightly. "Your instinct was spot on. It gave us the break we needed. Tell us about the standoff at the Tech Building."

"When we found the office and that it was locked, Morales went looking for a janitor or a public safety officer to learn whose office it was. The officer he found wouldn't tell us, so he suggested that, if we could just get in, we could find that out for ourselves.

"I think he meant it as a joke, but the guy went ballistic and called for backup, told us to stay where we were until this got sorted out. The next thing we knew, two more officers showed up and now the public safety sergeant they answer to is there as well. As soon as he heard the FBI was coming, he got on the phone with someone, probably an attorney."

Agent Williams chuckled. "This should be fun. Just the mention of the FBI and people call their lawyers. It won't do them any good today. On the way over, I requested a 'sneak and peek' search warrant for the office. With the information we have, I expect the Federal magistrate will already have approved the warrant. It should be here within the hour."

Drake was familiar with 'sneak and peeks'. He'd used them when he was a prosecutor in the D.A.'s Office. They allowed the search to be made and extended the time for providing notice of the covert search as much as thirty days after the search. That way, a person wasn't tipped off that he was under surveillance or a suspect. The warrants were mentioned in the Patriot Act legislation after 9/11, but they'd been used by law enforcement long before that. Terrorism didn't have to be involved to justify the warrant, just the belief that a Federal crime was involved. Like murder and kidnapping.

Sanchez led them through the lobby of the Technology Education Building and up the stairs to the third floor. Midway down the hallway, Morales was talking with the four public safety officers who were standing in a line with their backs to the door of the office he wanted to search.

Drake let Agent Williams take the lead when they approached.

"Gentlemen, my name is Special Agent Wayne Williams of the FBI."

He held out his FBI badge for inspection.

Public Safety Sergeant Billings stepped forward to look at the badge and make sure the photo matched the man holding it. "May I have your agent number, Special Agent Williams?"

Williams recited his FBI agent number and watched as the public safety sergeant wrote it down in his black pocket coil notebook.

"What's this all about, Agent Williams?"

"I'm here to search this office."

"You know I can't let you do that."

"You can and you will, Sergeant Billings. A search warrant is on the way."

"So is our attorney."

"Fine, I'll be happy to meet him, but you know that won't delay the search of this office."

"It will if he says it will."

Special Agent Williams smiled sweetly. "Sergeant, if you or your attorney impedes the search of this office for so much as one minute when the warrant is here, you will be arrested and charged with obstruction of justice. Do I make myself clear, Sergeant Billings?"

The public safety sergeant didn't respond other than to step back in line with his men and fold his arms across his chest.

The standoff at the office lasted for another fifteen minutes until five FBI agents climbed the stairs to the third floor and the covert 'sneak and peek' search warrant was handed to Special Agent Williams and a copy of it was presented to Sergeant Billings.

With the copy of the warrant in his hand, Sergeant Billings took a key from his key ring and opened the door of the office. Special Agent Williams led his men into the office and began the search of the office they quickly determined was the office of Professor Ari Ahmadi.

Chapter Thirty-Eight

PROFESSOR ARI AHMADI was enjoying a glass of chilled pinot gris in his luxurious room at the Fairmont Banff Springs Hotel in Banff, Alberta, Canada when the FBI conducted its 'sneak and peek' search of his office. If he had known what they were doing, he would have laughed.

Professor Ari Ahmadi no longer existed. He was now Allen Arnold Madison, an American-born Muslim from Chicago, Illinois. He'd had plenty of time to plan his escape after draining the accounts of the wealthiest Catholic parishioners, and now he had the expensive new identity along with the wealth he needed to live the life he'd dreamed of.

When he'd discovered Samantha's treachery, he'd only had to move up the timetable of his plan. There was a technical symposium in Vancouver, Canada he was already registered for that was scheduled for the weekend before Samantha's planned attacks. Instead of traveling to his ultimate destination in Central America after the symposium, he'd decided to take a short unplanned vacation.

He booked passage on the Rocky Mountaineer train, with Goldleaf Service, for the two-day, one-night trip to Banff, Alberta, Canada. Instead of attending the symposium, he picked up his packet of information and took a cab directly to the train station. While the college knew he planned on attending the gathering for computer science educators and researchers, no one knew of his little vacation plan.

And since no one, except the forger he'd purchased his new identity from, knew that he was now Allen Arnold Madison, no one would know he'd rented a BMW 328iX from Avis at Calgary International Airport for the sixty-seven-mile drive to Banff.

Allen Madison poured another glass of pinot gris from the ice bucket on the glass-topped coffee table and set it on the end table next to his blood-red leather chair. With his laptop open in his lap, he checked the balance in his offshore account in Panama one more time. Nineteen million, eight hundred thousand dollars! He felt like a kid on Christmas morning having a hard time believing he'd actually gotten the gift he'd asked for.

The problem was going to be finding out who Samantha was working with and silencing them, all of them, without letting the men he answered to find out about it. The more he thought about it the clearer it became that it wasn't his ISIS sponsors. He had agreed to train and help young women work as online recruiters if they had the ability or to be ISIS brides if they didn't. He'd done that and there was no need to bring someone in to handle Samantha.

He'd found her, recruited her and trained her. When she'd become obsessed with the idea of becoming a modern-day Nusaybah bint Ka'ab, also called Umm

'Umara, he'd faithfully sought approval of her plan and carefully monitored her planning for it. He'd coordinated the vetting of the others she had recruited and given each of them laptops he could access whenever he wanted to see who they were communicating with.

That's why he'd been so surprised to learn that she was working with someone else. How had anyone else, except those he answered to, known of her intentions, let alone had the opportunity or time to turn her?

Unless, of course, someone else was on to him. As careful as he was, it was always possible that, somewhere along the line, his name had been mentioned, with admiration he hoped, and a rival or a rival faction had investigated him. With the vast numbers involved in the underground of terrorism, it was certainly a possibility. But why interfere in the plans they were about to carry out?

The command to attack the Catholic Church was understood by all. Who wouldn't want cross worshippers to die by anyone's hand who was willing to make the sacrifice? There had to be more to this intervention, this betrayal, than that.

He thought back to the one aspect of their plan that Samantha had objected to, the draining of the bank and savings accounts of the wealthy parishioners. She had begged for them to be killed in their homes as they originally intended. She wanted to be the one to do it.

But he had carefully explained that the intent was to scare churchgoers all across America and the crucifixion of the attorney coupled with the demands to convert or die that would be delivered would do that. When she demanded to be allowed to select four of the Catholic churches to attack during mass, he'd gone to bat for her and obtained permission for that plan as well.

But she never stopped complaining about his plan to take their money. She wanted to hurt them but not by just hitting their pocket books.

Could that be the reason Samantha turned to someone else and betrayed him? But why? She didn't even know the names of the wealthy parishioners whose accounts he'd hacked into. She didn't have any way to identify them and administer Allah's justice, as she called it.

He picked up the glass of wine and sat staring at the screen of his open laptop, the account balance in his offshore account. And then it hit him, like a bucket of cold water being emptied over his head.

It was all about the money! Someone was using Samantha to get to the money he'd stolen. It had to be a rival faction within ISIS or even another jihadist group because Samantha would never help someone if it was just about money. They would have had to have something else on her to persuade her to betray him.

Ahmadi cursed and threw his wine glass across the room, hitting a painting of Lake Louise dead center and shattering. Someone was after his money and threatening his new life.

Chapter Thirty-Nine

ZAL NAZIR WAITED for Samantha Taylor or, as she demanded to be called now, Umara, at the same table at the Copper River Restaurant and Bar as before. It was close to his office at Intel and convenient for him, and it got her away from Portland where she was known.

It was also close to the farm north of the town of Helvetia where he'd told her to go and sequester her crew until they deployed on their mission the following week. The farm was an old dairy farm and, while the farmhouse wasn't much, the barn had been updated before he bought the place so that weddings and other events could be held there.

He'd purchased the farm several years before, when he had visions of building a house there and raising goats to make cheese like his ancestors had. That vision disappeared like fog in the morning when he learned that his uncle, who was an Iranian nuclear scientist, had been assassinated by the Jews of Mossad.

From that day forward, he'd dedicated his life to jihad,

against the infidels and their countries, especially Israel. He was the founder and leader of the Islamic Revolutionary Council of America (IRCA). Umara's coopted mission was the Council's first strike against the leader of the West, but it wouldn't be the last. The Council intended to wage a smarter war than the way the old leaders fought it, but the twenty million Professor Ahmadi had planned to steal was too good to pass up.

Today, Umara was early. She was also upset. He could tell by the way she punched the air with her motorcycle helmet as she walked into the restaurant and marched across the floor to his table.

She turned her chair around and straddled it before she hissed. "How did they find the cabin? How? I lost two of my fighters!"

Nazir leaned toward her and put both hands flat on the table. "Take a deep breath and try to relax while we talk about this. Your anger will only cloud your thinking."

"Safiya martyred herself so she wouldn't betray us. The others would have done the same if it was necessary. How could they have known we were there? No one has talked."

"Think about it. You didn't give the woman a chance to send a message to someone, and yet she did. How do you think that could have happened?"

Umara massaged her forehead and then her chin as she thought. "We searched her clothes for a tracking device and didn't find anything. But we didn't search her body. An implanted tracker of some sort?"

"That's my assumption. Employers are using implanted GPS microchips to keep track of their employees these days. Maybe the people she works for did the same thing. The other possibility is they know about Professor Ahmadi and learned that it was his cabin."

"If they know about him then they know about me."

As Umara considered the implications of that, Nazir signaled to a waiter for two beers like the one he'd just finished.

"Do you want something to eat?"

Umara shook her head. "I'm not hungry."

"Let's run through the possibilities. The woman could have had a microchip and they knew she was missing. They followed the signal to the cabin to rescue her and got lucky. Or they might have known something about Ahmadi. But I'm certain they didn't know the cabin is his. The cabin is owned by a company registered in Panama, I checked. I believe it's his company, but you can't tell from the registration. So the most likely possibility is an implanted microchip."

"How do you know about the company in Panama?"

"It's my job to know, Umara. We've been watching him for some time, even before you started sleeping with him."

Nazir wasn't surprised to see that she wasn't embarrassed by the revelation, but he could also see that she didn't like it that he knew about her sex life.

"If you've been watching him then where is he now?"

The waiter brought two pints of the draft beer Nazir was drinking and set them down on the table.

"Would either of you like to order something to eat?"

'No, we're fine. Thanks."

Nazir took one of the new pints and raised it. "Cheers, because I know exactly where he is. When you failed to get him in his condo, I assigned a brother to watch him. He never came back to his condo. He checked into a hotel and then left for a symposium in Vancouver, Canada. From there, he took a train to Calgary and rented a car and drove to Banff. He's there now."

"Why didn't you kill him before he left Portland?"

"Because I want to know what he's up to. He may think ISIS doesn't trust him and he's on the run. He may be planning something against us if he's learned you're working with us. Either way, I need to know what he's planning so I can react accordingly. When it's time, Professor Ahmadi will be taken care of."

"What do you want me to do in the meantime?"

"Do as we planned. Stay out of sight at the farm. There are no neighbors close by, but they will notice anything unusual. The barn has been used for events in the past so seeing people there won't be that unusual. Do any practicing or preparing for next week in the barn with the barn doors closed. There's plenty of room in there. We'll meet again Monday."

"I'll have to change my plans for the four churches now that I'm two fighters short. Do you think I should just hit three instead?"

"That's up to you. You'll have the element of surprise on your side. You could use three fighters at three of the churches and you go to St. Patrick's. But it's your call. You have field command for this."

Umara downed the last of her beer and stood. "That's it then, until Monday."

She turned and started to walk away before returning. "When it's time to take care of Ahmadi, I want to be there."

Zal watched her leave the restaurant and stride to her motorcycle. Knowing what she'd done to the attorney before hanging him on the cross, he wondered if maybe he should consider taking her to see Ahmadi. He would surely be afraid of the things she could do to him.

He paid for their beers and left the restaurant thinking that if she survived the attacks on the churches, he would invite her to go with him to take care of the professor.

Chapter Forty

AGENT WILLIAMS CAME out of the office on the third floor of the Technology Education Building and walked over to Drake and the others.

"The office is pretty clean. Nothing in his desk except class schedules, outlines for the classes he teaches, computer science literature and mailers for symposiums and conferences. They're downloading everything from his PC, but it looks like everything on it is related to his classes, grades and college staff notices, etc.

"We're getting as much about him as we can from the college, but it's Saturday. The attorney is advising them not to volunteer any information until they see a search warrant or a court order. There are other ways to get what we're asking for, but it might take a day or so."

"Is there anything there that identifies the woman Sanchez saw at his door?"

"Not that I've seen. She might be a student of his. I'm asking for a list of all of his students for this last year. That might narrow it down some. I'd like Ms. Sanchez to look at the pictures of his students from the photos they use for the student ID cards. She might be able to recognize our woman. If not, we'll have to consider looking at the photos of all the female students at this campus."

Morales playfully slapped Sanchez on the shoulder. "Guess you won't have much time for our workouts any time soon."

"With the way you've been sparring, who says I need them?"

"Ha, ha, Chiquita. We'll see how you do next time."

Drake held up a hand to stop the banter for a moment. "Do we know anything about this professor? Where he lives? What he drives? What he looks like?"

"The college requires criminal background checks and fingerprinting of all new hires. I should have that information by the end of the day."

Benning was standing next to Drake. He leaned close and whispered in his ear. "I think I can get it faster. I'm going downstairs to make a call."

Agent Williams watched Benning leave and smiled. "Of course, if you come up with that information before then, I'm sure you'll share it with me."

Drake smiled back. "Of course."

They all turned at the sound of the other FBI agents coming out of the professor's office, followed by the public safety sergeant who had been taking notes of what was searched and what was taken.

Agent Williams nodded to his lead agent, who advised the sergeant that he could secure the office, that they had all they needed today.

The FBI agents moved past and Agent Williams reminded Drake of their agreement. "Let's keep the sharing going. I think we might have something here."

"I think so too. I'll be in touch."

Drake, Sanchez and Morales followed the FBI agents down the stairs and found Benning near the lobby's doors with his phone held to his ear. He waved them over.

"Professor Ahmadi lives not far from here. He has a condo in Sullivan's Gulch. I have the address. Like to see where the professor lives?"

"We should make sure it's the right address before I share the information with Agent Williams. Lead the way, Sherlock."

Professor's Ahmadi's condo was in one of the oldest neighborhoods in Portland. Benning was familiar with the area because he'd grown up in Northeast Portland.

"Sullivan's Gulch is named after Timothy Sullivan, an early farmer there. It sits on a natural gulch that runs east from the Willamette River. It originally was a riparian forested area with waterfalls and a spring. In the Great Depression, it was called 'Hooverville', a shanty town. Now it's got some of the great old homes in Portland and some great restaurants.

"Ahmadi's condo is pretty high end for a community college professor, twenty-eight-hundred dollars a month for a two-bedroom, two-and-a-half-bath spread. He's on the fourth floor and the building does have security. We might not get very far."

The building wasn't what Drake had expected. It was modern, a stained-cedar and glass cube of a building parked in the middle of a stately old neighborhood on a tree-lined street. With its black trim and a roof with copper trim and gutters, the building shouted luxury.

They parked on the street in front of the building and let Benning lead the way. In the lobby, a security guard sat behind an enclosed desk watching them.

Benning walked over and held out his hand. "Jimmy, how long has it been? Ten years since you retired?"

The old security guard stood to shake Benning's hand. "Detective Benning, nice to see you again. It's only been seven years, but it feels like twenty. Margaret died two years after I left the department and I needed something to keep me occupied. What can I do for you, Detective?"

"Does Professor Ari Ahmadi live here?"

"He does. Fourth floor condo. But he's not in. In fact, I haven't seen him for a couple of days. He travels a lot."

"Is he married?"

"No, but he has a young hottie that spends a lot of time up there. I figure she's one of his students, but it's none of my business."

"Is she up there, by any chance?"

"No, I haven't seen her since Wednesday night. Actually, I didn't see her. I saw her on the security tapes when I reviewed them. She went up with two other men, but he wasn't in, so they didn't stay long."

"Can I see the tapes? It's important, Jimmy. I'm working with the FBI on something he may know something about. This woman might know something too, if I can find out who she is."

"You know I'm not supposed to let anyone see those tapes. We guard the privacy of our residents here very seriously."

"I don't doubt that for a minute. I know the kind of man you are, Jimmy. But this is really important."

"I can't let you take the tapes with you."

"Just let this woman see them for Wednesday night. She's a witness and can identify the woman we're looking for. We think it might be the hottie that visits Professor Ahmadi."

Benning's old colleague struggled with his decision for half a minute and then waved for Benning and Carol Sanchez to follow him. He opened the door behind his desk and held it for them to enter the room.

Morales stood beside Drake and whistled. "That was slick. He's still got the moves, doesn't he?"

"Indeed, he does. We can both learn a thing or two from Detective Benning. He was the best detective in the Sheriff's Office when I was prosecuting in the D.A.'s Office. It appears he hasn't lost his touch."

Fifteen minutes later, the door behind the security guard's desk opened and a smiling Carol Sanchez was the first one out.

"It's her. Ahmadi's girlfriend is Umara."

Chapter Forty-One

ON THE WAY to Drake's office, he called Agent Wayne Williams and asked him to join them. They were meeting in his conference room and had new information to share.

Paul Benning called ahead to his wife, Margo, and asked her to head down to the office from the condo. Coffee was in order and maybe a platter of sandwiches from the deli nearby.

Drake also called Kevin McRoberts, the young hacker-cum-computer genius who ran the IT division of Puget Sound Security. Was there anything more that he'd uncovered about the missing millions stolen from the parishioners or about the company registered in Panama?

"I'm having a hard time following the money without breaking too many laws in the process, Mr. Drake. The money initially was deposited in an offshore account in Liechtenstein belonging to a shell company in Grand Cayman. From there, it was transferred to another offshore account in Singapore. That's where I am right now, working on the Singapore bank records.

"The company registered in Panama that owns the house in Vancouver and the cabin in Oregon is a similar story, a shell company that belongs to another shell company and so on."

"All right, keep digging, Kevin. We may have some information shortly that will help."

It was five o'clock Saturday evening when they all convened in the conference room at Drake's law office. Margo had coffee, soft drinks and a platter of ham and cheese and turkey cranberry sandwiches waiting for them.

Drake let his hungry crew eat while they waited for Agent Williams. Sanchez and Morales hadn't eaten since breakfast and Benning's new diet wasn't carrying him through the day without being hungry.

Agent Williams used the call box at the front door of the office to let them know he'd arrived and Margo escorted him to the conference room. When he saw that the others were eating, he grabbed a sandwich and a Pepsi and took a seat at the conference table.

"Paul did some digging while you were searching Ahmadi's office. He found the address for the condo where he lives and we stopped by on the way here."

Agent Williams put his sandwich down and raised his eyebrows.

Before he could stop chewing, Drake explained. "It was on our path home, sort of, and Paul knew the Sullivan's Gulch neighborhood where his condo is. We got lucky. The security guard for the building was a retired deputy sheriff and remembered Detective Benning. He let Paul see the building's CCTV security tapes for last week with Sanchez. She recognized Ahmadi's girlfriend. It's Umara."

Agent Williams choked on the food he was chewing and took a quick swallow of his Pepsi. "Are you sure, Sanchez?"

"One hundred percent positive. She's the one I followed. She's the one who gave me a ride to the house when I was kidnapped."

Drake summarized what they knew. "The woman I shot at the cabin identified Umara as their leader. She also claimed they killed Michael Brennan. Now we find that Umara is Professor Ahmadi's girlfriend and that he teaches computer science at the community college. He's a computer guy and may be skilled enough to hack the archdiocese and steal the twenty million."

"That's quite a leap, Drake. You're assuming he's involved with this Umara who you think was recruiting young women for ISIS. Why, just because he might be a Muslim and knows Umara? And why steal the twenty million?"

"That's why we need to find Ahmadi and find out."

"We're looking for him. We did learn from the college that he's attending a computer science symposium in Canada. They were willing to tell us that much. We're trying to track him down at the symposium."

Sanchez spoke up. "What about the other girls? A public safety officer told me she was a student I should talk to when she walked by. Maybe they're all students. We know what the two dead girls look like or looked like. Maybe someone on campus can ID the others in the group. One of them might lead us to Umara."

Margo Benning was leaning against the wall behind her husband, listening. "Can't the FBI get a search warrant to examine the college enrollment records to identify these other young women? When I worked with Adam in the D.A.'s Office, I obtained warrants for him with less information than you have now."

Drake backed her up. "She did and could do it again, if you need help, Williams."

"I can get the damn warrant. But can't it wait until Monday? I'm making a lot of people work on their weekends. Besides, I don't have the backing of my office yet. The only thing I can prove now is that the woman Sanchez saw, who was called Umara by a dead kidnapper, knows Professor Ahmadi."

"Agent Williams, the dead kidnapper also said they had something planned for the Catholic churches," Sanchez said. "The ISIS attack in France where the priest was beheaded occurred inside the church during a mass. What if the attack Umara has planned is scheduled for tomorrow and we waited until Monday?"

That sobering thought silenced the room.

Drake broke the silence. "She's right, Williams. We need to find Umara now. I know you have an office to convince, but we can help. Let's divide the work and get started. I know I'll have trouble sleeping if something happens that we could have prevented."

Agent Williams looked around the table and saw that everyone agreed with Drake. He got up and carried his empty paper plate and Pepsi can to the food service cart near the door.

"I'll do what I can. It would be helpful if you would write down everything you have collectively learned and get it to me. With your permission, I'll put it in my report and meet with my boss today. He's not going to like it that this contradicts everything he's been saying publicly. But I think he's a fair man and will act appropriately."

Chapter Forty-Two

AFTER DRAKE SENT everyone home to get a good night's sleep and prepare for a long day tomorrow, he retreated to his office in the loft.

Boats were parading up and down the river past the RiverPlace Marina outside his window as he took out a fifth of Jim Beam Black and a tumbler from his credenza under the window and poured himself two fingers of the amber bourbon.

The whirl of events in the last three days had taken a toll and he was tired. Maybe not tired, more like moody. He wasn't depressed, he remembered what that was like after Kay died and he struggled to live without her. He kept seeing the face of the kidnapper holding the rifle to Sanchez's head just before he shot her. And that brought on the guilt for sending Sanchez to the college in the first place.

Maybe it was time to quit getting involved in these things before someone close to him got killed. Time to stop being the soldier he was once and let the guys who got paid for doing the job take over.

Drake sat down at his desk and called Liz in Washington.

"Adam, I hoped you would call tonight. How are you doing?"

"Feeling tired, but I'm okay."

"When you tell me you're okay, it usually means you're not. What's going on?"

He tried to find the words to describe how he felt and failed. "I don't know, exactly. Feeling a little blue, I guess. Not sure why. Wish you were here."

"What's happened?"

"We're still looking for the woman who took Sanchez. We've linked her to a professor at the community college, but we don't know if she was just his girlfriend or if he's involved somehow. I met Wayne Williams. We're sharing information. He seems like a good guy."

"I worked well with him and he was well-thought-of in the FBI until he crossed swords with the director. When politics take over, your friends seem to disappear. How's he doing in Portland?"

"We'll find out. He's presenting what we've come up with to the SIAC about now. The investigation of the murder of Michael Brennan is over. The suicide of the man who allegedly took responsibility for the murder in a suicide note left on his laptop closed that out. It fit nicely with the FBI conclusion this was all just a cybercrime. Williams' report will cause them to rethink their conclusion. We'll see if they will."

She heard him swallow. "Are you having a drink right now? Without me?"

"Guilty as charged. I'll save some for when you get here."

"I think I'll be able to fly out in a week. Care to tell me about the little vacation you have planned for me?"

"It's a surprise. You'll have to wait until you get here."

"All right for you then. Good night, cowboy. Get some rest."

"You do the same."

Drake finished his drink and left the office feeling better after talking with her, but there was still something bothering him and he realized what it was. He was afraid they wouldn't find Umara in time to stop whatever she was planning.

He thought about what she could be planning all the way home to his farm in Dundee. He knew that terrorists like to strap suicide vests on women and children, but he didn't see Umara as that kind of terrorist. Sanchez said her kidnapper had bragged that Umara was as good a fighter as her namesake and that she'd trained them all as new female warriors for the final battle. She had to be planning something that fit her image as a female warrior, however she imagined that to be.

Despite the slow crawl on the drive home, he wasn't able to conceive of what she was planning. In fact, the purring of the opposed flat-six engine in his Porsche 993 was making him drowsy and that was not a good thing. On most days, the sound of the engine excited his racing instinct and made him want to drive faster.

When he turned onto the long drive that led past the rows prepared and waiting for the new rootstock to be planted, he saw Lancer running down to greet him. He honked once and shouted out the window, "Race you home."

Lancer beat him by fifty yards, as he kept the speed of his car at a sedate twenty-five miles an hour. After a hearty greeting from his dog, who thoroughly searched him for the steaks he'd stopped for in Dundee, he held the bag of promised treat over Lancer's head and led him into the house.

Before he had time to season and prepare the steaks for the grill, he received two phone calls in a row.

The first was from Agent Williams.

"How did your meeting with the SIAC go?"

"Better than expected. He's not willing to reopen the investigation of Brennan's murder, but he's given me the green light to investigate Umara and the kidnapping. I'll have the warrant I requested for the college tomorrow morning. We should be able to identify Umara and her crew shortly."

"That's good news, Wayne. Thanks for the call and let me know if you need anything from me. Do you have the number for Carol Sanchez, if you need her to look at photos at the college?"

"I don't."

"I'll text it to you. Talk with you tomorrow."

The second call was from Benning.

"I found the link between Brennan and Ahmadi. I was going over the report the Sheriff's Office got for the suicide that closed the FBI's case. The kid was a plaintiff in one of the suits against the archdiocese and Brennan was the defense attorney representing the archdiocese. It got me thinking about other cases Brennan handled that might have upset someone. Brennan also represented a wealthy donor to Portland State University who demanded that Ahmadi be fired for calling out the donor's son in class as a bigoted redneck who hated Muslims. Ahmadi lost his hearing and was terminated as a tenured professor at the university. That's how he wound up at a community college.

For a tenured university professor, that's a big blow and a huge financial setback."

"Good work, Paul. You need to get that to Agent Williams. Do you have his number?"

"I have his card."

"The stink on Professor Ahmadi is getting stronger by the day. See you tomorrow."

Chapter Forty-Three

ARI AHMADI NOTICED the young man the first time the day before at the Banff Upper Hot Springs. He was wearing a grey Patagonia T-shirt the same color as his. His hiking shorts and shoes looked new and Ahmadi assumed they had been purchased in the Patagonia store on Banff Avenue when the man arrived in Banff. He had done the same thing when he arrived.

Once, when he was soaking in the outdoor thermal pool and enjoying the one-hundred-and-four-degree water and the stunning alpine views, he caught the man looking at him across the pool. His first thought was the man might be gay. They were the only two single men in the pool at the time.

Then, at lunch today, on the Lookout Patio of his hotel that featured the rich fares of the Mediterranean, he saw the man sitting two tables away. He was wearing sunglasses and eating one of the wraps on the menu. When he'd turned away from the view of the nearby mountain peaks and picked up his wrap, Ahmadi was sure he was watching him from behind his sunglasses.

Now he was sure the man was following him. To confirm his suspicion, he was riding the Banff Gondola to the top of Sulphur Mountain and the man was in the same four-passenger cabin with him. Same clothes, same sunglasses and now a booney hat. He was turned away and looking back toward Banff, but Ahmadi knew it was the same man.

What he couldn't fathom was how he'd been found. The tickets for the train from Vancouver to Calgary were purchased using a credit card issued to his holding company in Panama. He was using his new name that only two people knew of, his expensive forger and himself. Allen Madison was the name he used to rent the BMW he'd driven to Banff and his room reservation was in the same name.

The only possible answer was that he'd been followed from Vancouver and the symposium he was supposed to have attended. But why and by whom? Surely the police weren't looking for him, yet. Samantha had no reason to follow him. She would be focused on her plan to attack the churches in two days. But if someone was after the money he'd stolen, it could be her new friends. He would have to find out.

When they reached the summit, Ahmadi got out and purposely strolled around the ridgetop boardwalk, admiring the view. He entered the summit facility and checked out the restaurants and stopped to examine several of the interpretive exhibits. When he couldn't locate the other man, he quickly walked to the line for the next gondola cabin leaving the summit.

The man wasn't quick enough to get into his gondola cabin, but as Ahmadi's dropped away from the summit, he saw the man was in line for the next one down.

When he reached the gondola terminal at the base of Sulphur Mountain, he hurried to his BMW in the parking lot and sped away, just as the next gondola cabin was pulling in.

Ahmadi was in two minds as he drove away. Should he keep on driving and ditch his belongings in his room? It would be the safer of the two options he could think of, but it would mean leaving his laptop behind. There was too much on it to leave it behind. The other option was to return to his room and think of a way to get the man alone and find out who he was and why he was following him.

He didn't think of himself as a violent man, although he knew how to be one. He'd just never needed to be one. The one time he wanted to be, Samantha had volunteered to do it for him when she'd badly beaten the bully in his class. This time, he was on his own.

At the hotel, he had the valet service park his car and went straight to his room to decide how he was going to get the man alone. It had to be somewhere isolated and private. He didn't need witnesses for what he had in mind and certainly didn't want to wind up in a Canadian jail.

It was four forty-five in the afternoon when he closed the door to his room and sat down at the writing desk to open his laptop. A quick search established that sunset was ten minutes after nine that evening, which would give him time to have a light dinner back on the Lookout Patio, where he could be seen, and then a hike up to the summit of Sulphur Mountain.

The hike to the summit of Sulphur Mountain required three hours for the average hiker, the brochure he picked up in the lobby advised, but he didn't need to reach the summit. The switchbacks that began soon after you left the Upper Hot Springs parking lot and started up the trail would offer several opportunities to surprise the man and get him alone.

And then he would see how fast the man would talk when his Benchmade Infidel dagger was pressed against his neck. It was his favorite and only weapon; a fast-action, automatic-opening, out-the-front tactical knife. He carried it every day and felt safe with it in his pocket. He'd never had to use it, but tonight would provide him the opportunity.

Ahmadi took off his hiking shoes and lay down on his bed to visualize the evening. He would leave at six o'clock to have dinner on the Lookout Patio then drive to the Upper Hot Springs parking lot. When he was sure he was being followed, he would start up the trail and find the right place with no one around and spring his surprise.

When he had the answers he needed, he would drag the man's body far enough from the trail that he wouldn't be found for days. Then, the next morning, he would decide whether to leave for his ultimate destination or make sure his business was finished in Oregon.

Chapter Forty-Four

AHMADI SELECTED roasted steelhead trout and a glass of chardonnay from the Lookout Patio's menu for dinner. He took his time enjoying his meal until he saw the man come out on the patio and ask for a table.

As soon as the man was seated and looking at the menu, he got up and abruptly left the patio. At the valet service desk, he presented his ticket and stood patiently while his car was brought around. When he saw the man rush up behind him, he told the valet where he was going.

"Seems like a good evening for a sunset hike up the trail to Sulphur Mountain. Can you tell me when the last gondola will leave from the summit?"

"The service runs until nine thirty each night during the summer. You might have to hurry up the trail, sir. It takes most people two and half to three hours to make it to the top."

"I'd better hurry then."

He didn't know if the man had a car, but it didn't

matter. He would be up the trail waiting for him, however long it took him to get there.

Ahmadi tipped the valet and got in his car. The man was talking to the valet and motioning for him to hurry up and get him a cab.

A satisfied smile spread across Ahmadi's face as he drove away. It was going just as he had planned. The man had been caught off guard and was hurrying. He would be thinking about catching up and not worrying about what he might find around the next bend in the trail.

He parked the BMW in the Upper Hot Springs parking lot and started up the trail. When he reached the first switchback, he couldn't see if the man was on the trail yet. But it was too close to the trailhead and there wasn't enough cover there to conceal his position. He continued hiking.

It was a decent hike to the next switchback, with lodgepole pine, spruce and fir trees lining the path. The ground dropped off steeply to the left and in places was perfect for tossing a body over and letting it roll far enough so that it couldn't easily be seen from the trail.

When he was out of view around the switchback, he searched for a hiding place. The mountain sloped steeply up on his right, with a cluster of trees near the edge of the trail. To the left, the ground was rocky and barren for the first thirty yards or so down the steep slope. The location wasn't perfect, but it would have to do.

Ahmadi climbed up the bank and hid behind two pine trees that were growing close together. His position was four feet above the trail and a short leap down on the man when he passed below.

He took his dagger out of his pocket and squatted down behind the trees. From there, he could see up and down the trail. He hadn't seen anyone coming back down from the summit so far on the trail and prayed that his luck would hold out.

Ten minutes later, he heard the footfall of an approaching hiker. He was hiking at a rapid pace and Ahmadi could hear his heavy breathing as he came around the switchback.

It was the man who'd been following him. Head down and arms pumping, moving fast.

There was no one else that he could see on the trail in either direction.

Ahmadi waited until the man was even with the first of the two pine trees and stepped around the second one to his right and jumped down. He landed on the man's back and knocked him down. Before the man could react and get up, the blade of his Infidel dagger was at his throat.

"I've been wanting to meet you. This seems like a good time. Who are you?"

"Let me up and I'll tell you."

Ahmadi was straddling the man, sitting on his back with his knees pinning the man's arms down on the dusty trail.

"Sorry, can't do that. I'll ask again. Who are you?"

"No one you know, Professor. What do you think you're going to do if I don't tell you? Kill me? You're a desk man, not a fighter."

Ahmadi pressed the tip of the dagger into his neck deeply enough to draw blood.

"Whoever sent you must not know me very well."

"We know everything about you, Ahmadi. Your girlfriend says you're a little old for all the things you try to do in bed."

"Samantha will get what's coming to her, don't worry about that. One last time, who sent you?"

The man tried to roll and throw him off his back but

Ahmadi dug the blade a little deeper in his neck and stopped the attempt to escape.

"Your time is over, old man. ISIS and the caliphate are just a dream. We're the future and you don't even know we exist. But you will. Kill me and the Council will hunt you down wherever you go. Go ahead."

Ahmadi didn't hesitate and gave the man his wish. He lifted the man's head by his hair and drew the blade deeply across his neck before jumping off his back to avoid any blood spray.

He looked up and down the trail and saw that he had time to roll the body across the trail and down the rocky slope. Grabbing his ankles, he turned the body over on its back, dragged it to the edge and rolled it over with a shove.

The body kept rolling and sliding across the rocky surface until it came to rest against a gnarly snag of a tree thirty yards down. In the shadows of the late evening, it wouldn't be noticed until morning.

Ahmadi scuffed dirt over the pool of blood where the man had been lying and checked to see if there was a trail of blood to the edge of the trail. He didn't see one and turned to walk back to his car, wiping the blade of his dagger clean on a napkin he'd taken from his table on the Lookout Patio.

His immediate problem was solved, but he still didn't know who was after him. The 'Council'? A rival group critical of ISIS and the caliphate? He couldn't conceive of a group foolish enough to challenge ISIS. If it did exist, he would have to find it and make sure it was eliminated. It appeared his future might depend on it.

Chapter Forty-Five

DRAKE LEFT early Sunday morning and drove back to Portland. The traffic was light at eight in the morning and the parking garage closest to Mother's Bistro and Bar still had parking available on the lower floors.

Mother's was a favorite breakfast spot in downtown Portland and Agent Williams was buying. He'd called an hour ago and wanted to compare notes before he set off for the community college and a busy day.

Williams was sitting at one of the outside tables with a cup of coffee halfway to his mouth in his right hand and a menu in his left. When Drake pulled out a chair to sit down, he didn't look up. Breakfast for the FBI agent appeared to be serious business.

"I can't decide between the wild salmon hash and the stuffed frittata."

"Can't go wrong with either one."

Williams handed the menu to Drake. "The salmon hash then. Thanks for driving in to meet me. Benning called last night and told me about Ahmadi and Brennan. I'm getting a lot of resistance in the office when I ask for anything that relates to Brennan's murder. I may have to investigate that on my own."

"Let Benning help. He's on good terms with the Sheriff's Office."

"All right. What do you have planned for today?"

"I'm going to my office. You haven't found Ahmadi, have you?"

"No. He picked up his registration packet, but no one remembers seeing him after that."

"I thought I'd have my guy at PSS see if he can track him down. He's been searching for the twenty million the archdiocese would like to recover for its parishioners."

A waiter came out to take their orders and refill Williams' coffee cup. Drake held up his hand, with his finger crooked like he was holding a cup, on the waiter's way past a service stand. It would be his second cup of coffee for the day, but he didn't think it would be the last.

He couldn't shake the feeling that they were running out of time.

Williams ordered his wild salmon hash and Drake made it simple, ordering the omelet du jour.

When the waiter left, Williams continued. "We're serving the search warrant at the college at ten. If Carol Sanchez could meet me at Parking Lot One, I'll get her started looking for Umara. We know where the two dead women lived and teams are on their way there to search their apartments. When we identify Umara and find out where she lives, would you like to join me when I go there?"

"Call me and I'll meet you."

"Can you think of anything else we could be doing?"

Drake watched a bike courier ride by and thought about what they were all doing. Umara and Ahmadi were the key and they didn't know where they were.

"Have you reached out to the CIA or NSA to see if there's anything about ISIS and these women on campus? You'd think someone would be talking about it."

"I checked everything our Counterterrorism Division had last night and there's nothing about the community college or Oregon. We know ISIS is active online. We know how they identify individuals and vet them before they ever meet someone in person. But there's nothing about activity here."

"Then we focus on what we have, Umara and Ahmadi."

When their food arrived, the two men made small talk until they were finished. Drake asked about Williams and any family he had, what he'd done in the FBI and where he'd found to live in Portland. Williams was interested in Drake's service in Delta Force and his vineyard.

Then it was time to go to work. Williams stayed to pay for their breakfast and then drove to the FBI field office near the airport. Drake walked to the parking garage and drove to his office at RiverPlace on the Willamette River.

Paul Benning was in the break room making coffee when Drake got there.

"Thought you might be coming in early."

"I met Agent Williams for breakfast."

"You're getting kind of chummy with the FBI. You've kept your distance in the past."

"Williams is different. He doesn't seem to care about protecting his turf or making sure the FBI gets all the credit. But he's having trouble getting full cooperation from this field office. They aren't willing to investigate the Ahmadi/Brennan connection. I suggested that you could help with that and he agreed."

"Good. I'll head over to the Sheriff's Department and see if one of my old friends will let me use his desk for a while. What are you planning on doing?"

"I need to call Sanchez and have her meet Williams on campus. We need to identify Umara and find out where she lives. Williams is going to call me when they find out who she is and where she lives. I'll join him when they search her place."

Benning filled his twenty-ounce Yeti stainless steel insulated coffee tumbler and raised it in a toast. "Here's to happy hunting. I'm off. Call me if you find her."

Drake poured a cup for himself and walked upstairs to the loft. Sanchez was on speed dial and answered on the second ring.

"Agent Williams would like to meet you at ten in the parking lot where you met me yesterday on the campus. If they can narrow your search down to students who identify themselves as Muslim, it might not take you long."

"I'll be there."

Drake heard a voice in the background.

"Marco wants to know what you want him to do."

He started to ask where they were when other voices and someone asking how she wanted her omelet told him they were having the continental breakfast in their hotel.

"Take him with you to the campus. When we know where Umara's friends live, we'll need to question as many of them as we can. See if Agent Williams will let you help him with that. And tell Morales he's there to assist you until I tell him otherwise. He should like that."

"Does that make me the boss for now?"

Drake had to laugh. The two of them were getting along well, but telling Marco she was the boss could change that.

"Tell him whatever you want. Just don't wave the red cape in front of him when you do it."

Chapter Forty-Six

ZAL NAZIR DIDN'T APPRECIATE BEING SUMMONED to a meeting with his FBI contact. But with only two days left before Umara's attacks on the Catholic churches, he needed to know what the FBI was doing.

He knew the FBI had closed its investigation into the death of the attorney when the suicide note left by the city employee was discovered. Umara performed that brilliantly and the FBI had swallowed the deception hook, line and sinker.

But there could still be an investigation into the kidnapping and shooting in Ahmadi's cabin and that concerned him.

His contact was a thirty-eight-year-old Saudi American named Daniel Khan. Born in San Francisco to Saudi immigrant parents, he had a law degree from UC Berkeley and joined the FBI right after graduation. He was condescending and arrogant, like many of the Saudis he knew, and too fond of pastries.

They always met at Ken's Artisan Bakery on NW 21st

Avenue in Portland, convenient for Khan but quite a drive for someone he thought of as his eyes and ears in the Portland Muslim community, which was humorous given that Khan was a Sunni Muslim and he was Shia.

Nazir also found it humorous that the bakery where they met was just two avenues away from the Catholic church on NW 19th Avenue that was the main target for Umara's assault.

Khan was at the counter ordering his pastries and coffee when he walked in. "You want something?"

"Just coffee, thanks."

Nazir saw a small table next to the wall and headed there, leaving Khan to bring his coffee to him. He suppressed a smile as he watched the man balancing a plate and two cups of coffee as he walked across the bakery to the table.

"What's so important that they have you working on Sunday?"

Khan was already stuffing his mouth with what looked like a raspberry croissant, the first of two on his plate.

"We haven't talked in some time. Thought it wouldn't hurt to catch up."

Nazir let it go because it hadn't been that long since their last meeting.

"Nothing new on my end. It's been a quiet summer so far. How about for you?"

Khan washed the last of his croissant down with some coffee and shook his head. "Same thing for me until the new CTD guy arrived and is stirring things up. Have you heard anything about someone who calls herself 'Umara' and a band of women she's trained to be fighters?"

Nazir raised his coffee cup to hide the twitching he felt

at the corners of his mouth. How did they know her nom de guerre or the women with her?

"Where did you hear something like that?"

Khan gave him a funny look before answering. "She's someone we're looking for. Do you know anything about her?"

"Why would I know anything about her? I'd never heard the name until just now. Who is she and why are you looking for her?"

"The other CTD came across the information during an investigation of the kidnapping of an undercover operator working for a private security company. She's believed to be a student at a community college here and maybe even has ties to ISIS."

"I'm shocked. You think ISIS is operating here in Portland?"

"Why wouldn't they be? Portland has had its share of terrorist activity since 9/11. Probably as fertile a place to recruit as any."

"You sound like there are terrorists everywhere. I thought the government reassured us that ISIS was on the run and it's just a matter of time until they're defeated."

"I know, I know. It's still my belief, but there's a different wind blowing from Washington. Look, I've got to get back to the office. Is there anyone you can think of who might know something? Maybe someone on a community college campus that might have an ear to the ground."

"I'm afraid I can't help you, Daniel. I don't know anyone at the Cascade campus. I need to run as well. Thanks for the coffee and, next time, try not to call me on a weekend."

Nazir left as quickly as he could. *Stupid, stupid, stupid.* How could he have been so careless? As he looked in the window of the bakery from the sidewalk, he saw that Khan was watching him. The FBI agent never mentioned the Cascade campus of the community college. He fought the urge to run and walked as quickly as he could to his car parked around the corner, a block away from the bakery.

Khan was lazy, but he wasn't stupid. He needed to do something and do it quickly. The only thing he could think of was silencing the FBI agent. He looked to see if Khan was out on the sidewalk yet. Hopefully, he was still finishing the second croissant.

He had to chance it. He crossed the street and stood in the shade of the awning of a clothing store, where he could watch Khan leave the bakery. While he waited, he called a brother who lived nearby and worked at the Good Samaritan Medical Center.

"Brother, leave immediately and get in your car. I'm across the street from Ken's Bakery. There's a man who will be leaving there soon. I'll follow him to his car and send you a photo of him and his car. He must never reach his office out near the airport alive. Do whatever it takes to make sure he has a fatal accident. If you can't find a way to do that, kill him when he gets out of his car to go inside. Everything depends on this, my brother. Don't let us down."

Nazir stayed on the other side of NW 21st Avenue and tailed Khan as he walked north. Three blocks from the bakery, Khan crossed the street at NW Irving Street and walked east. When Nazir reached the corner, he popped his head around the corner of the building and saw Khan at the door of his car, a Chevrolet Impala.

He leaned around the corner and took a quick photo of Khan and his car. He hadn't been able to get a good full-face of Khan, but it shouldn't matter. He got the car and its license plate.

He ducked back around the corner and sent a text and photo to the brother. Just as he sent the text off, he saw the black Ford Mustang coming his way south on NW 21st Avenue. He stepped to the curb as Khan's car pulled out of its parking space and headed east. The Mustang slowed to let a woman cross the street at the corner and then followed the Impala.

Allah willing, peace be upon his name, it would be the last he would see of the FBI agent.

Chapter Forty-Seven

AGENT WILLIAMS CALLED Drake at ten minutes after eleven o'clock. Finding Umara had been easier than they had expected. Her given name was Samantha Taylor, age twenty. She was a computer science student, had taken a number of classes from Professor Ari Ahmadi and was the founder of the Muslim Women's Empowerment Club.

"Sanchez is looking for the women she saw in the house in Vancouver. She's already picked out five of them from the Muslim Women's Empowerment Club. They all share a common address about fifty blocks from here on NE Killingsworth Street. I'm heading over there in twenty minutes or so. Meet me there and we'll ring the doorbell and see if anyone's home."

"Make sure you're armed. The last time I went to knock on one of their doors, they shot at me with an AK-47."

"We'll be prepared. Might save me the trouble of getting a search warrant if they try that again, exigent circumstances and all."

"Did you learn anything else about Ms. Taylor?"

"She grew up in Reno. She said in a letter that accompanied her college application that she left home when she was seventeen and wanted to start college so she would have a better life than her parents. I've asked the field office in Reno to send someone to interview them."

"How in the world did she get from there to wanting to be a jihadist in three years?"

"On her application, she listed employment as a nanny for a Muslim family here in Portland. I've got someone going to interview them as well."

"All right, give me the address on NE Killingsworth and I'll meet you there."

Drake jotted down the address and retrieved his backup Kimber from his go-bag before he left. No use going in unarmed with this group.

When he approached the address Williams gave him, he was afraid he was going to miss the party. NE Killingsworth Street was blocked by a patrol car with its overhead lights flashing. Fifty feet ahead, two cars had collided and were blocking the traffic in both directions. On down the street, he saw another patrol car blocking traffic from the other direction.

Drake turned his Porsche onto the side street where traffic was being detoured and pulled to the curb. When he got out to walk back to NE Killingsworth, he saw Agent Williams waving to him from the corner.

With all the commotion caused by the accident, it didn't look like they would be searching Umara's house any time soon. Williams stood in the middle of a group of officers, quietly giving orders as Drake got close enough to hear.

"Get the street cleared on both sides. I don't want any

of her neighbors getting hurt. SWAT will wait for that to be done. We have access to her house from the rear. Be casual as you can with the neighbors. Tell them we have reason to believe one of the cars may be carrying explosives and that's why we're clearing the street."

When the officers dispersed, Williams walked over. "Fake accident was the best I could do on short notice. We'll have the neighbors out shortly and then we'll go in."

"You weren't kidding when you said you'd be prepared. How many men do you have here?"

"Six from the field office. The rest are Portland police."

"Which house is Umara's?"

"Six houses east of here, middle of the block."

They watched as neighbors were escorted out of the closest homes and walked toward them. Skirting around them, one of the officers stepped into the street and ran toward them.

He stopped in front of Agent Williams and pointed back down the street. "Agent, a neighbor says she knows Samantha Taylor, but she says they're not home. They all left several days ago."

"Did she see them leave?"

"She said they came out with duffel bags and got in a big SUV. She hasn't seen any of them since."

Agent Williams turned to Drake. "Shall we have a look? I don't want to bring all these people out of their homes if she's not there."

"Do you have the search warrant?"

Williams patted the pocket of his tan suit coat. "Right in here."

"It's your call. If you have someone at the rear of her house, why don't you send them in? They can open the front door for us."

"Why not?" Williams left to speak with the police sergeant in charge. He stood beside him as he held a tactical radio to his mouth and ordered his men to enter from the rear.

Three minutes later, Drake saw the sergeant listen on his radio and nod to Williams, who motioned for him to join them.

"The house is empty. Let's have a look."

Umara's house was an old, two-story craftsman with a full porch along the front. Williams led the way in and thanked the officers who stood inside the door.

The ground floor consisted of a living room with two old couches and a beat-up coffee table. The room across from it was a dining room that opened into a kitchen. The dining table was bare and the kitchen was clean and everything put away. At the back of the first floor were three rooms, a bedroom, a bathroom and a library.

There was nothing on the walls of the bedroom except a calendar on the back of the bedroom door. One bed, a footlocker at its foot and an empty closet furnished the room.

The library had two cots along two of the walls with a foot locker at the foot of each.

Drake followed Williams up the stairs to the second floor. It was equally sparse, with three smaller bedrooms and a bathroom. Each of the bedrooms had three cots and foot lockers for storage.

After looking in the last of the bedrooms, Drake met Williams at the top of the stairs. "This looks like an army barracks. Cots and foot lockers. Not what I expected for a twenty-year-old college student and her roommates."

"Did you notice the lack of decorations? The only thing hung on any of the walls is that calendar downstairs."

Drake remembered the calendar in the large bedroom across from the library and its empty bookshelves. The calendar was for the current month of August. One day was circled in red, the fifteenth, a Tuesday just two days away.

Chapter Forty-Eight

ZAL NAZIR WAITED in his Orenco Station apartment for a text message confirming his FBI contact was dead. When his phone pinged with the confirmation, he quickly called Umara.

"I'm coming out. Keep everyone inside."

He ended the call before she had a chance to ask why.

The decision he had to make was critical to their plans. Not just the plan for this week but for all *their p*lans. Umara was the ISIS model for widespread attacks on Christian churches in America. When he acquired her services as a Council asset, he'd decided to use the Council's online presence to promote her as an inspiration for others to follow. With every church attack, fearful Christians would consider their alternatives; practice their faith in fearful privacy in their homes or consider openly practicing the fastest growing religion in America, Islam.

If Umara was now compromised, should he allow her to continue or abort the attacks and tie up loose ends? That would mean making sure none of the women on his farm ever left there and finding Ari Ahmadi. He knew he could accomplish the former with some help, but he wasn't sure he could accomplish the latter.

Professor Ahmadi was proving to be a worthy adversary. With the support of ISIS, he could be anywhere. It was unlikely, but he could have discovered that she was now working with the Council. Finding Ahmadi, therefore, before he and/or ISIS found him was imperative.

Nazir left his apartment with his gym bag thrown over his shoulder and took the stairs down to his BMW M5 in the building's underground parking. The bag was far heavier than normal and the shoulder strap was making his right trapezius hurt.

When and if the time came, he wanted to be prepared. The gym bag concealed a HK MP7 that fired nine hundred and fifty rounds per minute and a Glock 19. If he had to end things, he wouldn't do it alone. But Umara and her fighters were heavily armed and would be anxious for Tuesday. He wasn't going to underestimate them.

Nazir left Orenco Station and headed north on Cornelius Pass Road deep in thought and anticipation. What were the factors he needed to consider before deciding to move ahead or wait and fight another day?

If the FBI identified Umara because of the college student she took to Ahmadi's cabin, the trail would lead them to Ahmadi and Umara but not to the Council. He wasn't worried about the FBI finding Ahmadi any time soon if they didn't. And, if he decided to let Umara go ahead with the attack and she and the others didn't survive, the trail would end there.

But if any of them were captured and made to talk, what did any of them know about the Council, other than

Umara? Nothing. That's why he'd been careful and always met Umara far away from any of the others.

The deciding factor, then, was whether Umara was prepared to be a martyr and not allow herself to be captured.

When he turned off the road and started down the farm's gravel driveway, he saw Umara standing on the wrap-around porch of the old, two-story farmhouse. Built in 1919, it had been rewired and updated somewhat, but it was still an old farmhouse. He'd intended to tear it down and build a home for himself, but the path he was on now made that an unpredictable possibility.

Nazir stopped in front of the house and made sure the big barn door was closed before he got out. If Umara had disobeyed him, and any of the women were in the farmhouse with her, then she had sealed the fate of all of them.

He got out and climbed the steps to the porch without saying anything. What he had to say could wait until they were inside. He walked past her and headed down the hall, looking into the living room as he passed it and then checking the pantry and bathroom before going into the kitchen.

Umara was standing in the kitchen, leaning back against the sink counter with her arms folded across her chest and a puzzled look on her face. "Did you really think I wouldn't do what you told me to do?"

Nazir didn't answer. He pulled a chair out from around the kitchen table and straddled it.

"The FBI knows who you are and they're looking for you. How do you think that happened?"

"What, you think I'm responsible for that? Maybe they caught Ahmadi, and he gave me up. Maybe one of his neighbors told them about me. I was there often enough. How should I know?"

"And maybe it's the woman at the cabin you failed to kill."

Umara shook her head. "No way. Allacia and Safiya knew we were never to use our real names. If they slipped and referred to me as 'Umara', that wouldn't tell anyone who I really am."

Nazir considered her defense and knew she had a point. His FBI contact had said they were looking for someone calling herself 'Umara'. He hadn't said they were looking for Samantha Taylor.

"The plan has always been for Ahmadi and ISIS to be blamed for the attacks. Whatever happens Tuesday, it can never lead back to the Council. We're just getting started. Do you understand what that means?"

Umara smiled. "Now you're questioning my willingness to become a martyr if that's what's required? Why all the mistrust? What have I done that makes you not trust me?"

Now it was his turn to shake his head. "That's not it. This is bigger than either of us. You know that. I have to decide whether we should go ahead as planned or wait until we know how close the FBI is."

"You mean how close they might be to learning about you and the Council. Because if we die as martyrs, as we're all prepared to do, there's nothing that leads back to you. I'm the only one who knows who you are. The decision you have to make is whether you're willing to trust me when I tell you I won't be taken alive. Isn't that right?"

Nazir met her unwavering and fierce gaze and knew he could trust her. Her goal had always been to be remembered as a great woman warrior for Islam. Dying in battle, even if it was her first, would guarantee that.

"Yes, you're right. If you willing to swear on the name of Allah, peace be upon him, that you won't be taken alive if it comes to that, then let's go forward. Strike the first blow and make America realize this is a war they can't win because we're willing to die for our cause and they're not."

Nazir spent the next hour going over some last-minute changes they needed to make. They needed different transportation for Tuesday, four vehicles that couldn't be traced to any of them or to Ahmadi. He would buy used vehicles and pay cash. They would be driven to the farm tomorrow.

Prepaid phones would be in each of the vehicles to allow them to coordinate the timing of the attacks.

And he would bring everything for their last meal when the cars were delivered, including something that would bolster their warrior spirits for their mission.

Nazir left his farm satisfied that Umara would die a martyr if necessary.

Chapter Forty-Nine

DRAKE WAS in his office Monday morning by seven o'clock. Paul Benning had called the night before and told him the Chief Administrative Officer of the Portland Archdiocese, Kelly Johannsen, wanted to see them as early as possible Monday morning. Benning had agreed to an eight o'clock appointment.

They had a lot to talk about and had made progress but not enough for an arrest to be made for the threats and the stolen money. The FBI was sticking to its story that they'd found Michael Brennan's murderer and weren't about to reopen its investigation, despite the reports Agent Williams was turning in.

The CAO met them at the door of her office with a cup of coffee in her hand.

"Would you like some coffee? I know it's early, but it's the only time I had open today."

Both men thanked her but said no.

When the door of her office was closed and they were

seated in front of her desk, she didn't waste time with pleasantries.

"The FBI tells me that Tyler Murphy killed Michael Brennan and confessed to stealing twenty million from our parishioners. Case conveniently closed. What do you think?"

Benning deferred to Drake to answer.

"I don't think he killed Brennan or stole the money."

"Why?"

"I agreed with your early assessment that ISIS was behind the threats and Brennan's crucifixion. I had PSS do a little digging on the dark web and found a thread talking about ISIS recruiting young girls on a community college campus here in Portland. We narrowed it down to the Cascade campus of Portland Community College. Mike Casey, the CEO of PSS, let me borrow one of his employees and we sent her onto the campus undercover. She was kidnapped and, while she was being held, was told by one of her captors that she'd been involved in killing Brennan. Unfortunately, she was killed when we rescued our employee, but she mentioned the name of the leader of her group. We're working with the FBI to find the leader."

Johannsen set her coffee cup down and sat back in her chair. "That's quite a story, Mr. Drake. Why is the FBI continuing to tell me it's closed the investigation into Michael Brennan's murder? And how are you working with the FBI?"

"One of the agents from the counterterrorism division agrees with us that Tyler Murphy's suicide is too convenient a way to end the investigation. He's able to keep investigating the kidnapping of our employee and search for the people responsible."

"How's that going?"

"The two young women involved in the kidnapping are both dead. One was killed in the rescue operation and the other woman hung herself in her jail cell. We've identified them and discovered the name of the leader. But we can't find her or any of the young women who belong to something called the Muslim Empowerment Club she started on campus."

"Is it your belief that these young women have been radicalized and pose a threat to us here in Portland?"

"It is, and that's something Paul wants to talk about."

Johannsen turned to Benning. "Go ahead, Paul."

"Kelly, we touched on this briefly when we first met, but I'm recommending that you hire security for your parishes. These women have automatic weapons, AK-47s, and aren't afraid to use them. I believe, as you do, that jihadists are behind the original threats and the crucifixion of Michael Brennan. I also believe that the leader, who calls herself 'Umara' after the female warrior who fought alongside Mohammad, has targeted the Catholic Church and would like to kill as many Christians as she can. I'll help arrange for the security, if you approve."

Johannsen leaned forward on her outstretched hands on her desk and put her head down. "I'm afraid that's just not possible, Paul. Even if I had the authority, and I don't, where would I start? We have one hundred and twenty-four parishes, fifty schools, two colleges and a seminary in the Portland Archdiocese. When would we need to have security present? All the time? When any mass is held? It's too big to cover it all and we don't have any idea where these jihadists will strike, do we?"

"What if we could narrow it down to the most likely targets?" Drake asked. "Terrorists look for targets where they can kill as many people as possible. We could protect the larger parishes until we eliminate the threat that Umara presents."

Johannsen grinned at his euphemism. "By 'eliminate', you mean kill, Mr. Drake?"

"If that's what it takes."

"Paul, when you said you would help arrange for security, did you mean private security or law enforcement?"

"Kelly, I don't think you can count on the FBI to help with this, but I can see if the Portland Police Department will help. I know most of the sergeants there from my time in the Sheriff's Office."

"I would consider that approach, if you can get local law enforcement involved, but I'll still need the archbishop's approval. He won't be back until later in the week. I'll explain your recommendation to him."

Benning stood and Drake joined him. "I'll get started today. Let me know as soon as you talk with the archbishop."

Johannsen ushered them to the door and shook each of their hands. When she shook Drake's hand, she looked him in the eye and nodded. "I wish you well, Mr. Drake, in 'eliminating' this threat to our church and our people."

"Thanks, I'll do my best."

"I'm sure you will."

Drake followed Benning down the stairs from the second-floor offices to the lobby. As he was passing through it, a poster on the wall caught his eye. It announced the Assumption Mass for the Virgin Mary, a holy day of obligation. He didn't know much about the Catholic Church or what a holy day of obligation was but he made a mental note to ask Benning about it.

At the bottom of the poster, the date for the mass was Tuesday, August 15, 2017. The next day.

Chapter Fifty

THEY RETURNED to Drake's office to coordinate their work for the day.

Benning was going to Portland Police Department headquarters to talk with a detective he knew there. Detective John Ellison had risen through the ranks of the PPD as Benning was doing in the Multnomah County Sheriff's Office. Ellison's rank was now commander in the detective's division, high enough to be listened to if he was convinced the parishes needed police protection.

Drake wanted to meet with Agent Williams and see if the FBI could add weight to the request for security for the parishes that might be at the greatest risk. When Benning let Margo know what they were doing and left the office, Drake called Agent Williams.

"Wayne, Adam Drake. Do you have time this morning to bring me up to speed on what you've learned about Umara and the others?"

"It's pretty hectic here. How about meeting me at

Shari's on Airport Way? I can't be out for long this morning."

"Why, what's going on?"

"One of our agents was killed yesterday. He was shot in his car, stopped at a red light. Some guy pulled up next to him and shot him through an open window."

"Sorry, Wayne. Was it anyone I might know?"

"Daniel Khan. He's the other counterterrorism guy from CTD here in Portland."

"I don't think I ever met Agent Khan. Give me twenty minutes and I'll meet you at Shari's."

Drake slipped his phone in the front pocket of his khakis, left his coat hanging on the back of the door and walked down to tell Margo he'd be gone for an hour or so. It was nine thirty in the morning and the temperature was already eighty, headed to ninety-five, too warm for a coat, even his summer-weight blue blazer.

Driving to meet Williams, he thought about what he'd said about the other agent, the one from the counterterrorism division. As far as he knew, Williams was the only agent in the Portland Field Office investigating Umara and the kidnapping of Carol Sanchez. Williams had said he didn't know of any terrorist activity in the area when they first met. What was this other agent working on when he was killed? Maybe Williams would tell him because he didn't want to consider the possibility that Umara knew the FBI was looking for her. If she did know, was she so reckless that she would kill an FBI agent to keep from being caught?

Williams was getting out of his Impala in the parking lot of Shari's when Drake drove in and parked next to him.

As they walked to the entrance of the restaurant, he couldn't resist asking, "Wayne, what was the agent who was killed working on? Is that something you can tell me?"

"Same thing I was, trying to find Umara. His notes say he was reaching out to one of his contacts yesterday but didn't say which one. He kept the names of his contacts within the Muslim community to himself. He felt he could protect their privacy better that way. At this point, we don't have any idea who he met with."

Inside, they were waved to a booth by the windows and they asked for coffee and Williams asked for a menu.

"I skipped breakfast, but a pastry or toast will get me through. Have you learned anything new?"

"No, not since we left Umara's house. What about you?"

"We've identified all the women in this Muslim Empowerment Club. All of them gave the same address to the college, Umara's. Professor Ahmadi's SUV, a late model Ford Excursion, has the same license as the license Carol Sanchez got when Umara picked her up in it. We have the license of the motorcycle Umara has a campus parking permit for. But we haven't found the SUV or her bike. In short, we've got squat. We can't find Umara, her friends or the professor."

Williams ordered a side of buttered toast when their coffee arrived.

"They're out there, Wayne. I don't think they've left the area. Remember Sanchez reported that the woman I shot said they were planning something for Catholic churches. I believe she meant churches here in Portland. It ties in with the convert or die warnings, the murder of Michael Brennan and the twenty million that was stolen."

"Drake, this thing's too big for a bunch of young college students to have planned and pulled off without help. There has to be someone else, like Umara's boyfriend, who's involved."

"We'll find him too. I have someone working on locating the money and he hasn't let me down yet. But until we catch up with the professor or Umara and her friends, there is something we can do.

"Benning and I met with the chief administrative officer of the archdiocese this morning and recommended security for the Catholic parishes. There are too many to protect all of them, but we suggested asking for law enforcement's help with the most likely targets. Is that something the FBI can help us with?"

Williams shook his head. "We don't have the manpower."

"Do you think the SIAC would ask local law enforcement to help out?"

"Our special agent in charge has ruffled too many feathers, from what I understand. Until he agrees to reopen the Brennan case, I don't think there's much chance of that. He'd be admitting the FBI was wrong."

"I had to ask."

The waitress brought Williams' toast and he asked her if she could put it in something so he could take it with him.

"Adam, I'm as frustrated as you are."

After agreeing to call each other if either of them learned anything new, they left to return to their offices. Drake hoped Benning had better luck with the Portland Police Department than he had with the FBI.

Chapter Fifty-One

BENNING DIDN'T. He stomped up the stairs to Drake's loft, letting his heavy footfalls announce his angry mood.

Drake watched him slump down in a chair in front of his desk. "No luck?"

"He wouldn't listen. I thought I knew the man."

"Why wouldn't he listen?"

"You know how political this city has become. He said that if they started protecting one religion, they'd wind up protecting them all. 'What about the mosques?' he said. 'They've had threats. What about the synagogues? They get threats and have swastikas spray-painted on their doors.' And then he said I should understand how the government can't favor one religion over another, separation of church and state and all. What BS."

"And yet we protect the Pope when he visits. He's forgotten that it's the state's duty to protect us all, regardless of race, religion and all the other identifiers we Americans like to use."

"What do we do now?"

"I don't know, Paul. Kelly Johannsen's right about one thing, we can't protect all the parishes. I don't know where you'd start to figure out which ones might be targets."

"I've been thinking about that. The warnings were posted in and around St. Patrick's on Northwest Nineteenth Avenue. That has to be a target. It was also Michael Brennan's parish."

"But where do we go from there? That leaves another one hundred twenty-three parishes."

"Let me go get a cup of coffee and think about it."

Drake considered the possibilities while Benning was gone. Terrorists like to maximize the number of people killed, so the largest parishes could be targets.

He knew from living in Portland that St. Patrick's was built in 1891 to serve the Irish Catholic lumber and dock workers. In the late twentieth century, it was chosen to serve the needs of the Hispanic community in Portland. Today it was a large and flourishing church serving every Portland community. He'd been there for a several funeral masses. But terrorists didn't seem to choose which Christians they killed based on race. Protecting a parish based on the race of its parishioners was a nonstarter.

What else did they know about the Catholics who had been targeted so far? The Catholics who had threats posted on their doors seemed to have been randomly selected. Benning might need to check to see if there were similarities among them.

And there were those targeted by the size of their bank accounts. Could the parishes with the wealthiest patrons be the targets?

Benning came back with his coffee and said, before he

sat down, "I think there are two likely possibilities, the largest parishes and the wealthiest parishes."

Drake enjoyed a smile from within at his friend's brilliance.

"Can you get that information from Kelly Johannsen?"

"Shouldn't be a problem."

"Paul, while I'm thinking about Catholics and their parishes, what is Mass for the Assumption of the Virgin Mary and why is it a day of obligation?"

Benning looked puzzled. "Where did you come up with a question like that?"

"Just something I've been meaning to ask you."

"Some Catholics have been debating that for centuries. You want the short answer or the long one?"

"You choose."

"Okay. In the fifth century, the Roman Emperor requested the body of Mary, the Mother of God, be brought to him. According to St. John of Damascus, the bishop of Jerusalem replied that Mary died in the presence of all the Apostles, but when her tomb was opened at the request of St. Thomas, her tomb was empty. The Apostles concluded that the body was taken up to heaven, St. John of Damascus recorded. It's a tradition of the church and mentioned in the meditations of the saints for centuries.

"Pope Pius in nineteen fifty declared it to be the dogma of the church that the Virgin Mary, having completed her earthly life, was assumed body and soul into heavenly glory."

"I've never heard that."

"You wouldn't unless you're Catholic."

"What's a holy day of obligation then?"

"It's a day when Roman Catholics are required to attend mass."

"Aren't all Catholics required to attend mass every week?"

Benning chuckled. "Are you trying to see if I remember catechism? Yes, the first precept of catechism is, 'You shall attend Mass on Sundays and holy days of obligation'."

Drake stared at the calendar on the wall behind Benning as the realization hit him. The only date circled on Umara's calendar was August 15th, 2017, the next day—the day of the Mass of Assumption for the Virgin Mary, a holy day of obligation when all Catholics were required to attend the mass.

"I know when she's going to attack the churches. It's tomorrow, the day of the Mass of Assumption. The 15th was the only date circled on the calendar in Umara's room."

"No, no, not tomorrow…"

"Paul, it makes sense. Umara's out there somewhere getting ready to attack. She got out of town so we wouldn't find her before she acts. It's an obligation mass that guarantees the parishes will have maximum attendance. She's going to do it tomorrow, I'm sure of it."

"What can we do?"

"If the PPD won't help, we'll have to do what we can to protect the churches. Get Kelly Johannsen to identify the largest and wealthiest parishes. Choosing them as targets makes sense. We'll try to narrow it down based on location and ease of access. I'll call Mike and see if he'll send as many VIP Protection team members as he can muster on short notice. We'll protect the parishes we think she's likely to hit and pray that she's selected the same ones."

"Shall I tell Kelly what we're planning?"

"I'll do it, when I know what Mike's able to do."

Benning left to call the archdiocese and Drake called his friend. If he was wrong about what Umara was planning, it would be a costly mistake, one that he would pay for out of his own pocket if necessary. But if he was right and lives were saved, it was worth the risk and much more.

Chapter Fifty-Two

DRAKE WAITED an hour for Benning to return with the information they needed. Two of the parishes had the highest number of parishioners who'd had money stolen and another had the largest attendance of all the parishes in the city. With the addition of St. Patrick's, Michael Brennan's church, there were four churches they agreed were the most likely to be attacked.

"What if we're wrong, Adam? If we send security to these four and other churches are attacked, we'll be blamed for any loss of life."

"I realize that, but what alternative do we have? Look, I'm trying to think like Umara when she planned this. If we're right, she has ten women left from her Muslim Empowerment Club and they all lived with her. In France, ISIS sent two gunmen into the Catholic church in Normandy and, at this point, that's the model I think she'll follow. That means she can send five teams of two, or four teams of two with herself and maybe a getaway driver as backup.

"Planners plan and see that plots are executed. Umara may be willing to martyr herself, but I think she'll want to hang back and coordinate the attacks. She wants to be remembered like her namesake, and being killed on her first outing isn't going to get her the recognition she wants.

"I think she'll target four churches. We just have to pray she's selected the same four that we have."

"Did you call PSS?"

"Not yet, I needed to know how many PSS personnel to ask for. Four armed protection team members per church, plus Morales, Sanchez and me should be enough. What do you think?"

"I think you're forgetting someone."

"Paul, I can't ask you to do this. I'm already in enough trouble with Margo."

"I'm not asking, Adam. The archdiocese is my client too."

"Then you discuss that with Margo, before tomorrow."

"Now's as good a time as any."

Benning went downstairs to talk to his wife while Drake called Casey at PSS. He wanted to be busy in case Benning's discussion with Margo became heated.

Mike Casey had been his best friend since their time in Delta Force working as a hunter/killer team in the Middle East. But Casey was also the man who had an international company to manage, with responsibility for the livelihood of thousands of men and women. He had always backed the play of his friend and now corporate special counsel, but Drake was asking a lot of him this time. Sending armed security to protect four Catholic churches, when local law enforcement had refused to do so, was sure to be criticized and second-guessed. But what choice did they have? He couldn't stand down and let innocent people be slaughtered.

"Adam, glad you called. Are you coming up Wednesday?"

Wednesday was the day each week that Drake spent at PSS headquarters, fulfilling his duties as PSS special counsel. Whatever work he didn't finish there, he brought back to his Portland office.

"It depends, Mike. That's what we need to discuss."

For the next fifteen minutes, Drake briefed Casey on the investigation into Umara and what he thought she was planning.

"What position is the archdiocese taking on this?"

"The Archbishop is in Rome, but his chief administrative officer is willing to consider using private security. I needed to talk with you before getting her approval."

"How many security personnel are you thinking?"

"Four per church, sixteen in all, plus Morales, Sanchez and me. Benning wants to be included, but I'm letting him work that out with Margo."

"Give me a minute. I'll see who we have available."

Drake knew he was looking to see how many armed security personnel were licensed in Oregon. No other state met Oregon's licensing requirement, so armed personnel sent to work in Oregon had to have their Oregon private security professional certification as well as an armed security upgrade. PSS had its own Oregon approved instructors, but not all personnel had attended the classes, taken the exams and been firearm qualified. Drake had made sure that anyone deployed on armed security assignments in Oregon and every other state met each state's licensing requirements.

"I have sixteen I can send. Do you want me to have a contract prepared for this or are you going to take care of that?"

"That's a bit of a problem. The CAO says she doesn't have the authority to approve this herself and she doesn't think she can get the archbishop to approve it until he returns."

"And you think whatever this woman is planning will happen tomorrow?"

"Yeah."

Drake waited ten long seconds for Casey's decision.

"All right. When is this mass?"

"Five thirty p.m. in all the parishes."

"They'll drive down early tomorrow morning. What will they be facing?"

"We know they have AK-47s, but that's all we know for sure."

"We'll send them with heavy armor. I'll book them rooms where Morales and Sanchez are staying and have them call you when they reach Portland. You'll have to take it from there."

"Thanks Mike."

"Just remember, I'm doing this on the advice of counsel."

"Roger that."

Drake understood what his friend was telling him. We're sticking our corporate neck out here a mile, you'd better be right. He prayed that he was and called Kelly Johannsen.

"Kelly Johannsen."

"Adam Drake, Ms. Johannsen."

"I thought we were on a first-name basis, Adam."

"Sorry, Kelly. We've talked with the Portland Police Department and the FBI. They're not going to provide any security. I'd like you to authorize Puget Sound Security to provide security for four parishes for tomorrow's Assumption Mass."

"Why tomorrow?"

"It's a holy day of obligation, it's a special mass and it'll be heavily attended. The people we suspect have gone into hiding and I think they've done that to prepare. We need to be prepared as well."

The pause this time was longer than the one waiting for Casey's decision.

"I can't officially authorize this, but I can ask that you eliminate the threat to our churches the best way you see fit. Is that enough?"

"It is for me, Kelly."

Chapter Fifty-Three

ZAL NAZIR CALLED Umara Monday afternoon before leaving for the farm.

"I'll be there in twenty minutes. As before, have the others wait in the barn. I don't want them to see the drivers or myself as we deliver everything you asked for."

"Fine."

He'd spent all morning scouring used car lots to buy four older minivans. They didn't look like much, the two Ford Aerostars, a Dodge Caravan and an ancient Toyota Previa, but he'd driven them and they would do.

It had taken longer to find the food Umara had demanded for their noon meal the next day. For some of them, probably all of them, it would be their last meal and she had polled the others to ask what they wanted. He'd been surprised at the list; fresh wild salmon that they would steam, wild rice, Caesar salad, garlic bread and chocolate chip cookies and ice cream for dessert.

It sounded more like the meal a young woman would get at home when she visited her parents from college. Of course, none of these women had families that approved of them or their newfound religion. That was one of the things he looked for when he'd vetted each of them for Umara.

The other item he'd told Umara he would supply for tomorrow was an adequate supply of Captagon, the terrorist's drug of choice. It improved the performance of combatants and made them resistant to fatigue and fear. It also removed any form of empathy they might have. Witnesses would describe the effect of Captagon as producing empty stares and expressionless faces, looking like the 'walking dead'. For these women, it would be their only battle and he had to make sure they performed well.

Nazir led the way when his small caravan pulled off the road and drove down the farm's long gravel driveway. When he parked the black Suburban with darkened windows he was driving in front of the farmhouse, he got out and directed the drivers of the four minivans to park in a line next to him.

When the minivans were parked as he wanted, he had his drivers get in the Suburban and wait for him. His drivers didn't need to see Umara and her women didn't need to see his drivers.

Umara was standing just inside the front door when he walked onto the porch and continued past her.

"Nice rides. You sure they'll get us there?" she said over her shoulder before she followed him.

"The keys will be in the driver's seat, along with a prepaid phone for each car. Use the phones only to communicate between you and the person in charge of each car."

"Did you bring the food I asked for?"

"I'll bring it inside in a minute. Tell me what your schedule is tomorrow and how the others are doing."

"I will go over our plan with them mid-morning and

then we'll prepare the meal to be eaten at noon. When we finish, we'll prepare ourselves and leave the farm at five o'clock. It's only sixteen miles to Portland and shouldn't take thirty minutes to get where we're going. With traffic at that hour, we'll give ourselves forty-five minutes. We'll reach our targets by a quarter to six at the latest. On my command, we all enter at the same time. The churches will be full by then."

"Excellent. Stay here while I bring in the things you asked for."

He was pleased with the way she calmly described the day ahead. No questions and no hesitation. Her plan was simple and, if they weren't stopped on the way for some unforeseen reason, should be successful. Regardless of the number that died, it would paralyze churchgoers for a long, long time with the fear it would create.

Nazir made two trips to and from the Suburban to haul in two large coolers with all of the food Umara wanted. When he'd set them on the floor near the refrigerator, he motioned for her to sit with him at the dining table.

"You've done well, Umara. Tomorrow will be your reward for all the hard work and sacrifice you've made. Have you made the videos for tomorrow?"

"We're making them tonight. We'll leave them here for you to post later."

Nazir took a baggie out of his pants pocket and put it on table before them. "Each of you take two of these when you leave the farm. They will give you courage and strength."

"I have plenty of that, as do the others."

"I'm not questioning that. I want you to have every advantage possible for tomorrow."

"I won't let you or the Council down. Thank you for honoring me with this."

"Your sacrifice honors Allah, peace be upon him, and all true Muslims. You will be remembered as a true warrior, worthy of the name you've chosen."

"Inshallah, Zal, inshallah."

When Nazir returned to his SUV, he got in and turned to the man sitting beside him in the passenger seat. "Did you get a good look at her?"

"Yes. She's attractive."

"She is, indeed. Her target is St. Patrick's Church on Northwest 19th Avenue. Find a spot where you can see her when she's not inside the church. If the police haven't killed her, make sure she keeps her promise and isn't taken alive."

Umara was the only one who could identify him and put a target on his back. The other women thought they were jihadists fighting with ISIS. Only Umara knew the truth, and it had to die with her.

Chapter Fifty-Four

PAUL BENNING RETURNED to the loft not long after Drake's conversation with Kelly Johannsen. He wasn't smiling, but he wasn't frowning either.

"Margo understands why I have to do this. She hoped that when I retired from the Sheriff's Office, her nights spent worrying that I was safe were over. But these are my people, and if the police won't protect them, she knows we have to."

"Good, Paul. Glad you're coming. I spoke with Kelly Johannsen. She didn't officially authorize PSS to provide security, but she did ask that we eliminate the threat to her churches the best way we see fit. Mike's agreed to send sixteen security personnel here tomorrow morning. We'll meet them at the hotel where Morales and Sanchez are staying."

"Do those two know what we're planning for tomorrow?"

"Not yet. I thought I'd head over there later. Before

then, do you have time to take me to St. Patrick's and show me around?"

"Be my pleasure."

Drake had driven by the church countless times in Portland, but he'd only been inside to attend funeral mass for people he knew. Maybe because of his reason for visiting the historic landmark on those occasions, he had never taken the time to admire the old church.

Benning drove them across town to the corner of Northwest 19th Avenue and Savier Street and parked in front of the church. It sat impressively on the corner of the two streets, built of stone with a red roof and hipped dome with a spire.

The church was exposed on two sides with a street in front and another running along its side. The main entrance had stairs that circled around to the front door, protected by an outer half-wall that curved around with the stairs.

Drake got out and walked to the corner to sight down the side of the building. Then he walked back and sighted down the other side.

Benning waited for him beside his Ford F-150. "The easiest way inside is the front door. There's the entrance on the side near the rectory, but someone here to the left of the stairs could cover the front and the side entrance."

"They'll want to come in the front door behind people to catch them by surprise. It's the easiest way in. Two guards on each side of the stairs will be able to cover a frontal attack."

"I agree. If they stay back against the side of the building, they won't be spotted until it's too late."

"Are you familiar with the layout of the other three churches?"

"I've been to two of them over the years, but I need to visit them again."

"Run me back to the office and go check them out. I'll go see Morales and Sanchez."

On the drive back across town, Benning brought up the likely confusion and panic that would follow an attack like they were preparing for. "Kelly needs to speak with the priests so they're ready to deal with this. Do you want me to call her?"

"I thought each parish would have an emergency plan in place, but let's make sure. Even if they do, knowing they might need to implement it tomorrow will give them an advantage. Thanks for reminding me. Give her a call."

Benning dropped Drake off at his car in the parking garage adjoining his office.

Before he drove away to check out the other churches, Drake tapped on his window. "Let's meet in the office tomorrow at seven to go over your ideas for the other churches. We'll go together to brief the PSS security personnel when they get here, but that will give us a chance to fine-tune our plan."

Benning gave him thumbs up and drove on. Drake took out his phone to call Morales and Sanchez.

When Morales answered, he heard people laughing and talking in the background. "Am I interrupting something?"

"No, we're just soaking in the outdoor hot tub. What's up?"

"Morales, it's seventy degrees and you're in a hot tub?"

"Great way to relax and things, boss."

"It's the 'things' I'm worried about. I'm headed your way. You and Sanchez meet me out front and I'll take you to dinner."

"What makes you think I know where Sanchez is?"

"Because I heard her ask you what I just said."

"She must have slipped in when I wasn't looking."

"Twenty minutes, Morales."

When Drake drove under the portico of the Best Western, Morales and Sanchez were standing near the front door. They didn't recognize him in his Porsche 993 until he rolled down the passenger-side window and whistled. They'd been too busy talking to each other to notice his classic sports car.

Morales sheepishly walked over and leaned his head in the window to look inside. "You want us to call a cab?"

"There's room. Sanchez can squeeze in back."

Morales held the door open and watched a little too admiringly as Sanchez ducked her head and slid in behind the passenger seat Drake had leaned forward.

"Evening, Carol. Have you had a relaxing day?"

Drake watched her smile in the rearview mirror before she answered. "R&R appreciated. Thank you."

Morales got in and they were off. "Nice car, boss. What year is it?"

"1998, last of the air-cooled 911s. I'll drive it until it quits on me then rebuild it and drive it some more."

"It's a beauty, Mr. Drake."

"Thanks, Carol."

Ten minutes was all he needed to drive from the Best Western at the Meadows to Stanford's Restaurant and Bar on Hayden Island. When they were seated in a booth, he told them what they would be doing tomorrow and why.

"We think Umara will take advantage of a special mass the Catholic churches celebrate tomorrow, the Assumption of the Virgin Mary. It's a holy day of obligation, which means all Catholics are supposed to attend. Umara had only one date circled on the calendar in her room, August 15th, tomorrow.

"The Portland Police and the FBI won't provide any security for the churches, so we're doing it ourselves. Sixteen PSS members of the VIP Protection detail are driving down in the morning from Seattle and have reservations at your Best Western for tomorrow night. We'll use the conference room at the hotel to brief everyone when they get here.

"We've chosen four parish churches to protect, the church Michael Brennan attended and three others. You two, Paul Benning and I will supplement the PSS detail. Any questions?"

"Why only four churches?"

"We can't protect them all, Marco, but we think these four are the most likely ones to be hit."

Sanchez sat back in the booth and crossed her arms across her chest. "The last time I had the pleasure of meeting Umara, I wasn't armed. Will I be this time?"

"That's a problem, but I'm working on it. You haven't been with PSS long enough to complete the classes to be licensed in all states, and you don't have a concealed carry permit that's honored in Oregon. We'll figure something out."

A waiter stopped at their table to take their orders. None of them had opened their menus and she left with only their drink orders.

As they looked at their menus, Drake knew he had to find a way to protect Sanchez. He'd already thrown her into deep water without a lifeline. He wasn't about to do it again.

Chapter Fifty-Five

DRIVING HOME after dinner with Morales and Sanchez, Drake tried to think of a way to arm Sanchez. Oregon was an open carry state because of its Constitution. But cities and counties had the authority to restrict that right. Portland was one of six Oregon cities that prohibited loaded firearms in all public places.

She could openly carry a knife, but what would that do against an AK-47 in the hands of a terrorist? She had a black belt in Krav Maga and could defend herself, but he didn't want her close enough to Umara or any of the others to have to use those skills.

He was still frustrated with the problem when he drove up the driveway of his farm and saw Lancer, his German Shepherd, running down to greet him. He rolled down his window and whistled loudly twice, their signal to meet at the top behind his house for a proper 'thank you' for guarding the farm while he was away.

Lancer raced ahead and was sitting patiently in front of

the steps leading into the mud room and kitchen when Drake pulled up.

He got out and walked over, kneeling in front of his dog and rubbing behind his ears. "Did you keep the bad guys off the farm today? Of course, you did. What idiot would want to tangle with one hundred and ten pounds of muscle and fangs? Let's go and get you something to eat."

Drake led them inside and stopped in the mud room to measure out Lancer's dry dog food. He added a spoon of canned dog food on top and a little warm water to mix up a tasty meal, and took the dog dish into the kitchen where Lancer liked to eat.

Lancer sat next to his dish, looking up at Drake until he heard the command he was waiting for. "Go ahead."

He'd trained Lancer as a protection dog as a puppy and won a handful of medals with him in the Schutzhund competition in the Northwest. But he was still amazed at how a dog could sit so patiently with a dish of his favorite food before him until he was given the command to eat.

Drake scratched Lancer's shoulders as he walked past, poured a glass of the new pinot noir he was trying, and sat down at the kitchen table to call Liz. She needed to know what he was planning to do and he needed her assurance that he wasn't doing it foolishly.

"I know it's late, do you mind if we talk for a while?"

"You know I don't. I'm reading in bed and this *New York Times* best seller is putting me to sleep. You're rescuing me from boredom."

"Glad that I can help. How was your day?"

"It was fine. During the August recess, things slow way down in the Senator's Office, so I had time to finish up a couple of things I needed to do before I leave."

"Will you still be here by the end of the month?"

"Maybe a little before. Why, missing me?"

"Yes, and, uh, Lancer says he does too."

"You sound distracted. What's going on?"

He tried to think of a way to tell her that he was asking Sanchez to confront the woman who kidnapped her unarmed without making it sound too dangerous, which, of course, was exactly why he was calling her, to find a way to keep Sanchez safe.

He couldn't think of a way to put lipstick on the pig.

"We identified the woman behind the crucifixion of Michael Brennan and the stolen twenty million. She's the same one who kidnapped Carol Sanchez, the woman I sent undercover and unarmed to the college campus where we thought she was recruiting for ISIS. I think she's going to attack one or more of the Catholic churches here and we're going to stop her because the police and FBI won't help us. I can't find a way to keep Sanchez protected and armed and I need her tomorrow."

"When did all this happen, finding out who this person is and what you think she's planning to do?"

"Yesterday and today. I didn't have time to call."

"Don't worry about that. I just wish I'd had time to try to help some way. Does Carol Sanchez have to be involved tomorrow?"

"She's the only one who's met this woman. We have a photo of her from her student ID, but you know how misleading those can be."

"Is Sanchez licensed for Oregon or have CCP?"

"No, that's the problem."

"You're not doing this alone, are you? Please tell me that isn't what you're planning on doing."

"No, Mike's sending down members of the VIP Protection detail. We're guessing at which churches they'll hit, so we've selected the four most likely to guard."

"Can't one of them protect her?"

"Not very well, if they show up with their AK-47s firing on full auto."

"Then I don't see how you can guarantee that she'll be safe, unless you can put her somewhere to spot this woman without being in the line of fire."

"She won't like it, but that might work."

"If you put her somewhere she's isolated, make sure she has backup of some kind. She's still going to be unarmed, but you can't leave her in a danger zone alone."

"I'll find a way to make that happen."

"Promise me you'll be safe. I'm not moving across the country because I like Seattle better than Washington."

"I'll be here when you get here. I can't go on the little vacation I have planned by myself."

"Are you going to leave me guessing again tonight?"

"Yep."

"Good night, cowboy. I love you, so call me as soon as you can tomorrow."

"Good night, Liz. I love you too."

Drake put his phone down and saw Lancer stretched out at his feet. Liz was right, Sanchez could be their lookout. And he had the perfect backup lying right in front of him.

Chapter Fifty-Six

THEY LEFT the farm early Tuesday morning to drive to Drake's office. The rear seats in the 993 were folded down and Lancer was lying with a commanding view of the road ahead from behind his right shoulder.

He'd decided that the best protection he could provide for Carol Sanchez was his German Shepherd. They needed a lookout at St. Patrick's, with the church on a corner and streets on two sides. Situating Sanchez unarmed in a car with Lancer to protect her was the best solution he could come up with.

The traffic was light and they made the commute in less than his usual early morning thirty-minute drive time.

Paul Benning was sitting at Margo's desk when he came down the stairs from the parking garage with Lancer behind him.

Benning looked up with raised eyebrows. "Are you feeling a little insecure this morning?"

"Sanchez isn't licensed in Oregon and doesn't have a

CHL permit. Lancer's going to be her backup today. We'll post them as our lookout at St. Patrick's."

"Good idea. I'm ordering food for the PSS guys when they get here; coffee, juice, bagels and doughnut. Anything I should add for Lancer?"

"Filet of terrorist, rare, if they have it. Anything new this morning?"

"I just checked with the Sheriff's Office. No one's seen any of the women we've identified or any of their vehicles."

"They're smart, staying out of sight until they strike. I'm going to get a cup of coffee and go up and call Williams to see if the FBI has anything new. Join me when you finish and let's go over our plan for the churches."

Agent Williams and the FBI didn't have anything new either. "Not a whisper about Umara or any of the others. Maybe they left town?"

"If they did, I don't think they would go far. If the date circled on her calendar means what I think it means, we'll see them today somewhere. I just hope we're there to greet them."

"What are you planning, Drake?"

Agent Williams hadn't been involved in the decision to protect the Catholic churches privately because he didn't want the FBI interfering. But Williams didn't seem to care what the Portland Field Office thought about him or the way he went about his work. He was the counterterrorism expert and he was going to do his job the way he saw fit. Until they transferred him again.

"Meet me at the Best Western at the Meadows at ten o'clock. I'll be in the conference room and explain, if you promise not to interfere in what I have in mind."

"If it's not illegal, you have my word."

"See you at ten."

Drake reached down and scratched Lancer behind his ears. "Let's hope I'm not making a mistake with Agent Williams."

Benning started up the stairs and Lancer rose up until he saw the top of his head.

"Did I hear you invite Williams this morning?"

"He promised not to interfere, if we're not planning something illegal."

"That's comforting, letting the FBI decide what's legal or not. I remember the way the FBI went after the underground in the seventies. A lot of the things they got away with weren't legal."

"I think Williams won't interfere and he might come in handy if the FBI gives us a bad time after the fact. He'll be able to confirm our stories about what we're doing."

"About that. Margo wants to be reassured that I'll have body armor if I'm going with you."

"Mike said he'd send down gear for us. Tell me what you're thinking about the other three churches."

"If we have four men for each of the churches, I think we should let them position themselves after they've been to check out their assigned church. The mass isn't until five thirty. They'll have plenty of time to scope things out. This is what they do, let's let them do it."

Drake agreed the VIP Protection division knew what it was doing. PSS hired the best people with military experience and tactical skills and paid them the highest salaries in the industry. Because of that, maybe they didn't need four operators at each church.

"What about reducing the number to three at each church? Keep four as a rapid-response team in case she hits some other church?"

Benning tilted his head back and looked at the ceiling

for a second. "That's not a bad idea. If we're right about the number of women with her, she has ten remaining. If she sends two to a church, as ISIS likes to deploy its crazies, she could hit five churches."

"Any way you look at it, we're playing a guessing game. She could send them all to the same church and our operators would be outnumbered. We'd still win. Our guys are better trained and equipped, but it's still a crap shoot."

"Agreed, it's still a crap shoot. Margo's cooking my favorite breakfast, so I'm going to head upstairs and spend time with my wife. When are you leaving for the Best Western?"

"I'm meeting Sanchez at nine to break the news that she's going to be our lookout. She needs some time to get comfortable with Lancer and learn his commands. Meet me at ten, that's early enough and you need the time with Margo. If she's cooking your favorite breakfast, you know she's nervous."

"All right, see you at ten."

Drake wished there was a way to ease Margo's concern, but there was no getting around the fact that they were putting themselves in harm's way. Umara might just be a young wannabe terrorist with unknown skills and training, but put an AK-47 in her hands and she was as deadly as any other terrorist in the world.

Chapter Fifty-Seven

UMARA STOOD in front of two wooden benches in the old barn. Eight women she'd chosen to fight with her sat on the benches, subdued but listening eagerly as she gave them their orders for the day.

"This is the day we live for, to prove our total submission to Allah. Two sisters have gone before. Two more chose to serve the caliphate as brides. We are the chosen ones who remain to strike the first blow against the crusader church in America. We are the ones who will lead the way for other sisters to pick up the sword and fight side by side with our brothers.

"Like lions, we hunt alongside our brothers. The male lion may hunt differently, using stealth to make his kills, but it's the lioness that hunts in the open, using her speed and skill. Today, we will use speed and skill to kill our prey.

"We are ready. You know the routes to our targets. You know where each van is to stop, and you know how quickly you must strike. One minute from the time you leave the van until you enter the church.

"You will have the element of surprise, but don't be slow to make sure you kill everyone. Move quickly down the aisles side by side, shooting as you go. Reload quickly and keep moving. When you reach the altars, make sure the priests die. Turn and walk back, shooting anyone you missed on the way to the altar. No one lives.

"If the police aren't there yet, get in the vans and drive away. You know where our meeting place is. Inshallah, we will live to fight another day.

"If Allah wills it and we are martyred, you know the reward that awaits us and that we will be remembered forever.

"Begin your cleansing in shifts, sharing the bathrooms in the farmhouse. When the first of you have finished, come to the kitchen and help me prepare our meal. Everything we asked for is there and more.

"After we've eaten, take time to meditate and pray. If you haven't finished your videos, do it then.

"We leave at four thirty this afternoon. If you have any questions, ask them now."

Her fiercest young fighter raised her hand. "May we shave our heads as well as our pubic areas and under our arms?"

"No, don't shave your head. We don't want to be recognized before we reach our targets. Someone who sees us may be familiar with the Quran and know that we're told to enter the Sacred Mosque with heads shaved and without fear. 'Taqiyya' permits our deception."

Another raised her hand. "Will you be coming with us?"

Umara looked angry for a moment and then composed herself. "I am your leader. I will lead the way into St. Patrick's, the church of the attorney. I want our message to be understood. We will finish what we've begun in America by killing the attorney and then at St. Patrick's and the other churches where we'll kill his fellow believers."

There were no more questions and Umara dismissed them, leading the first two women back to the farmhouse to begin their cleansing. When she got there, she went to her room and sat on the edge of her cot.

When they wrote about what she would accomplish today, she wondered what her parents would think. Would her father finally understand she wasn't someone to be ignored because she was a woman, like he'd ignored her mother and herself? He'd never touched her, like the boys she'd beaten in high school, but his rejection and drinking hurt just as much.

She wished she could see his face tomorrow.

Chapter Fifty-Eight

WHEN DRAKE STOPPED the Porsche under the portico of the Best Western, Sanchez was standing next to the door.

He waved her over. "Get in, there's someone I want you to meet."

As she walked toward the car, Lancer raised up onto his front legs. His head was scrunched against the roof and turned to the open window.

Sanchez leaned down to look inside and then stepped back.

"He won't bite. Come on, get in."

Easing herself into the passenger's seat, she never took her eyes off Lancer.

"Carol, meet Lancer."

She turned to her left, putting her head a foot away from Lancer's. "He's so big."

"That he is. Delta Park and the Owens Sports Complex is a couple of blocks from here with trails and green space. I'll drive there so you can properly meet Lancer."

Drake shifted into first gear and drove out from under the portico and onto North Denver Avenue.

"Why did you bring your dog along?"

"I'll explain in a minute. Have you been around working dogs before?"

"Sure, in Denver. But I never worked with the K9 unit, except on drug busts, and that was before I went undercover."

"I've had Lancer since he was six months old. He's Schutzhund trained, which means he's trained as a protection dog and has won competitions all over the Northwest. He saved my life when three terrorists paid me a visit one night on my farm, and I know he'll do the same again if it's necessary. I brought Lancer along because he's going to be your backup today."

Drake drove into the Owens Sports Complex and parked next to the nearest soccer field. Before Sanchez had a chance to ask why she needed backup, he got out and leaned his seat forward for Lancer to come out.

Together, they walked around the bonnet of the Porsche and waited for Sanchez to get out. Lancer quickly sat down next to Drake's left heel. When she did and faced the two of them, he answered her question.

"Carol, I couldn't find a way to arm you for this afternoon. Portland has a very strict ordinance against having a loaded gun in any public place, unless you have a concealed handgun license. The possible penalty is six months in jail, and I won't risk that for you.

"When we split up to protect the four churches we think are the most likely to be hit, I want you to come to St. Patrick's with me and be our lookout. Lancer will be with you to make sure you're safe if things go sideways.

"We're thinking of posting operators from the VIP

Protection division at each of the four churches and have one team available for a rapid response if Umara hits a church we haven't protected.

"If that happens and we have eliminated the threat at St. Patrick's, I want you to come with me and we'll augment the rapid-response team.

"You're the only one with first-hand knowledge of what Umara looks like. If she shows up wearing a mask or some other disguise, you might still recognize her. They'll all have to be stopped, but especially Umara. She can't escape to do this again somewhere else."

Sanchez was standing at ease with her hands clasped behind her back. "I appreciate you bringing Lancer to protect me, but I don't know the first thing about working with a dog. What if I mess up and he gets hurt?"

"You won't mess up and Lancer knows how to take care of himself. Let's go out onto the soccer field and run through some commands. You'll be surprised how easy it is with a well-trained dog."

Drake handed her a three-by-five card with six commands written on it.

"These will be the only commands you'll need for today. They're all in German, but the English pronunciation is there in parenthesis. Go ahead and start with the first one. Say Lancer's name followed by the command."

Sanchez looked at the card as Drake stepped back leaving Lancer sitting in front of her.

"Lancer, sitz!"

Lancer looked to Drake and then walked forward and sat in front of Sanchez, who had a big smile on her face.

"Lancer, fuss!"

Lancer moved around and stood with his shoulder beside her left leg.

Sanchez looked at the card again. "Lancer, platz!"

Lancer lay down on the grass.

"Try one more, the fourth one on the card, and when he obeys, walk over to me."

"Lancer, bleib!"

Lancer stayed down as Sanchez walked over and stood beside Drake.

"How long will he stay there?"

"Until you tell him to do something else."

"That's amazing! How long did it take you to train Lancer?"

Drake smiled and told Lancer to come to him. "Lancer knew those basic commands when I got him from the breeder when he was six months old. The last two commands on your card, the command watch, or pay attention, and the next command took longer. Only use the last two when you want him to leave you and go help someone else."

"Thank you. With Lancer, I'm not really unarmed, am I?"

"You won't have 'weapon' per se, but you have something just as good, in my opinion."

Chapter Fifty-Nine

ON THE WAY back to the hotel, the head of the VIP Protection division called.

"Drake, David Bryce. We're at the hotel. Where do you want us?"

"Go ahead and get everyone checked in. I have the conference room reserved at ten. Let's all meet there and get acquainted."

Drake knew David Bryce. Casey had hired him when he heard that Bryce was leaving the Secret Service after fifteen years. Bryce quit the federal law enforcement agency, now a part of the Department of Homeland Security, disgusted by the way a former first lady treated him and the other agents. He was charged with developing the private protection service for PSS and quickly began hiring the best people available, especially those with military service or law enforcement backgrounds. His division was filled with SEALS, Marine Security Guards, also known as Marine Embassy Guards, and Secret Service personnel. He'd also helped Casey put together a hostage rescue squad, like the FBI's HRT, for kidnap and ransom cases.

They stopped under the portico at the hotel and Drake got out. "Why don't you stay with Lancer while I go see if the hotel will let me take him to the conference room? I'll be right back."

It took longer than a minute to convince the manager that Lancer was a necessary part of his presentation to the men gathering in the conference room. When he explained that the men were all employees of Puget Sound Security and that Lancer was a guard dog, the manager agreed. He would let the dog enter the hotel, provided that he went straight to the conference room and left the same way when the presentation was over.

Drake went back to his Porsche and told Sanchez to take Lancer with her and go straight to the conference room. He would park his car and join her there.

Lancer waited until Sanchez told him to heel, looked to Drake to see if it was okay and jumped out to walk beside her. Seeing Lancer with Sanchez reminded Drake of the walks Kay and Lancer used to take without him.

He was pulling into a space in the guest parking lot when Benning drove in and parked his truck two spaces away.

"How's Lancer getting along with Sanchez?"

"Lancer's fine and she's getting over being nervous around him. She's okay with being a lookout. Did you bring printouts of the locations of the four churches?"

Benning patted the bison leather messenger bag hanging from his shoulder. "In here. Locations and directions."

Drake knew that the messenger bag also had a

concealed carry pocket for his .40 caliber Glock 23 and two extra thirteen-round mags.

"Let's go meet the team then."

The conference room was crowded when they got there—sixteen operators from PSS, twelve men and four women, half of who were standing around Morales, Sanchez and Lancer. Agent Wayne Williams stood off by himself at the sidebar getting a cup of coffee.

David Bryce walked over and shook hands with Drake.

"David, meet Paul Benning. Paul, David heads the VIP Protection division for PSS. David, Paul is a former detective with the Sheriff's Office and now works out of my office as a private investigator. The Portland Archdiocese is his client."

Bryce and Benning shook hands. "How long have you worked for the archdiocese?"

"They hired me just after the 'convert or die' notices were put on the doors of some of its parishioners."

"Hell of a deal, threatening to behead people in their homes and then crucifying that attorney. You ready to tell us what we're doing here, Drake?"

"Yes, let's get started. Ladies and gentlemen, get something to eat or drink if you want and then take a seat. My name is Adam Drake, if we haven't met, and I serve as special counsel for PSS. Standing next to me is Paul Benning and, in the back, that's Agent Wayne Williams of the FBI. He's working with us to track down a cell of young women who think of themselves as female Muslim warriors.

"We have reason to believe they're planning an attack on Catholic churches this afternoon here in Portland. Local law enforcement won't provide security for these churches, so we're doing it for them.

"At five thirty this afternoon, Catholics are obligated to

attend the Assumption Mass of the Virgin Mary. Some of you might be Catholics and know what that is. The fifteenth of August was the date circled on the calendar in the bedroom of the leader of this cell, the date of this special mass. Carol Sanchez was kidnapped by this group last week and heard one of them say they were planning something against the Catholic Church.

"We don't know which church or churches they're planning to hit. We've selected four churches we think might be targets, and we need to determine the best way to protect these four churches.

"In case we've picked the wrong churches, we'll need a rapid-response team to go to a church we missed. Bryce might have a better solution, but I'm thinking four teams of three and a four-person response team will work. Carol Sanchez will be with me and serve as our lookout at the church we feel they'll most likely hit, and Morales and Benning will be available to complement the other teams.

"We've printed out information for the four churches. This is your area of expertise, so I won't presume to tell you how to best protect them. We have time and I suggest that you split up, however Bryce assigns you, and go visit each church. Then we can meet back here and finalize our plan. You have questions, I'm sure; so fire away."

"Do we know what weapons they'll be using?"

"They have AK-47s. That's all we know about."

"Do we know how many of them there are?"

"We believe originally there were twelve. Two of them are dead."

"Are these churches aware of what we're doing?"

"The priests have been told and will be prepared to activate their emergency plans if needed. But they will not have security themselves at any of these churches."

Drake waited to see if anyone else had a question. There were none.

"We have this conference room reserved for the day. I'll hand things over to Bryce now to organize you. We'll meet here again at three o'clock. That gives us four hours to decide how we're going to do this. If you need anything from me, Bryce knows how to get hold of me."

He stepped out into the hall and motioned for Morales and Sanchez to join him.

"There's not much we can do here. This is what they do best. I'll take Lancer with me back to my office. If you want to stay and see how they can use you, you can. Otherwise, be back here at three."

Drake turned to leave when Morales spoke up. "Boss, you didn't say anything about the rules of engagement."

"I'll go over it at three. But it's simple. If we reasonably believe they're about to use deadly physical force against anyone in those churches, we stop them."

Chapter Sixty

DRAKE WAS DRIVING across the Fremont Bridge on the way back to his office when Kevin McRoberts, the young tech guru for PSS, called.

"Mr. Drake, Kevin McRoberts. Mr. Casey asked me to continue monitoring social media for terrorist activity in Portland. I thought this might be important."

"What might be important?"

"What I just saw on Twitter."

"Kevin, what did you see on Twitter that you thought might be important?"

"Is it okay if I read it to you?"

"Kevin, what is it?"

"Okay. This is it. Quote: Watch the Portland news tonight. As the Prophet said, peace be upon him, 'Kill the one who sodomizes and the one who lets it be done to him.' Inshallah, it shall be done tonight as Allah commands."

Drake's mind raced into hyperdrive. Was Umara targeting the LGBT community and not the Catholic churches? Portland did have the second highest percentage of LGBT residents of all the metropolitan areas in America.

"Kevin, I haven't been watching the news lately. Is there an LGBT event taking place somewhere in Portland?"

"I checked and the Portland Pride Expo starts tonight at six o'clock at the Oregon Convention Center."

"Thanks for keeping an eye on this for us, Kevin. Let me know immediately if you see anything else about this."

"Will do, Mr. Drake."

He hit speed dial for Paul Benning. "Are you still at the Best Western?"

"Yep, I didn't want these doughnuts to go to waste."

"Is Williams still there?"

"He's sitting right beside me. Why?"

"We may have screwed up. Kevin McRoberts found something on Twitter that makes it sound like Umara may be targeting the LGBT convention and not the Catholics' mass this evening."

"That's not good. Let me put this on speaker so Williams can hear. What exactly did Kevin find?"

"Someone's advising people to watch the news tonight from Portland and quoting, maybe the Quran, something about killing the sodomites."

"Drake, Williams here. Could this be a head fake? Everything's been aimed at the Catholics; the warnings, the crucifixion, the twenty million that's missing. Now we get a very public social media tweet to make us think it's not about the church. It's awfully convenient."

"It's happened before, something on social media warning of an attack hours before it happens. How do we know?"

"I'll check with CTD in Washington and see if they've heard anything. What do you want us to do now?"

"I'm almost at my office. I'll grab my go-bag and laptop and come back to the hotel. We've got to decide if this is a head fake or not and real soon. Paul, check with the Sheriff's Office and see what kind of security they have for this Expo. See if they've gotten wind of threats being made lately against the LGBT community here. We might be late to this party, if that's where she's heading."

"Shall I call Bryce and get his people back here?"

"Not yet. I still think she's planning something for the Catholic churches. I agree with Wayne, everything points to the obligation mass tonight. But if this Expo starts tonight, that might be the reason she circled the fifteenth. Let's find out as much as we can before we recall the troops."

When he rushed down the back stairs from the parking garage to his office, Margo was at her desk. "What's happened? Is Paul okay?"

"He's fine. He's at the hotel. Someone just put something on Twitter that makes it sound like there's an attack planned for the Portland Pride Expo and not the Catholic churches. We're trying to decide if the threat is real or not."

"Is there anything I can do to help?"

"Not that I can think of, Margo. If the target really is the Expo at the Oregon Convention Center, the police will handle that. They respond to threats of a possible hate crime, just not if the threat is to Christians."

Drake ran up to his loft, grabbed his go-bag and stuffed his laptop inside and ran back down. "I'll have Paul let you know the minute we decide what we're going to do."

"Be safe, both of you."

Five minutes after parking the 993 with Lancer stretched out inside, guarding it with the windows down and the keys in the ignition, he was behind the wheel driving back to the Best Western.

He was sure that he was right about Umara planning to attack the churches. Everything pointed to it. And yet, he remembered reading that the Ayatollah Ali Sistani, who was praised for being such a moderate Muslim, said that "sodomites should be killed in the worst manner possible." If that was truly the belief of a moderate Muslim, Umara would feel obligated to kill as many as possible, especially when they were conveniently gathered in one place so close at hand.

His gut instinct, though, told him Umara would hit the Catholic church or churches and do it today. But his left brain was still suggesting his trusted instinct might be wrong. Until he was convinced otherwise, even if it meant giving the local FBI office even more reason to continue thinking he saw terrorists under every rock, he had to trust the tingle he was feeling in his gut.

Chapter Sixty-One

BENNING AND WILLIAMS were waiting for him in the conference room when he marched through the lobby with Lancer. Agent Williams had a phone to his ear and threw a sloppy salute in greeting. Benning leaned down to pet Lancer.

"Do you want me to call Morales and Sanchez?"

"In a minute. Did the Sheriff's Office have anything?"

"They haven't heard anything unusual, and nothing specific about this tweet."

"Did Williams get anything?"

"He's talking with someone now back in Washington, but it doesn't look like he's having any luck either."

Drake went to the sidebar and poured a cup of coffee and picked up a bagel. His stomach was a little queasy and he thought the bagel might help, but he knew it wasn't because he was hungry. It was the way he always felt before a football game or right before leaving on a mission.

He pulled out a chair at the conference table and sat

down. Benning took a seat on the other side and watched as he tore a big hunk of the bagel off and started chewing.

"Is there a way to trace the IP address of the tweet?"

Drake swallowed and took a sip of his coffee. "Luke warm. I should have tried it before I sat down. As far as I know, you can't trace the IP address. Twitter can do it, but they'll want a subpoena before they'll give it to you. I believe there's a way to do a search and find the geographical area where the tweet originated, but that won't get us to the IP address of the person who sent it."

"How do we determine if the tweet is real or if someone's trying to scare the LGBT crowd away from the Expo or like a kid who calls in a bomb threat to avoid taking a test he's not going to pass?"

Williams pulled out a chair beside Benning.

"My friends in the CTD in Washington took a look at the tweet, but they have no way to determine if it's real or not. They did say that it's the first time that they know of that terrorists have said anything in advance of an attack on an LGBT gathering. The shooting in Orlando did happen during Gay Pride Month, but the shooter didn't announce his attention before he called 911 and pledged allegiance to ISIS."

"Any ideas, Wayne?"

"Look, I think we're all on the same page here. Everything points to Umara planning something against Catholics. The Assumption Mass is a perfect time to hit a church. The way I see it, if we're wrong, you called in security that wasn't needed. My office alerted the Portland Police Department, but they already knew about the tweet. They're doubling the number of officers who will be there and they'll be prepared if it happens. Everyone's safe all the way around."

"Why would she announce an attack?" Benning asked. "She had to figure the Expo would have security."

"But she doesn't know PSS will have operators guarding these churches," Williams said. "By causing the police to double security at the Expo, she's diverted some of the cops she might have encountered to a different location on the other side of town."

"You're right, it is a smart move if it is a head fake," Benning said.

Drake looked across the table and shook his head. It was a smart move. "But if she's that smart, maybe she's smart enough to pick churches that we haven't thought about. Maybe she's going to storm the archdiocese and take hostages or something. What if we're wrong?"

"Then we're wrong, Adam, but it's the best we can do. Remember when we recommended security for the parishes and Kelly Johannsen told us there are too many of them, they couldn't protect them all. We knew going in that we might be wrong, but we have to try to outguess this crazy woman jihadist."

He knew that doubting his gut instinct was buyer's remorse. The decision had been made and forces deployed. Every general going into battle probably worried that he'd put men in the wrong places to win. But you make your move and hope the other guy didn't anticipate it.

"All right, we stick with the plan. It's almost noon. I'll give David Bryce a call and see how they're doing. Paul, call Sanchez to come and take Lancer for a while and then we'll go have lunch somewhere. I have a feeling it might be late before we're finished tonight."

He didn't have to elaborate. Benning and Williams knew, as well as he did, that if Umara showed up and tried to storm the churches, there were going to be causalities—

hopefully all of them terrorists. But since the police and FBI weren't officially a part of the plan, they would be answering questions well beyond tomorrow's sunrise.

Chapter Sixty-Two

UMARA SAT with her two team leaders at the kitchen table after their final meal before leaving the farm. The others were in the barn praying and resting.

The women sitting with her were twin sisters and had chosen the Muslim names of two legendary warriors who were also sisters, Dhiraar ibn Azwar and Khawlah bint al-Azwar.

"Dhiraar, the gay pride marchers will walk over the pedestrian walkway on the lower deck of the Steel Bridge on their way to the convention center. It's spontaneous, so they didn't get a permit and the police aren't supposed to know about it. The police will be out in force at the convention center after the tweet you sent, but not on the bridge. Stop your van in the middle of the bridge and send one sister east toward the convention center and the other is to go west. You go behind them and kill anyone left standing in the direction where most of the walkers are.

"The marchers on the pedestrian walkway will be penned in by the railing on their side, so you're shooting fish in a barrel. Traffic will stop and block the police from reaching you, so you will have plenty of time.

"The march will start at five o'clock so they have time to get everyone across for the opening speeches at the Expo at six o'clock. Wait until five fifteen before you drive across. Khawlah and I will wait until five forty-five to attack the two churches.

"Between us, we will kill more Americans in one day than anyone ever has, except for 9/11. Be proud of what we will accomplish as models for young women everywhere. It's a noble thing we're doing and we will always be remembered for it."

Umara reached down and took two bags of pills out and set them on the table.

"We leave here at four thirty. Have everyone take two pills at four o'clock. Each van has a hand-held GPS navigator, and you've memorized the routes, but if traffic's a problem, use the alternate route we picked.

"Dhiraar, you'll be the first to leave. Is there anything you have a question about?"

"The man who comes to the farm, does he know that we're not attacking the four churches as originally planned?"

"Why is that important?"

"Because I don't trust him. He doesn't trust us; otherwise we wouldn't have to stay in the barn whenever he comes."

Umara shook her head. "No, Dhiraar, he doesn't know we changed the plan. He still thinks we're attacking four churches. That's why I had him bring four vans. We will surprise everyone, including him."

Khawlah picked up one of the bags of pills and slipped it into the pocket of her camo shorts. "What about the professor? Did he know what you were planning before he disappeared?"

"Don't worry about him. He might have guessed I was working with someone else, but he didn't know what I was planning. Even if he did, he won't tell anyone. He's hiding somewhere and doesn't want to be found. The Council will find him and he'll get what's coming to him."

Khawlah bowed her head and sighed. "I'm afraid I didn't do a very good job with my video. I said all the right things, like we talked about, but I didn't say the right things to our family. They'll never understand."

Dhiraar laid her hand over her sister's. "They don't share our faith, Sister. But by seeing how faithful we are to Islam, maybe they'll see Islam differently and join us someday."

Umara waited patiently for them to finish talking about their family. She knew how hurt they'd been when they were disowned by their precious family after submitting themselves to Islam. But people like their parents would never understand, not in a thousand years. They valued their fancy home and luxury cars and bank accounts too much to adopt a faith that rejected those values. The only way people like their parents would ever become Muslims was when a sword was held over their heads.

She stood and waited for them to do the same. "Go pray and find the peace Allah will give you. You will receive your reward this day and that is something to rejoice in."

Chapter Sixty-Three

PAUL BENNING SUGGESTED lunch at the Island Café, a floating restaurant at McCuddy's Marina on Hayden Island. They were looking over their menus when David Bryce called Drake.

"We've scouted the four Catholic churches. Where do you want to meet to go over our recommendations?"

"Where are you?"

"I just left St. Andrew's and I'm headed back to the Best Western."

"Put the Island Café in your GPS and come join us for lunch. I'm here with Benning and Agent Williams. You're close, we'll wait to order."

"On my way."

While they waited for Bryce, they ordered ice tea and watched the water traffic coming in and out of McCuddy's Marina across the way.

"Wayne, have you found out what happened to your agent who died last Sunday? Benning asked. "I heard the accident is under investigation."

"A witness who was following his car said the shooter just opened fire at a stop light. The witness didn't get a license but said it was a black Mustang."

"What was he doing on a Sunday?"

Williams snorted. "What, you think a federal crime fighter doesn't work weekends?"

"Well…"

"We're looking into that. He was meeting one of his Muslim contacts, seeking information about Umara. The notes on his laptop don't identify the contact."

"Any chance he was shot because he was asking about Umara?"

"That's probably a stretch, but who knows?"

"Well, sorry you lost one of your own. I know how it affects an office."

Drake saw Bryce coming through the café and waved him to their table on the back deck.

"I could get used to this," he said as he pulled out a chair. "It's like being in the Caribbean."

Benning passed him a menu. "Then you'll like what's on the menu. Are the rest of your teams back at the hotel?"

"They're stopping somewhere for lunch and then going there. We're ready to meet whenever you are."

A cute, young waitress came to their table, looking very tropical wearing cut-off jeans and a tied-off shirt that allowed a peek at a tattoo descending below her belly button.

"Anyone care for a margarita or a daiquiri?"

When she saw they were all shaking their heads no, she started around the table taking their orders. Two burgers, a pulled pork sandwich and grilled chicken teriyaki bowl. The teriyaki bowl was Drake's.

While they waited for their orders, Bryce gave them a

quick report. "The four churches are spread out, as you know, two on the west side of the river and two on the east side. We made a diagram for each church showing positions and fields of fire. You'll have those when we get back to the hotel.

"I would like to position four operators at each church, but that doesn't leave anyone for the rapid-response team you wanted. We'll be dressed in street clothes and wearing body armor, but weapons will be out of sight, obviously. We shouldn't attract too much attention.

"Every situation is different, and these are all public places, so we'll need to be clear on the rules of engagement. I'll go over the rules we're used to operating with later, if you want to make any changes."

Drake thought a minute. "Bryce, if we add Paul, Morales and me to the mix, we could have four at each church and use three operators for rapid response. Carol Sanchez isn't licensed for Oregon, so I want her to be with me at St. Patrick's as a lookout. We have the student and driver's license photos of Umara, but Carol's the only one who's seen her up close."

"Sure, that would work."

"Paul, are you okay with joining one of the teams? I know how concerned Margo is."

"I wouldn't miss it, but I did have to promise her I would wear armor."

"Bryce brought body armor for everyone, including us."

"Drake, where do you think we should position the response team?"

"Somewhere midway between the four churches, maybe either end of the Steel Bridge. That would give them a quick way to get across the river. Maybe someplace near China Town or Union Station."

"All right. Are we still meeting at three o'clock in the conference room?"

"Unless you think we need more time to go over things with your operators, three's fine."

Their food arrived and the men dug in like they had to finish lunch before the cute waitress returned to refill their ice teas. It reminded Drake of eating in an army mess hall in basic training, with a drill sergeant prowling around making sure you were in and out in under five minutes.

It was also the way soldiers ate before leaving on a mission, which was precisely who they were and what they were doing, minus the uniforms.

Chapter Sixty-Four

BEFORE LEAVING THE ISLAND CAFÉ, Drake called Sanchez to find out how she was getting along with Lancer and to tell her to find Morales and meet him at Delta Park. He had a feeling she wouldn't have to go very far to find her PSS compatriot.

When he drove into the park and stopped beside the same soccer field where Sanchez had practiced giving Lancer commands, Morales was there but Sanchez wasn't.

"Where's Sanchez?"

Morales hooked a thumb over his shoulder. "She's exercising your dog."

Drake looked where Morales pointed and saw Sanchez jogging around the next soccer field over with Lancer trotting at her side.

Sanchez waved when she saw him looking at her and started across the empty soccer field toward them.

"They seem to be getting along all right."

Morales turned around to watch Sanchez and Lancer. "Oh yeah, they're best buds."

Drake suppressed a grin. It sounded like Morales was jealous.

Sanchez sprinted the last fifty yards and couldn't pull ahead of Lancer.

"It's a race you'll always lose, Carol. Believe me, I know. Thanks for taking him for a run."

She leaned down and scratched with both hands behind Lancer's ears. "I think I'm going to get a dog like Lancer. I didn't know they could be this much fun."

Drake thought he detected a slight grimace on Morales' face.

"Let's sit down and talk for a minute."

They followed him to the edge of the soccer field and sat down cross-legged across from him. Lancer lay down next to Sanchez.

"We're going to split up to guard the churches, with Carol staying with me at St. Patrick's. One three-man team will be stationed midway between the four churches, with Marco and Paul Benning filling in at two of the other churches. I'm going to have Agent Williams stay with us at St. Patrick's to act as our spokesman, if we need to explain what we're doing with law enforcement or the FBI.

"Marco, I'll go over this when we meet in the conference room, but I want any question asked by the Portland police or the FBI to be handled by Williams, David Bryce or me. If deadly force is required, there will be an investigation and possibly lawsuits filed. Bryce and his operators are here as Oregon licensed armed security. The three of us aren't. Identify yourself as an employee of PSS and direct any questions to me, as special counsel for PSS.

"The FBI agents in the Portland Field Office aren't my biggest fans and I don't want to give them any reason to start poking around in what we did to find Umara. They're already curious about how we found Carol in the cabin at the coast.

"You have your choice of carrying your handgun or using one of the HK416s Bryce brought. I think you'll be okay with either weapon, but maybe a little better off with a handgun. The media and the thought police go nuts whenever they hear someone's carrying an 'assault rifle'.

"Be ready to defend yourself and do what's required to protect anyone in harm's way if these women show up, but let Bryce's operators take the lead. I might be overly sensitive about this, but we don't need them coming after us with a hate crime investigation by the FBI's Civil Rights division, alleging that we acted against these unfortunate young women solely on the basis of their religion."

"No problem, boss. If they show up, it will be obvious who the bad guys are."

"It will be, but that doesn't stop the gun haters and lawyers from getting involved. If you shoot someone in your home and they're there to steal or rape or kill you, you will still be sued by someone. It's just the way it is."

Sanchez uncrossed her legs, stretched them out in front of her and leaned forward to touch her toes. "What happens if I use Lancer as a weapon and order him to attack someone?"

"Lancer's there to protect you, Carol. But if it's necessary to protect someone else, send him."

"What if the someone is you?"

Drake reached over and petted Lancer. "If the someone is me, Lancer knows what to do. You won't have to send him; he'll be on his way."

He got up and stretched, twisting left and right. "Keep Lancer with you until the meeting at three and get something to eat, if you haven't already. I'm going back to my office to check in with Margo and call the new PSS vice president for governmental affairs. She needs to be up to speed in case we need her."

He didn't think Liz would need to get involved, with Agent Williams knowing what they were doing, but you never knew. The real reason he was calling her was just to hear her voice—and remind himself he had something to live for, beyond the adrenaline rush he seemed to crave more and more these days.

It hadn't always been that way. When he left the army, and worked as a prosecutor, he was never really in danger. The closest he'd come to it was skiing black diamond runs or driving too fast in the 993. But after Kay died and he lost interest in his law practice because he was drinking too much, he'd been dead inside.

Until he'd been asked to help a friend of his father-in-law's and crossed swords with the terrorist assassins preparing to kill a list of American VIPs. The fire that had been lit in him by 9/11 that led his to joining the army after law school, instead of working for the law firm in Portland, was rekindled by the threat from the same enemies he'd hunted and killed in Afghanistan and Iraq.

And here they were again. And he would do everything in his power to defeat them again.

Chapter Sixty-Five

DRAKE'S VISIT to his office was brief and bittersweet. He'd been able to assure Margo that her husband would be wearing body armor and that he'd been told to let the trained professionals do what they were trained to do. She knew him well enough to know that he was sugarcoating it but appreciated him doing so.

He wasn't able to reach Liz and headed back to the hotel wondering where she might be. It wasn't like her to not answer her phone because she always had it with her.

Bryce had everyone assembled in the conference room when he got there. Agent Williams was there, talking with Sanchez who had Lancer sitting beside her. Benning and Morales were waiting in line at the sidebar for coffee or one of the soft drinks he'd ordered for the meeting.

Bryce tapped his coffee cup with a spoon. "Let's get started, people."

He walked to the head of the conference table and stood next to Drake. It was Drake's meeting, but they were there to hear his recommendations for the security PSS was asked to provide.

Drake led off. "In my role as special counsel for PSS, I'll take a minute to remind you of our policy regarding the use of deadly force. You are authorized to use deadly force only when necessary. It will be necessary when you have a reasonable belief that someone is about to use deadly force and poses an imminent danger of death or serious injury to another person, in this case, to one of the people you're there to protect, a civilian walking by or a fellow operator. You've heard me say all this before, and I know you understand the restraint we're required to demonstrate in situations that we might face today. So, with that out of the way, I'll let Bryce review the plan for protecting these churches."

Drake went to the sidebar for a cup of coffee and stood aside to hear what Bryce had to say.

"You scouted the church you're assigned and met with me to tell me where you feel you need to be positioned to provide security in each location. I don't need to go over that now, unless you're having second thoughts about what we agreed on."

Bryce waited to see if anyone had anything to say. "It's imperative that we are as discreet and inconspicuous as possible. The people coming for this mass do not expect to see armed security at their place of worship. We don't want to make them anxious or afraid because we're there. Smile at people as they pass by, mingle and move around your chosen position. No sunglasses. Let them see your reassuring eyes.

"I've decided to make a change with the weapons we'll be carrying. The HK416 is harder to conceal when we're wearing suits, so we're going to go with the SIG MCX

Rattler SBR. Keep them slung under your coats and out of sight the best you can.

"We've all used the Motorola two-way radios. You'll have the Sentry 2-wire earpiece accessory with the 'push to talk switch' to be worn down your sleeve. Nothing new there.

"Instead of putting four of you at each church, we're going to hold three of you back to serve as a rapid-response team, in case we guessed wrong on which church these people will attack. We'll break into teams before we leave here and I'll tell you where we'd like the response team to be stationed.

"Drake, Morales and Paul Benning and I will be with you to make four operators at each church. In case you're wondering, Carol Sanchez hasn't been with us long enough to become licensed for armed security, so she will be our lookout at St. Patrick's."

Bryce checked his watch. "It's three thirty. Dress in your rooms and we'll meet out front in one hour. That's all for now."

The operators filed out, taking most of the remaining soft drinks with them.

Sanchez came over with Lancer. "Is Lancer leaving with you?"

"Tired of him already?"

She turned her head toward the front desk. "No, but I think management feels he's overstayed his welcome."

"I may have implied Lancer would only be here for a short time. I'll talk with the manager on my way out. Keep him with you and follow the operators going to St. Patrick's in Paul's truck. We'll find a good place to park it for you and Lancer as our lookout. I'll meet you there."

Agent Williams and Benning were waiting for him when he left the conference room behind Sanchez and Lancer.

"Where do you want me to go, Drake? You're not going to deny your friendly FBI agent the chance to be in on this, are you?"

"That's up to you, Wayne. I'd like to have you with me at St. Patrick's, to explain everything when the police or your office shows up. But I don't want to cause you any trouble in case your presence isn't authorized."

"Let me worry about that. If this turns out the way we think it might, my presence will give the FBI bragging rights with the locals."

"Okay, ride with me if you want to St. Patrick's. Paul, are you staying here?"

"I think I will. Saying goodbye to Margo again will just make it harder for her. I'll get with Bryce, find out where he wants me and then ride with that team to the church."

With an hour to kill before leaving for St. Patrick's, Drake left Williams and Benning trading war stories in the lobby. He wanted to walk around Delta Park to clear his head and call Liz again.

Chapter Sixty-Six

AT FOUR THIRTY, the first van left the farm with Dhiraar driving. She was followed by Khawlah, her sister, ten minutes later. Umara waited for five minutes and followed the second van up the long gravel driveway to the highway.

The three vans, a green Dodge Caravan, a gray Toyota Previa and a tan Ford Aerostar were spaced far enough apart that no one would think they were together—or remember the ten, serious looking, young women wearing black headscarves.

This last hour was the culmination of one year of planning, recruiting and training women to be warriors and martyrs prepared to die gloriously in the service of Allah. Two had already gone on ahead, carrying out Umara's orders. And now the remaining members of the Muslim Empowerment Club were about to do the same.

She thought about the irony of how the college had helped her by blessing and supporting the club. They praised it up as a peaceful model for oppressed minorities attending universities and colleges in America. Weren't they in for a surprise? Right under their noses, she'd been able to organize a cell of believers that stood for everything the college didn't believe in. They didn't tolerate gays and lesbians, they hated them. They didn't march for women's rights; they cherished their honored place in the world the Quran afforded them. And they certainly didn't believe in multiculturalism. There was only one culture in the world worthy of supremacy, and that was the Muslim culture.

She glanced in the rearview mirror to see how the two women sitting behind her were handling the Captagon pills she'd given them. They looked serene and calmly composed, alertly looking straight ahead as they contemplated their actions when they reached the church. She knew they were unafraid and would act without empathy as they gunned down the cross worshippers. That's what Captagon did; it turned you into the perfect warrior.

She didn't need the drug herself because she was never afraid. Her pills were still in her pants pocket and would stay there for another time. There would be other battles to fight after this one.

Her cell phone buzzed and she saw that it was Dhiraar.

"Approaching the onramp for the Sunset Highway. Traffic as anticipated and we're right on schedule."

"Let me know if there's a slowdown so I can decide if you need to take your alternate route."

"Will do."

Her cell phone buzzed again.

"Umara, there's a state police car following me. He's been back there for the last couple of miles."

"Take a deep breath, Khawlah. There's nothing wrong with your van. I checked it. Have you been speeding?"

"No, I've been holding steady at the speed limit."

"Just keep going. You'll follow Dhiraar onto Highway 26 in just a minute. Let me know if he turns with you."

There was nothing they could do if one of the vans got pulled over for some traffic thing, but if the van was searched and the weapons found, Dhiraar and Khawlah were ordered to kill the cop and proceed to their targets.

She knew that in every famous battle her namesake had fought in, something unexpected had happened. You just had to be prepared to react intelligently. That's why she hadn't taken the Captagon. She needed to be clear-headed.

Khawlah called. "He kept on going. I'm on Sunset Highway, just passing Tanasbourne."

"How's traffic?"

"Heavy as always but moving okay."

"Keep me informed."

As she followed Dhiraar and Khawlah onto the Sunset Highway, she wondered what Zal Nazir was doing. He'd be watching the evening news somewhere, at his place in Orenco Station or maybe a bar somewhere. He'd be excited and nervous for them but also proud. Her only regret was that she'd never been able to get him in bed. Professor Ahmadi had been easy, but Nazir had made it clear that their relationship would always be professional. She'd have to wait for paradise to satisfy all her desires.

She drove on, thinking about what her reward would be if she went to paradise today. She didn't have a husband and knew that she would be able to marry any man she wanted when she got there, but she wondered if there would be more. If paradise was a place of sensual delights for men, surely there would be something similar for women, especially for martyrs who sacrificed themselves just like men, even if the Quran failed to mention such a reward specifically.

Well, she might know soon enough.

Her phone buzzed again.

"I just passed Barnes Road. Traffic slowing but as expected."

"Thanks, Dhiraar. Proceed to your staging area near the bridge. Send as many of the sodomites to hell as you can and, inshallah, clear the way for us to do the same to the Christians."

Chapter Sixty-Seven

THE PSS OPERATORS dressed in their rooms, putting on body armor under the dark gray, blue or black suits they had selected for the assignment.

Drake and Benning used the room Morales was in to don the protective vests Bryce gave them. They were dressed more casually, wearing summer-weight blazers and slacks that were more appropriate for the eighty-five-degree, late afternoon temperature of the day. They didn't look as intimidating as the PSS guys, but they were degrees more comfortable.

Morales didn't have the luxury of returning to his apartment in Seattle. He only had jeans and an untucked long sleeve, black T-shirt that covered the inside-the-pants holster and the SIG P320 X-Carry pistol he preferred.

Carol Sanchez was waiting for them in the lobby when they got there, wearing a pair of khaki shorts and a dark blue polo. Bryce didn't bring a protective vest that would fit her, but she argued that, staying in Benning's Ford F-150 with Lancer as their lookout, she didn't need to wear one.

Drake didn't like it because Williams could have found one for her at his office but didn't argue with her.

They assembled in the lobby of the hotel, getting curious looks from the front desk and guests who walked by, until they loaded into five silver GMC full-size Yukons parked out front under the portico.

Drake and Agent Williams got in the first SUV with two of the PSS operators for the ride to St. Patrick's Catholic Church. Sanchez would follow them in Benning's truck.

Benning and David Bryce, the head of the PSS VIP Protection division, and two PSS operators got in the second SUV to go to St. Mary's Catholic Cathedral.

Morales and two PSS operators were assigned to security for St. Andrew's Catholic Church and four operators were assigned to St. Stephen's Catholic Church. Both churches were located across the Willamette River and their two SUVs pulled out before the two leaving for St. Patrick's and St. Mary's.

The last silver Yukon, designated the rapid-response team, would carry four PSS operators and position itself at Union Station just west of the Steel Bridge.

Drake and Williams sat in the second row of seats in the lead SUV behind two PSS men, Parker and Thompson. Thompson was riding shotgun and turned around to face them.

"I'm curious, what are you carrying, Drake? I know Williams will have a 9mm Glock Gen 5 the FBI issues its agents."

"A Kimber .45. Got used to the 1911s in the army."

"Don't you find the eight or nine round capacity limiting?"

"Never had to use more than that."

When Drake didn't elaborate, Williams did it for him.

"He's trained to put a bullet between your eyes at a full run. Eight's probably a luxury for a guy like Drake."

Drake shot an angry look across to Williams. His records were supposed to be sealed to protect the privacy of the Army's elite soldiers.

Williams leaned over. "Don't worry; no one else in the Portland Field Office has seen your records. I called in some favors in Washington after we met in the Sheriff's Office in Warrenton. I was curious about how you took down the woman at the cabin."

"I'd appreciate it if you'd keep my not-so-sealed records to yourself. Some of the guys in your office already think I'm too gung ho. If they know I was an operator, my relationship with the FBI will only get worse."

"Anything I can do to help with that?"

"Maybe there is. If this goes down like we think it will, why don't you take credit for tracking down Umara and figuring out what she was planning? Getting credit for it isn't going to help me any, but your office will know we worked together on this. Maybe it will earn me a little respect if they see I'm willing to work with you."

"Sure, if that's the way you want to handle it. What's been the problem in the past?"

"Getting someone to listen to me. I have experience in dealing with terrorists. I know how they think. Just because I'm a civilian now doesn't mean I can't help out when I see something."

"You sure saw something this time. If you hadn't sent Sanchez to the college, we wouldn't have a clue who Umara is or what she's up to."

"Let's pray we got it right, Wayne. AK-47s in a crowded place like a church will kill a lot of innocent people."

"We won't let her get that far."

Their driver, Parker, turned his head and said, "We're almost there. Check your two-ways and make sure we can hear each other. We'll show you where we'll be and where we think the best positions for you are. I think I know a good place for your lookout. If you'd like me to show her where that is, I'm happy to do it."

Drake caught him grinning in the rearview mirror. Parker was a good ten years older than Sanchez, but he wasn't wearing a wedding ring from what he could see. Sanchez could take care of herself and was used to fielding advances from fellow cops, he wasn't worried about her.

It was what Morales would do to the poor guy if he thought he was poaching on his preserve.

Drake grinned back at Parker. "That's okay, you point out where you think she should be and I'll get her there. I need to make sure my dog knows what I want him to do."

Parker turned the corner and pulled to the curb in front of St. Patrick's.

It was time to get ready for an attack they hoped would never happen.

Chapter Sixty-Eight

DRAKE STOOD ON THE CORNER, looking south down Northwest Nineteenth Avenue and then up Northwest Savier Street to the east. He agreed with Parker's suggestion to park the Ford F-150 across the street on the northwest corner of the intersection of the two streets. From there, Sanchez would be able to see anyone coming down Northwest 19th Avenue in her rearview mirror and anyone coming from the east on Northwest Savier Street toward the church.

He pointed out the location to Sanchez and then crossed Northwest Savier Street to wait for her to drive around the blocks necessary to reach the vacant parking place he was saving for her.

When she pulled in, he motioned for her to roll down the passenger-side window. "Keep this window rolled down. Lancer will use it to get out to protect you, if necessary, or go help someone else if you tell him to."

"Where will you be?"

"Somewhere by the church where I can see you. Do you remember your signal for help?"

Sanchez thought for a second and then smiled broadly. "Kimchi."

"That's the one."

Drake crossed the street and joined Agent Williams at the bottom of the stairs in front of St. Patrick's. Several parishioners walked by, early arrivals making sure their favorite pews were available. They didn't seem to pay any attention to them or the two PSS men standing back a little on either side of the stairs.

"Where would you approach from?" Williams asked.

"I'd come down Nineteenth. Straight shot and I wouldn't have to worry about turning at the intersection."

"I was thinking the same thing. I think I'll go over and be in front of the bank across the street. There's an ATM there. I'll look like I'm waiting to use it."

"I'll be here at the corner. I can keep an eye on Sanchez and see both approaches to the church."

Drake waved to Sanchez and found a shady spot on the sidewalk under a tree near the corner.

It was a quarter after five and the number of people entering the old church had quadrupled. The parishioners were scrutinized for any of the telltale signs of a nervous terrorist; the thousand-yard stare, sweating more than normal or softly repeating a prayer or verse from the Quran. None of the Catholics he saw came even close to looking like a terrorist. They were older, for the most part, and smiled if you made eye contact with them.

Across the street, Williams had his phone to his ear. He looked at Drake and jogged over.

"Someone's stopped in the middle of the Steel Bridge

and started shooting people. Some sort of flash mob gay pride march over to the convention center. They didn't have a permit, so no security along the route. These marchers are sitting ducks on the pedestrian walkway on that bridge. Looks like the tweet about killing the sodomites was genuine."

Drake shook his head and swore through clenched teeth. Was he wrong about Umara hitting the churches? Everything he knew about her, what Sanchez heard at the cabin and the fifteenth circled on her calendar made it the logical possibility. He'd missed something.

"Can we get the response team there to help? They're at Union Station."

"What I'm hearing is that traffic's at a standstill in both directions. The police are trying to get there on foot from the convention center and a police helicopter is airborne."

"What did we miss? I was sure she'd attack one of the Catholic churches, that the tweet was a head fake, a feint to get us looking there when she was coming here."

"She fooled all of us. Should we pull security?"

"How many shooters are on the bridge? Do we know?"

Williams got his phone out. "I'll check."

Drake walked away and then pivoted back. If the march to the convention center was a flash mob event, how did Umara know about it in advance? She and her crew didn't strike him as the LGBT types.

Williams covered the phone's speaker with his hand. "They're reporting just three shooters on the bridge."

"Where are the others? If there were twelve women in her Muslim Empowerment Club, two are dead and three are on the bridge, that's not all of them. She's still coming, Wayne."

Chapter Sixty-Nine

UMARA WATCHED the coverage of the attack streaming live to her Samsung Galaxy from the traffic and news helicopter hovering over the Steel Bridge. Bodies were lying everywhere on the pedestrian walkway on the side of the bridge. People were running for their lives from cars that were stopped and couldn't go anywhere. Some of the sodomites were even jumping from the bridge into the river to escape the merciless fire being laid down by her warriors.

She would wait ten minutes for the police to respond to the attack on the bridge before leaving for the two churches. Their two vans were parked innocently side by side in the parking lot of the Rose Garden and needed fifteen minutes to drive down to the two churches in Northwest Portland. It wasn't critical when they arrived; the Christians weren't going anywhere until the mass they were attending ended. They would have plenty of time to enter and add to the number of casualties they would tally for the day.

The two women riding in her van were sitting calmly, watching people stroll among the roses and stopping to lean down and smell the fragrant flowers. It was good to be reminded of the beauty that awaited them in paradise.

Umara checked the time and started her van. Khawlah turned at the sound of the engine starting and flashed a thumb up as she started her engine as well. It was time.

Umara backed up and drove out of the parking lot onto Southwest Lewis and Clark Way. From there, she knew the route to the churches by heart. Once they reached Southwest Vista Avenue to the east of the Rose Garden, it was a simple drive north, first crossing West Burnside and then continuing on Northwest 23rd Avenue..

Kwahlah would follow her and turn east on Northwest Everett Street. St. Mary's Catholic Cathedral was only ten blocks away and Khawlah would pull over and wait until she signaled her to proceed.

St. Patrick's was farther north, up Northwest 23rd Avenue to Northwest Raleigh, where she would turn right and drive to Northwest 18th Avenue, take a left then another left on Northwest Savier Street and the church was one block away.

Locating the church on a street that was called "Savier" was a joke, not only because it wasn't the way you spelled "Savior" but because no one was going to be saved at that church today.

Traffic was moderately heavy, as people headed home, but she had driven the route at the same time of the day often enough to know how long it would take. They were right on time.

When she approached the intersection of Northwest 23rd Avenue and Northwest Everett, she turned her right turn signal off and on three times. Kwahlah flashed her bright lights three times in response and turned right onto Northwest Everett.

They were almost there and the anticipation of what lay ahead was doing a number on her stomach. The butterflies made her wish she had taken the pills with the others. But she knew that without the artificial stimulus Captagon provided, she would enjoy every person she sent to hell more than the others would. The nervousness was a small price to pay for that added pleasure.

"We're almost there. Uncover the weapons on the floor and be ready to hand one of them up to me in front. Don't forget the extra thirty-round mags you have. I want every round fired. No one should walk out of this church alive if we do what we need to do to, please Allah. You worked hard and you deserve every reward that's waiting for you. This is our time. Send a message to the world that Muslim women are to be feared, just like our men. As Allah wills it, so shall it be."

Umara slowed at the intersection and turned right onto Northwest Raleigh Street. The oldest symbol of Rome and its crusaders in Portland was only eight blocks away.

Chapter Seventy

TEN MINUTES after the Assumption Mass for the Virgin Mary began at St. Patrick's, most of the parishioners attending it were inside the church. A few late arrivals hurried along on the sidewalks toward the front stairs.

They didn't appear to pay any attention to the two men in dark suits flanking the curving stairs. Another man walked back and forth on the sidewalk, looking up and down the street as if he was waiting for someone to arrive.

Carol Sanchez clicked the push to talk button in her left hand. "A white van is coming down 19th Avenue behind me. I can't make out what it is."

Drake looked to his left down 19th Avenue and saw the van. "I see it."

Agent Williams saw it too from across the street in front of the bank. As it got closer, he could identify it. "There's lettering on the side. It's a mobility service for the handicapped."

The van slowed at the intersection and pulled to the curb in front of the church. The driver got out and came around to the sliding door and opened it. A white-haired lady using a cane stood inside, waiting to be helped down the steps that extended out from under the sliding door.

Drake walked over to help the lady up the stairs.

"There's another van approaching on Savier Street, tan in color," his lookout reported.

Sanchez raised her binoculars to get a better look. "One woman in front wearing a black headscarf. This could be her."

Drake was halfway up the stairs with the old lady. From his position, he saw the tan Ford Aerostar over the top of the mobility van as it pulled away from the curb. He took hold of the lady's arm and sat down on the stairs.

"Ma'am, I need you to sit down here and not move until I get back. Will you do that for me?"

She frowned and nodded yes, puzzled by the request. "Will you be right back?"

He saw the Aerostar slow and begin to turn left across the intersection. "Right back, I promise."

Drake crept down the stairs and crouched behind the curving outer wall. "This is it, guys. Let them make the first move."

He heard four clicks in his earpiece, acknowledging his reminder of the rules of engagement as he pulled his Kimber from its holster.

The van slid to a stop in front of the church. The side door slammed back, allowing two women to jump out. They carried their AK-47s at port arms and started toward the stairs, giving no sign they saw anyone guarding the church.

Drake let them reach the sidewalk. "Stop right there. Put down your weapons."

Two Kalishnikovs rose up and started firing in his direction from ten feet away.

Above the sound of gunfire from the AK-47s and the return fire from two SIG MCX Rattlers on either side of him, Drake heard Williams shouting in his earpiece.

"The driver's getting out. It's Umara. She's slipping around to the back of the van."

Drake was pinned down at the bottom of the stairs. Then the sound of gunfire abruptly stopped and there was silence.

"Two Tango's down," PSS Thompson whispered from his position on the other side of the stairs.

"Roger that," PSS Parker confirmed.

"Where's Umara?" Drake asked quietly into the microphone of the two-way radio he wore down his sleeve.

"She's trying to slip away," Sanchez said from the Ford F-150 across the street. "She's running toward the bank."

"I see her." Williams moved out from the side of the bank to stop her. "FBI, throw down your weapon. You're under arrest."

Umara fired a burst at Williams and turned to run across Savier Street toward the Ford F-150.

Sanchez saw her coming and hesitated. She couldn't stop Umara and she didn't know if anyone had a clear shot. Her only option was to send Lancer.

"Lancer, *fahs*!"

Lancer jumped out the window and took aim at the woman running toward him. From ten feet away, he launched into the air.

Umara didn't see him coming and didn't have time to get her hands up to protect herself before Lancer hit her, knocking her backwards onto the street. Barking loudly, he took hold of her right arm as she struggled to get up and use her rifle.

She was up on one knee when her head snapped back. A pink mist burst in the air as she fell backwards.

Drake didn't hear the shot and didn't know where it came from. He just knew it hadn't come from any of them.

"Did anyone see the shooter?"

No one had.

"Carol, call Lancer back and keep him in the truck with you. This is a crime scene and we want everything left where it is, except for Lancer."

Drake ran up the stairs to check on the old lady. She was sitting where he left her, with her hands resting on the top of her cane.

"What was all that noise?"

"Nothing to worry about, ma'am. Let me help you up."

The front door of the church opened slowly and a young priest looked out. Drake waved him over.

"Help this lady inside. Keep everyone in the church until the police arrive. They'll decide if they want anything from any of you."

"Is this what we were warned about?"

"Yes, but it's over now."

Drake walked down to where Williams was standing, looking down at the two dead bodies on the sidewalk. He turned with his phone to his ear.

"They hit St. Mary's at the same time. Three shooters, just like here. No one hurt on our side. I called it in. I'll handle it when the locals get here."

"Did you hear anything more about the shooters on the Steel Bridge?"

"Three shooters, all of them down. It took S.W.A.T. a

little time to get there, but they ended it when they did. Don't have a casualty count yet, but it's going to be high."

Three on the bridge, three at St. Patrick's and three at St. Mary's. Eight women, plus Umara and the two at the cabin. That left two unaccounted for, if they were correct that originally there were twelve of them. He'd wait a little longer before he called in the three other PSS teams.

Bryce answered on the third ring. "Dave, let's wait thirty minutes until we call in the men from the two other churches and the rapid-response team. I think it's over, but, by my count, there could be two more of them out there, if everyone in her Empowerment Club was in on this. Then we can wrap things up tomorrow and get your guys back to Seattle."

"Williams told me what happened. You got it right about her targets."

"Two of them anyway. I didn't see the one on the Steel Bridge."

"No way you could. I've got someone here who would like to talk with you, if you have a minute."

"Sure, put him on."

Benning was at St. Mary's and probably wanted to know if his truck was all shot up.

"Are you all right?"

He was stunned. "What are you doing in Portland?"

"Making sure the man I'm moving across the country for is alive. We thought you'd be at St. Mary's with Paul."

"Margo's with you?"

"She met me at the airport and we came straight here. Can I come and see you?"

"There's nothing I'd like better, but I might be busy for a while."

"I'll wait. I'll be there as soon as I can call a cab."

Williams saw him smiling. "I could use some good news. Care to share why you're smiling?"

"Because I'm a lucky man, Wayne. Liz flew out from Washington. She's headed this way."

Chapter Seventy-One

AGENT WILLIAMS KEPT his word and dealt with the Portland Police captain in charge of the scene at St. Patrick's. He and Liz had been able to slip away at eight thirty with Paul and Margo for dinner at Paley's Place on Nob Hill.

The parishioners at St. Patrick's had exited the church using its emergency evacuation plan and been spared the sight of the bodies. But they couldn't help but notice the police cruisers with lights flashing all around the church. Northwest 19th Avenue and Northwest Savier Street were blocked off for two blocks in each direction. The parishioners who parked in the parking lot and on nearby streets were sent on alternate routes away from the church by uniformed police officers.

Paley's Place was Drake's favorite restaurant in the city and he made every effort to attend Wine Wednesdays as often as he could. A mystery wine was complimentary with each wine flight to accompany the special offerings from the kitchen on those nights.

He'd called without a reservation and crossed his fingers when he asked to speak with Chef Vitaly. The restaurant was booked solid throughout the evening, but Chef Vitaly promised there would be a table available for Drake and his friends whenever they arrived. The Victorian home and restaurant was close by on Northwest Twenty-First Avenue, but it was too far to walk and they drove there in Benning's F-150 XLT.

They were personally escorted to their table on the front porch by Chef Vitaly, a perfect seating for a warm summer evening.

"I haven't seen you for the last several Wine Wednesdays, Adam. Have you left me for one my competitors?" Chef Vitaly asked as he pulled out a chair for Liz.

"You have no competition, Vitaly. I've just been busy."

"Keep that in mind, my friend. Now, let me recommend Wagyu beef tartare or the hazelnut roasted king salmon. They're both especially good tonight. Your waiter will be Sevie. Please enjoy your evening."

Sevie introduced himself and told them about the night's special offerings. Before he left the porch with their drink orders, Drake sat back and recognized the early signs of the post adrenal dump slow down. His body was beginning to wind down from the adrenaline rush that kicked in when Umara drove up. He'd been flying at forty thousand feet, and like the jet Liz flew in to Portland, he had to slow down to land.

He reached over and took hold of Liz's hand. "I'm glad you're here."

Margo interrupted the tender moment. "I am too. Now maybe you'll get some work done in the office."

"That's what I've been doing, Margo, just not in the office. In fact, I'm thinking of taking the rest of the month off to recuperate from the stress and strain of the last week."

"Well, clear your desk if you do. I didn't work all those files for them to just sit there and gather dust."

Thankfully their drinks arrived and ended the not-so-gentle reminder that he hadn't been in the office much lately.

Benning raised his glass of lager and proposed a toast. "Here's to the safe conclusion of a very ugly day."

They raised their glasses and drank thankfully. Seventy-eight marchers on the Steel Bridge had died and a dozen more who jumped were missing. The churches had been spared, but the city was now learning it would be remembered as the city where the worst terrorist attack since 9/11 happened.

FBI Agent Williams was being hailed as a hero for his role in uncovering the plot of the young women terrorists in time to protect the Catholic churches. The Portland Field Office wasn't saying anything about the crucifixion of Michael Brennan by the terrorists and Agent Williams was going along with the decision for the time being. When things quieted down, he promised Drake he would demand the investigation be reopened in that case as well as the suicide of the city employee accused of his murder.

Drake laid down his menu and looked around the table. "Would anyone mind if I order a dozen chilled oysters on the half shell?"

No one objected, but Benning was struggling to keep from smiling. Both men knew that one of the post adrenal stress effects was horniness. When they face danger and survive, people often become hypersexual. Benning didn't know where Liz was spending the night, but he would gladly help his friend with the oysters he'd ordered because he knew who would be in his bed.

When they finished eating what Liz proclaimed was the best food she had ever eaten, Drake suggested they call it an evening. It was ten o'clock, one o'clock on the east coast, and he'd seen Liz covering her mouth a couple of times to hide a yawn.

Drake paid for their dinners and had Benning drive him to the Best Western Inn at the Meadows where he'd left his Porsche. Carol Sanchez had offered to keep Lancer for the night after learning the hotel was pet friendly. Apparently, the ban on pets only applied to the business and conference wing of the hotel.

After stowing Liz's suitcase in the bonnet of the 993, they were headed home to the farm with soft instrumental jazz accompanying the hum of the flat opposed six-cylinder engine in the rear of the car.

Before they reached the exit to Pacific Highway West, Drake saw that her eyes were closed and her head was back on the headrest. He squeezed her hand and told her to go ahead and sleep.

The evening wouldn't end as he had thought it might, but the day hadn't either. Tomorrow was a new day. There were things he wanted to show her and things they needed to talk about, including the vacation he'd arranged for them.

Chapter Seventy-Two

DRAKE LEFT Liz sleeping when he got up at sunrise the next morning. The sky was an eerie reddish orange from the smoke of a hundred forest fires burning in British Columbia. He missed the sunset the night before, but knew it would have been as spectacular as this sunrise.

He made coffee and was sitting in an old rocker on the front porch when Liz padded out barefooted and wearing an Oregon T-shirt of his.

"Good morning, sleepy head."

She leaned down and kissed him on the cheek. "Why is the sky red?"

"Smoke from forest fires in Canada. Want some coffee?"

"Stay put, I can get it."

Drake pulled the other rocker on the porch closer to his and waited for her to return.

"Where are the coffee cups?" she shouted from inside.

"Cabinet on the far left."

Liz walked out to the porch carrying a mug of coffee in both hands and sat down beside him. "It's beautiful here."

"We can go for a run later. You'll see some of the neighboring vineyards along the way, and at the top of the run you can see all the way down the valley."

"Thank you for letting me sleep on the way home last night. I couldn't keep my eyes open."

Drake got up to refill his coffee cup. "You had a long day. You look good in my shirt, by the way."

She looked up with a mischievous grin. "I don't remember getting undressed or putting it on."

He grinned back. "You wouldn't. You lay down on the bed when I was in the bathroom. You were sound asleep with your clothes on when I got back. Letting you borrow my T-shirt was the least I could do."

"We're you a gentleman?"

"I was as gentle as I could be. Are you hungry?"

"Should I be?"

"If you're not, I can think of something that might help with that."

After they shared the shower an hour later, they decided to postpone the run and have breakfast instead.

Liz was toasting bagels and pouring orange juice, while Drake made two smoked salmon and cream cheese omelets with green onions.

"I didn't know you could cook."

"A guy would get pretty hungry if he didn't know how to fix a few things."

He slid the omelets onto their plates and carried them to the breakfast table in the kitchen. As he looked around to see if he'd forgotten anything, he realized that he hadn't had breakfast with a woman here for almost three years. He also realized he wasn't uncomfortable about it.

He pulled out her chair and waited until she sat down before sitting across from her. "Let me know if you're not a fan of smoked salmon. I can use bacon or sausage or crab or whatever you want next time."

Liz took a forkful of the omelet and nodded. "This is really good and I love smoked salmon. Did you just invite me to stay more than one night?"

Drake paused with his orange juice glass halfway to his mouth. "Liz, you can stay as long as you want. I thought I told you that."

"You did, but I had to know it wasn't just something you said in the moment."

"I meant it, Liz. I want you here for as long as you want to be here. I know you want to buy something in Seattle, but there's no rush."

"My things are being shipped to Seattle next week. I'll have to go get a few more things."

"Have them shipped here if you want. There's no need to pay for storage somewhere if you don't have to. There's plenty of room here. You remember how big the building is out back."

Liz had only been inside it once, when she was with DHS and helped him store the bodies of three dead terrorists for a while. They'd made the mistake of trying to kill him late one night here on his farm.

"Okay, I'll take you up on that offer, if you're sure we're not moving too fast."

"We'll know if we are soon enough. Let's try it and see."

They both knew what they were saying to each other and concentrated on finishing breakfast. Liz had never been married and, as far as he knew, had never lived with someone. He had been but was widowed three years ago. Living together on the farm was a big step for them both, even it was just for a while.

Drake got up to refill their coffee cups when his phone

vibrated and buzzed on the kitchen counter. He saw that it was Kevin McRoberts from PSS calling.

"Good morning, Kevin."

"I found him, Mr. Drake. Professor Ahmadi is on St. Helene, a small island on the east end of Roatan, Honduras."

Chapter Seventy-Three

THREE HOURS LATER, Mike Casey landed the PSS Gulfstream G650 at Hillsboro's general aviation airport with a hastily organized extraction team. The destination was six hours away, on the island of Roatan, thirty-five miles off the coast of Honduras, where Professor Ari Ahmadi was living.

Drake stood with Liz, Morales and Sanchez waiting in Global Aviation's passenger reception and waiting area for the G650 to taxi in and pick them up.

"The flight to Roatan will take us six hours. With any luck, we should be in the air with Ahmadi by midnight and back here by mid-morning tomorrow."

Liz slipped her arm around his waist. "I'll be waiting. Carol gave me a quick rundown of the things she does with Lancer. Is there anything special he needs?"

"Food, water and a little loving. I fed him this morning. Feed him tonight and again tomorrow morning. He'll be outside keeping you safe the rest of the time."

They watched as the G650 stopped outside and opened

its passenger door. Mike Casey came down the steps, waved and then pumped his arm, telling them to hurry up.

Liz pulled Drake's head down and kissed him. "Please be careful. Call me when you leave Roatan."

He kissed her again. "I will. Don't worry about me, I'm in good company."

He ran to catch up with Morales and Sanchez and greet his best friend.

Casey looked back to Liz, standing with her arms crossed over her chest. "Is she here to stay?"

"Her things are arriving next week."

"Arriving here or in Seattle?"

Drake shoved his friend up the steps. "We'll see."

Introductions were being made in the main cabin when they stepped inside.

Drake knew Steve Carson, Mike's pilot, and Kevin McRoberts. Two men he didn't know, but, by their looks, he guessed they were men with special operations force experience.

Casey introduced them. "Meet Don Borden and Nick Manning. They're both former SEALS. Thought they might come in handy because it looks like the only way to this guy's place is by water.

Drake shook hands with both men. "Is he giving you a bad time about being Navy?"

"Yeah but coming from a grunt we ignore it."

"Just remember this grunt's your boss."

Casey went forward and took the co-pilot's seat next to Carson. Drake sat down in the seat behind the bulkhead with McRoberts across the aisle and buckled in.

He turned to his left toward McRoberts. "Mike said the only way in is by water. How did you learn that?"

McRoberts held up his two hands and wiggled his

fingers. "Magic touch, Mr. Drake. Just kidding. I found that one of the offshore accounts Ahmadi uses transferred money to a realtor on Roatan. On his computer, I found a listing for the same amount as the price of a fishing cabin on Roatan, east end on St. Helene. The property listing from the realtor advertised it as an off-the-grid, Caribbean-style fishing fish cabin that's only accessible by boat. Here's a picture of the place from the listing."

Drake took the iPad McRoberts handed him and studied the picture of the cabin. It was a stilt cabin maybe eight feet off the ground. There were two docks, one with a thatched palapa at the end, and two screened porches at the front and rear of the cabin, each with steps.

"How do we get there?"

"That's a bit of a problem. St. Helene is on the eastern end and Roatan's forty-eight miles long. The roads aren't good, but we were able to charter a helicopter. Mr. Casey made a couple of calls and a friend of a friend of a friend flies tourists around the island sightseeing. He's going to fly us to a dock at the end of Old Port Royal Road. A local fishing guide he knows will let us use his Zodiac Hurricane for a deposit equal to the cost of a new one, plus an hourly rate of five hundred dollars. That's crazy, but Mr. Casey said to do it."

"You did all that in three hours?"

McRoberts smiled and held up ten wiggling fingers.

Drake unfastened his seatbelt and walked back to talk with the two SEALs and sat in the empty seat in front of Nick Manning.

"Do you have a plan to get us from the dock to Ahmadi's cabin?"

Manning handed his iPad over Drake's left shoulder. A satellite image of Roatan and St. Helene was on the screen.

"See the dock at the end of Old Port Royal Road?" Manning pointed. "It's a straight shot from there to this channel that separates Roatan from St. Helene. We'll come around this way and approach his cabin from the east. It should take us about an hour."

"Extraction is by helicopter at the dock where we get the Zodiac?"

"It's the only way. There's no place to land a helicopter big enough to get us all out of there. The ones with pontoons will only carry two passengers and a pilot."

"ETA at the airport?"

"Depends on how long we're at his cabin. If he's alone, we'll be back before sunrise. If he has some of his ISIS friends with him, who knows?"

"It sounds solid. Let's hope he's alone."

Drake walked back to his seat past Morales and Sanchez playing some game on their smartphones to pass the time.

He was looking forward to meeting the man who conspired with Umara to kill innocent people and then fled the country. He knew an FBI agent anxious to put cuffs on him and make sure he got what was coming to him. Of course, if he unfortunately resisted his return to America violently, he might get it long before then.

Chapter Seventy-Four

IT TOOK them two hours to get from the international airport in Roatan to the boat dock at the end of Old Port Royal Road. The fishing guide stood at the end of the dock beside his Zodiac with a handheld credit card reader and waterproof document bag. He wasn't letting them use his boat without the deposit he demanded and a signed rental agreement.

Casey had to use his American Express Centurion Black card to satisfy the old man.

The two SEALs waited until the key for the Zodiac was handed to Casey before they boarded and examined the boat.

Drake followed them and listened to their excited raving about the old Zodiac.

"I didn't think I'd ever get to drive one of these again! Zodiac Hurricane H-733, the same Navy Zodiac we used in SEALs," Nick Manning said. "Two 150 horsepower Evinrudes, color radar, VHF package, Echo Sounder, the works."

"This fishing guide's spent a lot of money keeping this in tiptop shape," Don Borden, the other SEAL, added. "I can think of a lot of things this boat could be used for other than fishing."

Drake agreed. "Let's hope he hasn't been using it for any of those 'other things'. Last thing we need is the Honduran Navy watching for it. Which one of you is going to drive it?"

Manning was the senior SEAL, but he pulled out a coin. "Heads or tails?"

Borden called tails.

It was heads and Manning moved to the center to check out the Simrad dual touchscreens and navigation systems he'd be using.

Drake took the duffel bags holding the equipment Casey brought with him from Seattle and held out a hand to help Sanchez and the others climb onto the boat. Everyone was going to Ahmadi's hideaway except Steve Carson, their pilot.

Manning fired up the Evinrudes and pulled away from the dock. When they were far enough away the guide couldn't see what Casey was passing out, he distributed the HK416s, the SIG P320s, FLIR NYX-7 night vision goggles and two-way radios, one each for all of them.

Except Kevin McRoberts, who only got a two-way radio and a tactical flashlight. His role was limited to securing Ahmadi's computer and searching for any information available about the missing twenty million and Ahmadi's terrorist network. He wasn't an operator, but his expertise would guarantee the success of their mission.

The eastern end of the island was sparsely populated. Thick mangroves lined the shoreline and added to the darkness of the moonless night as Manning brought the Zodiac up to plane and skimmed over the flat ocean toward St. Helene.

The satellite imagery provided the precise GPS coordinates of Ahmadi's fishing cabin. But Manning was heading to the narrow channel through the mangroves that separated Roatan from St. Helene. The channel was narrow and two hundred yards long with mangroves lining the way.

He slowed the Zodiac down off plane and slipped through the dark channel. At the other end, he pushed his push-to-talk button. "ETA ten minutes."

Six clicks responded.

When they came around the eastern end of St. Helene and turned toward the cabin, they saw there were lights on and could hear music playing.

There were no boats tied up at either of the two docks. Manning steered toward the far side of the shorter dock. At the end of it, across a narrow strip of sandy beach, was an equipment shed of some sort.

"When we reach the dock, Borden will slip over the side and move to the shed. He'll cover the rest of us until we're ashore. Drake and Casey, secure the Zodiac. If the water's shallow enough, we'll all follow Borden over the side. We won't know how much noise the dock will make. So stealth mode from here on."

Six clicks responded again to the lead of the head SEAL.

Manning slowed the Evinrudes to idle and drifted alongside the dock. Borden slipped over the starboard side and waded ashore with his HK416 held above his head. The water never reached higher than his chest.

When he waded ashore and crossed the sand beach, he took a position with a view of the front of the cabin. "All clear."

With the boat secured, they followed him through the water, with McRoberts making the trip with his laptop held aloft. When they were gathered around him in the shadows of the shed, Drake took the lead.

"Manning, Borden and Morales, go around to the back porch. Tell me when you're there. We'll make our way to the foot of the stairs on the front porch. We'll enter together on my signal."

The two SEALS and Morales split off to the right around the shed and stayed in the shadows on the way to the back porch.

Drake led them along the narrow strip of beach to the far side of the open area in front of the cabin. When they stacked up behind him, he sprinted to the side of the front porch and listened. The only thing he heard was music from *Les Miserables* playing softly.

Drake waved the others over and got ready to run up the stairs. "Remember, we need to talk with Ahmadi. If there are others inside, defend yourselves. Ready, on the count of five."

Two teams rushed the cabin from the front and rear with no resistance. Ahmadi was sitting at a small table in the kitchen with his laptop in front of him, startled by the sudden noise of their entry.

While he stared up at them in shock, Drake pulled him out of his chair and away from his laptop.

"Professor Ahmadi, I'm here to take you back to America to stand trial and recover the money you stole. You can come with us voluntarily or wait here for U.S. Army soldiers from the Soto Cano Air Base in Honduras to get here and fly you to Guantanamo. It's your choice."

Ahmadi regained his composure and smiled. "You have no right to be in my house, pointing guns at me. I haven't been charged with anything. What is it you think I've done?"

Drake shoved him back down in his chair. "Someone restrain him while I tell him what he's done."

Morales pulled out flex cuffs and pulled Ahmadi's hands around behind the chair and cuffed him. He did the same with double flex cuffs around his ankles.

Drake stood in front of Ahmadi while the others spread out to search the cabin. "To start with, you conspired with Samantha Taylor and supported her little band of women warriors in their jihad against Christians. You had her kill Michael Brennan and attempted to kill Catholics while they worshipped in their churches. You stole twenty million dollars from those same people and then participated in the slaughter of gay marchers over the Steel Bridge. There are probably other crimes associated with your ties to ISIS, but that's what we know at the moment."

Ahmadi glared up at Drake. "You can't prove any of that. What she did, she did on her own. And I'm not the one she conspired with. She was working with someone else and she tried to have me killed. That's why I had to get out of Oregon."

"Then you can prove all of that at your trial."

McRoberts shouted from the sitting area near the front porch. "It's all here. I've found all the offshore accounts. The rest will be easy."

Drake turned back to Ahmadi. "Have you decided to come with us voluntarily or shall I call the air base to come and get you?"

"I'll take my chances in Oregon."

"Then you agree that you are voluntarily coming back with us to Oregon?"

"If that's what you call this. I don't really have a choice, do I?"

"You have a choice, Professor. Trust the legal system in the country you must hate, to do what you've done, or take your chances as a terrorist and enemy combatant at war with America."

"Fine, I will go back to America voluntarily," he said and spit on the floor.

Casey recorded the whole thing on his smartphone, standing back with Morales and Sanchez. "That's it then. Let's get back to the airport and in the air. The sooner we give this man the homecoming he deserves the better I'll like it."

It was eleven thirty by the time they got back to the Gulfstream with Ahmadi. They were delighted to find their pilot had a local restaurant bring platters of fried fish, conch fritters, rice and beans and a case of Red Stripe beer for their dinner on the flight home.

By sunrise, they would be back in Oregon.

Chapter Seventy-Five

THE SNOW on Mount Hood was a light shade of pink from the sunrise and smoke from forest fires as the Gulfstream glided by Thursday morning on its path to Hillsboro Airport.

Drake admired the mighty mountain out the window to his right, home to twelve glaciers and six ski areas. He had skied them all and made a note to take Liz up for a ski weekend at Timberline Lodge. It had been declared a National Historic Landmark in 1977 and was everything you'd expect a historic ski lodge to be.

The two SEALs guarded their silent and restrained passenger in the rear, and Kevin McRoberts was playing a game on his smartphone. Sanchez was asleep with her head on the shoulder of a smiling Morales when Drake turned to look, and Casey and Carson were talking quietly in the cockpit as they prepared to land.

FBI Special Agent Williams was at the airport waiting to arrest Ahmadi and take him into custody. The Department of Justice had decided to charge him with only the cybercrime for stealing from the Portland parishioners for the time being. The attorney general wanted to make sure the case against him was airtight for his acts of terrorism, conspiracy and murder.

When they touched down and stopped on the tarmac at Global Aviation, Drake stayed inside while Agent Williams and three other agents escorted Ahmadi off the Gulfstream and walked him to the black Suburban idling nearby. This was Williams' show and he didn't want to be seen having any role in it. For all anyone would know, who didn't have a need to know, this was entirely the work of the FBI and one talented counterterrorism expert who would be commended for his work. That was the agreement Drake negotiated in exchange for publicly not criticizing the Portland Field Office for its hasty conclusion of the investigation of the murder of Michael Brennan.

As soon as the FBI agents were gone, Drake called Liz.

"I know this is short notice, but Mike wants us to return to Seattle with him. We just landed in Hillsboro and I'm renting a car to come and pick you up. Pack a bag for a couple of days and I'll be there in half an hour."

"How did it go? Did you find Ahmadi? Is everyone okay?"

"Everything's fine. Ahmadi is under arrest, the FBI just left with him. Now hurry, Mike's refueling the plane and wants to leave as soon as possible."

"Why do we have to go to Seattle? I was looking forward to spending time with you here."

"Liz, you know Mike. He wants to make sure we've covered all our bases about our trip to Honduras. Just trust me and be ready when I get there."

Before he left, he stuck his head in the cockpit. "I'm taking a rental to get Liz. We should be back in an hour. I told her you wanted her in Seattle to wrap up our Honduras adventure. Make something up if she asks."

"Go get your lady. We've got this covered."

Drake skipped down the steps and ran to the passenger waiting area where he picked up keys for the car he rented. A BMW 528 from Avis was waiting outside the building for him.

On the drive to Dundee, he called his vineyard manager who kept Lancer while he was away for more than day. The manager's German Shepherd and Lancer played well together and Lancer seemed to enjoy the break in his routine. Drake liked it because he knew his buddy was in good hands.

Drake sped up the long gravel driveway to his old stone farmhouse, leaving a cloud of dust behind him. Liz was standing on the front porch with Lancer.

He parked the BMW at the rear of the house and hurried inside, meeting Liz in the kitchen with a hug and a kiss.

"Ready?"

"What's going on, Adam? Are we really in this much of a hurry?"

"Yes," he said over his shoulder on the way to the closet in his bedroom. He came back with a black carryon and his laptop and picked up her carryon on the way back out to the BMW.

Liz followed him to the door with a frown on her face. "Would you like me to lock up?"

"I'll do it, thanks." He closed the trunk on their luggage and his laptop and opened the door of the BMW for her. "I'll just be a minute."

He made sure the front door was locked and knelt down in front of Lancer. "Thanks for being such a good sport with Liz. We'll be gone for a while, but she's coming back."

Drake gave Lancer a double ear rub and left a key on the counter for his neighbor to lock up when he came for Lancer.

Liz was looking at him with a puzzled look on her face when he got behind the wheel and started the BMW, but she didn't say anything. She'd never seen him rush around and act like he wasn't in control of everything. And she wasn't sure she liked it.

Drake told her about the flight to Roatan, the helicopter flight to the dock and the Zodiac ride across to St. Helene in great detail, dominating the conversation all the way back to the airport.

Casey was standing at the top of the steps of the Gulfstream when they hurried across the tarmac from the passenger waiting area.

"Sorry for the rush, Liz. I have an emergency that I need to take care of back home. I'd like you two to prepare a story about our involvement with the arrest of Ahmadi, in case we need it."

As soon as the steps retracted and the door closed, the Gulfstream started to roll. Five minutes later, they were airborne and turning north on the way to Seattle.

Thirty-five minutes later, they were on the ground in Seattle and Liz was more baffled than ever by Drake's behavior. He was nervous about something and that made her nervous as well.

When the two SEALs, McRoberts, Morales and Sanchez got off the Gulfstream and took the duffel bags carrying their gear for the extraction, Drake remained seated until Casey came out of the cockpit with a big smile on his face.

"Time for me to go to work. Steve is flying the Gulfstream to Hawaii, where I believe Adam has a surprise for you. Welcome to PSS, Liz. I'll see you both in the office when you get back."

Liz looked at Casey and then Drake. "I don't understand."

"Remember the surprise vacation I mentioned? This is it. We have a villa on the Hamakua coast on the Big Island for the next two weeks and nothing to do but explore and have fun. That okay with you?"

Liz jumped across the aisle and threw her arms around his neck. "I can't think of anything I'd rather do."

Drake winked at his friend as Casey headed down the steps. "Well then, let's get this bird in the air and go have some fun."

Next in The Adam Drake Series

vinci-books.com/tippingpoint

A shadowy figure funds Antifa anarchists, threatening to tear America apart with violent riots.

Adam Drake is tasked with uncovering the mastermind behind the chaos. Evidence points to a Russian oligarch in New York, but as Drake closes in, the Deep State intervenes to protect their own.

Turn the page for a free preview…

Tipping Point: Chapter One

THE VILLA SITTING on the edge of an oceanfront cliff on the Hamakua Coast of the Big Island of Hawaii had a panoramic view of the Pacific Ocean to the east. It was owned by a grateful client of Adam Drake's who had made it available to him for a short vacation. He had needed a little R&R after a particularly hellish week.

A band of radicalized female college students, recruited by ISIS, had planned to massacre Catholic parishioners while they worshipped at mass in Portland, Oregon. Drake and an FBI agent, aided by a team from Puget Sound Security where he served as special counsel, had uncovered the plot and stopped the terrorists.

The man who recruited the young women, a Muslim computer science professor at their college, had fled to Roatan, an island in the Caribbean, to avoid capture. When his hideaway was discovered, Drake and his team had flown there in the PSS Gulfstream. Allowed to choose between a trip to Gitmo, if they turned him over to the U.S. Army stationed in nearby Honduras, and voluntarily returning to face federal charges in the U.S., the professor had wisely agreed to return with them to Oregon.

An inquisitive press wanted to know why and how Drake and PSS had been involved, and taking a short vacation allowed him to avoid their questions. The Big Island was the perfect place to vacation. Lush tropical beauty surrounded the secluded villa and he was there in the company of the woman he loved.

Liz Strobel was sitting on the other side of a teak patio table on the villa's lanai, wearing a white bikini and eating a blueberry croissant. She was stunningly beautiful, and he knew he was staring, but he couldn't help it.

When she turned and saw him looking at her, she smiled. "Are you enjoying the view as much as I am?"

Drake winked. "Probably more so. I've always loved looking at beautiful things, the endless blue ocean … a woman in a white bikini."

"You're such a gentleman. What would you like to do today? We could stay here and relax or go to the botanical gardens."

"Let's see the gardens tomorrow. The guy who owns the best helicopter charter service here is a friend. He flew a helicopter in the 160th Special Operations Aviation Regiment, the NightStalkers. He was air support on some of the missions Mike Casey and I were on in Delta Force. His name is Riley Bishop, and he'll be here at ten o'clock to fly us over the volcano and that incredible lava flow."

Liz reached across and turned his wrist over to look at his watch. "We have an hour and a half. Why don't you get your swimsuit on and join me in the pool? You could use a little sun," she said with a smile.

It was Drake's turn to smile. He was wearing cargo

shorts and a blue polo shirt. He'd been wearing less than that the night before.

When he joined her minutes later, she was standing on the far side of the infinity pool. Her chin was laying atop her folded hands and seemed to be resting on the horizon. He dove in and came up beside her.

Brushing his hair back out of his eyes, he said, "Penny for your thoughts."

"I can't get the young women who died last week out of my mind. What makes college students want to be jihadists and kill people?"

"Terrorist recruiters offer them whatever they're seeking. If a woman sees herself as a victim, it's a chance to get back at whoever, or whatever, they feel victimized them—a society that doesn't value them or their religion; men who have abused them; friends who have turned their backs on them. ISIS does it, but terrorist groups have been doing the same thing for a long time."

"Will it ever stop?"

Drake slid his arm around her waist and pulled her close. "Not any time soon. In the meantime, why don't we get out? You could use a little sun to get rid of those tan lines that I've noticed. I'll be happy to put sun lotion on for you."

"Once again, you're such a gentleman."

Tipping Point: Chapter Two

TWO THOUSAND THREE hundred and nineteen miles away, in San Francisco, a huge counter protest had been organized to confront a "Free Speech" rally.

A conservative radio host and Fox news contributor had been scheduled to speak on the University of California Berkeley campus at an event sponsored by the student Republicans. The event had been canceled because the university was afraid there would be violence. The "Free Speech" rally was then rescheduled by supporters to be held at Crissy Field in San Francisco.

Counter-protestors had quickly hacked the SFPD and determined that the police were told not to actively confront any of the anarchist counter-protesters. Firearms and other obvious things that could be used as weapons were banned, but searches for them would be randomly made. Knives strapped to a counter-protester's leg would likely not be discovered.

Police barricades would be set up and manned, but they could easily be overrun with a sufficient number of counter-protesters. In recent protests to counter the hate of right-wing Nazi supporters of the president and other white supremacists, the counter-protesters had outnumbered the opposition ten to one. Overrunning police barricades with those numbers, especially if the police were being told not to interfere, wasn't seen as a problem.

On Saturday, at two o'clock in the afternoon, fewer than five hundred people were at Crissy Field to support the "Free Speech" rally organized by a group calling itself "We Are Patriots". Five times that number surrounded the patriots holding signs with black Nazi swastikas circled and crossed out in red. Other signs read, "Resist Racism," and "Haters Go Home."

Three leaders of Antifa, the violent anarchist movement, were in charge of inciting the riot. Counter-protestors were assembling in the parking lot of the nearby Sports Basement Presidio, a massive sports equipment store, from where they would march down Old Mason Street to Crissy Field and close in on the rally from three sides. There would be no way for anyone to escape, unless they jumped in the bay at the rear of the field.

The first three patriot speakers did little to stir up the counter-protesters, but the fourth was being loudly shouted down. As he tried to continue, scuffles broke out between the two sides.

It was time. The Antifa leaders were sent a message. "Go!"

It took five minutes for three hundred black-clad anarchists to run down Old Mason Street and out onto the field. The police on the barricades saw them coming and withdrew, standing behind their police cruisers in riot gear.

The black clads cut through the throng of counter-protesters, shoving them aside on their way to the "Free

Speech" patriots in front of the stage. Fighting erupted and the anarchists pulled out saps and collapsible batons to beat people to the ground.

Twenty of the anarchists, wearing black hoodies and balaclavas, also used their knives to slash and cut as many of the patriots as they could. Because the knives were silent weapons, the screams from the victims blended in with the other screaming that was heard.

It took the police take several minutes to react to the violence. Before they could reach the black-clad anarchists, they had to wade through the other counter-protesters. By the time they got there, the orchestrated violence was over.

Beaten and bloodied protesters were on the ground, but the riot police didn't stop to help them. They were chasing after the anarchists running from the field.

The massacre was witnessed live on every major television channel for all the world to see.

It was the first wave of violence the anarchists hoped would start a second civil war. The country was so divided, ideologically, politically and racially, that it wouldn't be long before all the factions would be armed to defend themselves. The more violence that was witnessed on television, like the coverage of the war in Vietnam, the sooner the streets would be filled with citizens demanding an end to it all. And when the government couldn't end it all, people would have to choose sides and try to do it themselves.

It was the way you started a civil war.

Tipping Point: Chapter Three

PRECISELY AT TEN O'CLOCK, a maroon helicopter circled around the villa to land on the paved driveway that ran across the property from the road. Drake and Liz had watched it fly along the coast from the back deck. By the time it took them to walk through the villa, the helicopter was down on the driveway with its rotors spinning slowly.

Riley Bishop walked over to greet them. He was wearing a white embroidered Hawaiian shirt, jeans, aviator sunglasses and a maroon baseball cap with gold letters. The letters matched the name on the side of the helicopter, Bishop Royal Charters.

He was shorter than Drake by a couple of inches, with broad shoulders and a barrel chest. He walked past Drake and greeted Liz the Hawaiian way, with a hug and a gentle kiss on her right cheek.

"Casey is right, you are a looker. I'm Riley Bishop, at your service."

Turning to Drake, he greeted him with a strong handshake. "Glad to meet you, Drake. If you're half as good as Casey says you are, this lady's in good hands."

"Mike told me to check and see if your flying skills were as good as his. He said he was worried about our safety flying with you," Drake said, returning an equally strong handshake.

Bishop snorted. "He was never as good as me. That's why he left us to join you ground pounders. Come on and get in. I want to show you my island."

Bishop's helicopter was an Airbus H130 Eco-Star, a single engine, light utility helicopter. Drake saw that it had the high-density cabin configuration with three front passenger seats in line with the pilot's seat. He helped Liz in and then climbed in next to her.

As soon as they were buckled in and had their headsets on, Bishop lifted off and headed out nose-down out over the cliff.

"My pilots have our charters covered for the rest of the day, so we'll take the scenic route over the ocean. It's quicker overland, but there's a petition to ban flights overland on the way to the volcano. It's an economic issue for the charters, but I understand where the petitioners are coming from."

"How long have you lived here?" Liz asked.

"I was born on the Big Island. I moved to the mainland for college and returned when I left the service. I've always considered it my home. Most tourists stay on the Kona side of the island. That's one of the reasons I like it here on the windward side."

Drake pointed down to his right at a large villa on a cliff. "Looks like you're getting a few of the uber rich staying on this side."

"That's the richest resident on the island, Mikhail

Volkov, the Russian oligarch. He's not here very often, but he has a lot of guests."

Bishop circled around so they could take a better look at the estate. "I've flown a number of them up here, landing on his helipad on the roof."

He flew back out over the ocean and headed south. When he got closer to Hilo, he descended to fly around the bay and show them the town.

"The bay front in Hilo's been hit three times in the last hundred years by tsunamis, once in 1946, in 1960 and then again in 1975. The one in 1946 was caused by an earthquake in the Aleutian Islands. One hundred and fifty-nine people died. A lot of the buildings closest to the bay were destroyed. The one in 1960 was caused by an earthquake in Chile. Sixty-one people died in that one. Two people died in the 1975 tsunami caused by an earthquake off the coast. There's a tsunami museum on the bay front you should check out while you're here. It's got information about tsunamis all around the world."

"There's a lot of green space and parks down there. Is that a statue of King Kamehameha?" Liz pointed ahead.

"Sure is. That area was called 'New Town' before the 1946 tsunami. It was a Japanese residential community. It was completely wiped out, everything except a Coca Cola bottling plant. It's all park land now."

Bishop flew back out over the ocean and followed the coastline and then turned inland south of the two lava streams pouring red hot lava into the ocean.

"Since the eruption in May, Madame Pele's lava has covered over eight square miles of land. You've seen the coverage on TV, but that doesn't capture the massive loss of land that's occurred. Kapoho Bay and the tide pools just disappeared when the lava reached there. Homes, farms, businesses, just gone."

Bishop's two passengers were awestruck by the fast-flowing streams of red lava that had destroyed everything in its path.

"How are people coping?" Liz asked.

"As best they can. There is some temporary housing, but a lot of the people who have lost their homes and their belongings have left. The state and FEMA have done what they can, but the government can't afford to make people whole again. It's tough, but we'll survive.

"The volcano is a national park and there's a great museum on the rim. Go at dusk or sunrise to enjoy it, if the park's open. There's also a place I recommend, the Kilauea Lodge, where you can stay. Rooms are usually reserved years in advance, but I can help with that, if you want.

"Lava's been flowing to the ocean since 1970, but not anything like this. There are boat charters that will get you close to where the lava flows into the ocean. That's something else I'd recommend."

Liz put her hand over Drake's. "I'd like to see the volcano before sunrise and the lava flow at night from a boat before I leave. This is just incredible."

"If you want, I can get started on that, if you'll give the dates," Bishop offered. "The lady that handles my charter reservations is a gem. She's also the woman I'm dating."

Drake looked over at Bishop, who was looking down at the lava flow with his lips pressed tightly together. He didn't know anything about the man's personal life. He appeared to be a man who enjoyed what he was doing and loved everything about the place he called home. But he was also obviously saddened by the loss of land below.

Drake thought of his old farm, and the vineyard he was working to restore, in the Oregon wine country southwest of Portland. He loved it, like Bishop loved his island. But someday soon, he knew he was going to have to make a choice.

He could stay on his farm in Dundee and risk losing Liz or move to Seattle. She had given up her career in Washington to take a job with PSS and be closer to him. It was up to him to make a similar sacrifice, if he wanted to continue their relationship.

Drake knew what he wanted to do. He also knew a part of him would be saddened when he did it.

Tipping Point: Chapter Four

ACROSS THE PACIFIC OCEAN in Oregon, Zal Nazir, a software engineer, left the Intel Hillsboro campus in his black BMW M5 to meet a man for lunch. The invitation for the meeting had come to him in a plain white envelope, left under the windshield wiper of his car the night before.

The name of a nearby restaurant and bar had been written on the back of an embossed business card, from the Iranian consulate in Ottawa, Canada. Below the name of the Copper River Restaurant and Bar was the time for the meeting, one o'clock in the afternoon.

Nazir wasn't unduly concerned about the meeting. In addition to his work as a software engineer for Intel, he was also the founder of the Islamic Revolutionary Council of America (IRCA). The Council was made up of a select group of Muslim hackers he'd recruited to wage cyber jihad. He had chosen American citizens with clean records and no affiliation with any radical imam or mosque in the country. Their names weren't on any watch list, and they were extraordinarily careful about keeping it that way. They all flew under the radar of the enemies of Islam.

He arrived at the restaurant twenty minutes early and waited patiently for a table to clear next to a window. He wanted to watch the envoy from the consulate arrive to see if he was being followed. From a window table, he would have an unobstructed view of the parking lot.

When he was seated and had ordered a cup of coffee, he watched as cars left the parking lot and looked for cars arriving. At five minutes to one, a white Ford Taurus drove into the lot and pulled into an empty spot. The rear bumper had an Avis rental car sticker on it.

The man who got out of the car looked to be in his late forties. He had dark, curly hair, a pair of round wire-rim glasses and wore a light gray suit. There was nothing about him that attracted attention as he walked to the entrance. But Nazir knew he was the man he was to meet by the relaxed but alert way he casually observed his surroundings. He had made sure there were no threats he had to worry about before he made his way to their table.

Pausing briefly at the door, he saw Nazir and walked to his table and sat across from him.

Nazir reached across the table to shake hands. "You obviously know my name, but I don't know yours. Who are you and why did leave your card on my car?"

"It's not important who I am, Mr. Nazir. I'm only a messenger. But, to put you at ease, my name is Dana Ghorbani. I work at the consulate in Ottawa."

"What do you do there?"

"Something similar to what you and the Council do."

Nazir sat back in his seat. "What do you know about the Council?"

"Everything. I represent your sponsor, Masoud Jihandar.

He has something he wants you to do. America is paying too much attention to us, since it decided to pull out of our nuclear agreement. We want you to create a distraction for them to correct that."

"How am I to do that?"

"We want you to work with someone to start a civil war in America. He's been recruited by our ally in the north and will think he's working for them. He has a relationship with the Antifa anarchists through the student group he founded, Students for Social Justice. You will support his efforts with the skills you and your Council have."

"Why would I want to do that?"

Ghorbani leaned forward and said softly, "Because your sponsor wants you to, Mr. Nazir. We'll be in touch with instructions for meeting your new partner."

Nazir watched him stand up without saying another word and walk out of the restaurant. The sponsor Ghorbani had mentioned was a high-ranking officer in the Iranian Ministry of Intelligence and Security, the MOIS, and the supplier of the resources for the Council.

Starting a civil war in America sounded crazy to him, but he wasn't in any position to refuse cooperation. Not with the consequences he knew that would swiftly follow, if he didn't do as he was told.

Grab your copy...
vinci-books.com/tippingpoint

About the Author

Scott Matthews got hooked on reading thrillers – especially the James Bond thrillers – as an escape from the required reading in his high school English class; *The Odyssey*, *The Scarlet Letter*, *The Great Gatsby* and all the other "great" literature meant to prepare him for college and life beyond.

But Bond was fun! When Scott studied for the Oregon bar exam, he rewarded himself after a long day of study, reading a dog-eared Fleming paperback for fifteen minutes before turning off the bedside light each night.

His collection of thrillers later expanded to include the novels of John MacDonald, Nelson DeMille, Barry Eisler, Randy Wayne White, Daniel Silva and Steve Berry. And when his favorite authors took too long releasing their next books, he started jotting notes for a thriller he would write someday.

Scott still lives on the Left Coast in Oregon with his beautiful wife, and now writes his own thrillers that carry on the tradition of a brave and patriotic hero battling evil enemies and terrorists to protect his homeland.